The Act of

Vengeance

Dennis Medbury

Trade Paperback
@Copyright 2021
All Rights Reserved

Library of Congress: 1-10337127141
ISBN: 978-0-9969593-7-7

Requests for information should be addressed to:
A Vegas Publisher, LLC.
www.vegaspublishers.com
vegaspublisher@gmail.com
First edition: 2021
Map Design: Adam Wolters

For my children, Hailey, Joey, and Breanna. You three may be the cause of many of my gray hairs, but I love you with all my heart.

Publisher's Note

When Dennis submitted his manuscript to A Vegas Publisher, we were intrigued. His writing style is unique and alluring. We were instantly transported into the world he created, filled with diverse, captivating characters and creatures engaged in action-packed scenarios. Dennis has a vivid imagination and his visual writing style allowed us to picture his magical world, with clarity, just as he envisioned.

We asked Dennis how he came up with the material because it was unlike anything we had previously read. It was his reply that caught us by surprise: Dennis struggles with PTSD and suffers from insomnia; a result of his 14 years of service in the United States Navy. Not wanting to become dependent on medication, Dennis started to write this story in his head to help him fall asleep. The story began to develop and take on a life of its own. He decided to put his story into words.

We applaud Dennis for discovering a coping mechanism that works for him. It is estimated that over 44 million Americans suffer from PTSD. Dennis is a role model for those suffering with this condition. Through creative writing, Dennis can share with others how his evolving thoughts and ideas have helped him relieve some of his symptoms. Dennis encourages sufferers to discover their unique creative outlet. It can lead to brighter days.

Dennis, thank you for your service.

Virginia Clark
A Vegas Publisher

Each case is different; it is not recommended to stop medications, procedures, or treatments without consulting your physician.

The following links contain valuable information for struggling veterans in need of assistance:

https://nvf.org/veteran-resources/

https://www.mentalhealth.gov/get-help/veterans

https://www.neptunesociety.com/resources/list-helpful-veteran-resources-support-groups

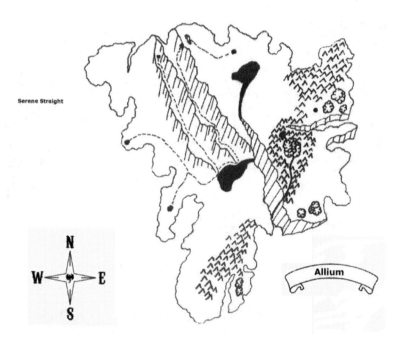

Serene Straight

N
W E
S

Allium

Elendor

Elendor marched to meet the orcs that stampeded toward him. The tusked warriors emerged from the city of Parvus Arbor, the home of the elves, his home. During his prolonged absence, the brutish race invaded his birth city. He did not know how, nor did he know if any of his people survived the attack, but he knew one thing: he would kill every last one of them or die trying.

Beyond taking the elven city, the hulking monstrosities committed a crime Elendor could never forgive: a set of orcs killed one of Elendor's oldest friends, Vaylon, just moments ago. He knew that his actions led to his friend's demise and the loss of Parvus Arbor, but at this raging moment, he could only think of revenge. Jocia and Galain, his surviving friends, begged him to stop the suicidal mission. The tone of their cries communicated their desire, but he lost the meaning of their words. Unable to decipher anything above his pulse's heavy beating and the adrenaline-filled blood rushing through his body, their muffled pleas barely registered. Everything in his line of sight seemed to take on a tinge of red, especially the usual tan-skinned warriors that drew closer with each passing step.

Cocking back his wooden arm, he intended to bury his fist in the dirt. From there, he would stretch out the appendage, forming it into three spikes that would burst from the ground beneath the orc's feet and impale them. However, before his magic-infused arm found its mark, Galain tackled Elendor from behind, drove him face-first into the grass, pinned his shoulders to the ground, and mounted him like a horse.

Elendor struggled against his friend's grapple to no avail. Keeping the wooden limbed elf pinned on the ground with his superior physical aptitude, Galain yanked his friend's face close to his own. "Are you a fool? You stand no chance! We must flee...now!" Galain shouted.

"They killed Vaylon! They have to pay! I have the power...I can..."

Galain punched Elendor in the face. "If we die here, who will give Vaylon his Rites of Passage? Who will ensure he returns to the Mother Matera? Do you care so little for his soul that you would risk this?"

Tears streamed from Galain's eyes. Elendor could see the rage and sorrow in his friend's expression. A part of him hoped that his friend redirected his anger to an undeserving target, but he knew better. Galain aimed his hostility at the elf he blamed for the loss of their mutual friend.

Elendor turned away, squeezing his eyes shut. He knew the truth behind Galain's words, but fighting a horde of giant-sized killers seemed easier than facing the consequences of his actions: the mutilated corpse of his friend.

Galain stood, yanking Elendor to his wooden feet. "If you care for any of us, especially Vaylon, you will help me get us out of here!"

"You are correct. I will go." Elendor took a deep breath to calm his rage and glanced over his shoulder. Soon the orcs would be upon them, but enough time remained to make it to their horses. He approached Vaylon's body, extended and split his wooden arm into four tendrils, wrapped them around his dead friend, and lifted him. He could not help but feel a sense of irony. For nearly a century, Vaylon transported Elendor on his back. Born missing an arm and both legs, only Vaylon, a half-elf, possessed the stout frame needed to carry his disabled body. He never complained about the burden nor showed a sign that he disliked the task. Now, after finally discovering the magic that allowed Elendor to operate wooden appendages, their roles reversed. He only wished Vaylon could enjoy the peculiarity of the situation alongside him.

After draping Vaylon on his saddle, Elendor climbed upon his steed and followed Galain and Jocia's retreat. With their horses galloping at full speed, he kept his hand on his dead friend to ensure he did not slip. Just as with the confrontation that led to his dear friend's death, Elendor looked behind to see the orcs gaining ground on the elven trio.

"This is not going to work!" Jocia began as if she read Elendor's mind. "They will catch us before we make it to safety."

"Not if we go south." Galain returned.

"Only the Nigereous Forest lies to the south," Jocia recalled.

"I know." Without further discussion, Galain

turned his horse in the direction of the cursed land, commonly referred to as Exiled Forest.

Following Galain's lead, Jocia strode beside him while Elendor trailed. He knew they discussed their course of action, but he could not make out their words above the stomping of their horse's hooves. He brought his horse closer, attempting to join the conversation; however, he doubted they cared for his opinion.

"The Exiled Forest is just as certain a death as facing the orcs!" Jocia protested

"Perhaps, perhaps not. Our chances of survival are far less if we are forced to face the orcs. If they know about the Exiled Forest's reputation, they may not follow. If they do not know, perhaps the forest itself will take care of our adversaries." Galain kept his eyes fixed forward

"If it does not take care of us first," Jocia whispered, barely loud enough to hear.

They soon arrived at the Exiled Forrest. The ash-colored trees stretched into the sky. Black fingers of an oozing substance snaked up the trunks. Gnarled, disfigured branches appeared ready to snatch anyone foolish enough to enter. No insects or woodland creatures called the cursed land home, leaving the forest soundless except for the cold wind whistling through the tight spaces between the trees.

"Hurry! They will be upon us soon." Galain ordered. "Stay close, do not get separated."

Elendor dismounted, keeping Vaylon's limp body wrapped in his grasp. The narrow gaps between the trees barred carrying Vaylon, forcing the grieving elf to create a makeshift harness to strap his dead friend to his back. Ripping his wooden arm from the harness with a yank, he reformed the remaining stump back into an arm and hand.

Elendor yelped in pain. His unique ability to connect with nature allowed him to feel the harness's wood until the moment he tore his arm away. The action felt as though he broke the arm of a natural-born limb. The agony did not last long yet left an impression he would not soon forget.

Extending his wooden legs to prevent Vaylon's feet from dragging on the ground, Elendor towered above his friends. Jocia and Galain craned up at him, wearing masks of fear as the orcs encroached. Neither cared much for his magical limbs nor the sacrifice needed to operate them. His arbormancy once allowed him to manipulate all manner of vegetation. Ever since he gained his limbs, he lost the ability to control plants beyond the hunks of wood attached to his body. His friends knew, just as Elendor did, that if he had not meddled in forbidden magic, Vaylon, and perhaps all their people, may not have suffered an untimely demise at the hands of the orcs. Had he not ventured to Tenbris for selfish desires, perhaps he could have learned of the orc's attack and used his arbormancy to defend the city.

Galain led the group into the forest. A chilling aura blanketed Elendor the moment he squeezed between the trees. A dark and ancient magic radiated from somewhere unseen, raising the hairs on the back of his neck. Chills ran up his spine as goose flesh traveled down his one natural-born arm.

Elendor turned around to peer out of the forest. As he feared, the orcs showed no sign of hesitation. They barreled in, weapons drawn, faces blazing red with rage.

Elendor turned to run deeper into the forest. Expecting to follow his friends, he found only empty space where they last stood.

"Jocia! Galain!" He called, but no answer returned.

Elendor's heart raced. His eyes darted from side to

side, desperate to locate his friends. His chest heaved with panicked breaths, beads of sweat formed on his brow. He searched for any impression in the dirt to determine which direction his friends fled but found no evidence that they even entered the forest in front of him. Turning back to gauge the orcs' distance, he peered between the trees to see them squeezing their massive frames between the gray trunks.

Elendor ran. His slight frame and nimble feet gave him a distinct advantage over the burly orcs. He hopped from side to side, leaped over raised roots, and ducked beneath low branches. Making his way deep into the forest, he turned back to observe the span he put between himself and his pursuers. What he found left him in shock.

The orcs barely entered the tree-line when an unexpected ally assaulted them. Gray branches and roots snagged each orc. Whips of wood wrapped around their torsos, squeezing until blood spouted from their mouths, nostrils, ears, and eyes. Pointed timber stabbed through flesh and bone. Roots tore the limbs from their bodies, leaving a gruesome display of carnage.

Grabbing a nearby tree, Elendor steadied himself

as he deeply panted. The world seemed to spin as his breathing grew rapid. The threat of his friends falling to the same fate as the orcs left him panicked and distraught. Scanning his surroundings, he searched for any signs of their presence but found no clues to their whereabouts. He wanted to call out to his friends again, but the icy claws of fear snatched the words in his throat.

Unanswerable questions flooded his mind. He did not understand how his friends disappeared without a trace. He hoped the two remained together but could not deny the possibility that they became separated from each other. The thought of Jocia finding herself alone in the dangerous Nigereous Forest left Elendor anxious and fearful for the well-being of her physical and mental state.

The magic of the forest felt dense and potent. He could not determine if the power came from a specific source or if the forest itself emitted the energies like a singular living entity. The trees seemed to expand and contract as if they breathed, but he could not be sure his eyes weren't playing tricks on him in his current state. The forest seemed indifferent to Elendor's presence, but his senses picked up another sensation that spiked the hairs on the back of his neck and left his skin cold, clammy.

He felt a distant gaze fixed upon him from an indeterminable direction. Without spotting the observer, he knew precisely who watched him. Since he left Parvus Arbor, a specter appeared to him during stressful situations. Its hollow, armor-clad body and red eyes floating above its hooded, headless frame burned its visage into his mind. Most encounters occurred during his sleep and presented each meeting in identical situations. The nightmares began with him finding himself mysteriously transported to the Exiled Forest. The ghostly figure approached Elendor and tortured him with a high-pitched wail. Ordinarily, the simple act of waking saved him from the specter, but no such reprieve existed this time.

The creak of hundreds of trees emerged from behind him as if a maelstrom threatened to split every tree of the forest in half, yet no wind blew. Turning to find its source, Elendor saw the trees of the forest moving. The trunks parted the ground as easily as flowing water. No mounds of dirt piled, and no roots rose above the ground. Each tree avoided each other as though they followed a choreographed dance. Forming two walls, they created an unescapable path leading to a circular-shaped grass field in the distance.

Elendor's body trembled. Even with elven eyes, he could not see anybody in the clearing, but he knew the faceless phantasm waited for him there. He wanted to turn and run, but the trees blocked his path in all directions. With no options remaining, he slowly stepped forward. Each step increased the pounding in his chest. Air entered and exited his lungs in rapid spasms, and his jaw vibrated as if he traversed through a frigid tundra. Intense magical energy surrounded him like water, making the journey feel as though he walked upon the bed of a deep lake. He rapidly blinked his dried eyes as though he walked against the gale of a storm, yet no wind blew.

Taking his first step into the clearing, Elendor released a grunt as his wooden foot met with sharp, bladed grass. He knew this place. In his dream, the apparition provided the runic symbol for activating his wooden limbs in this very spot. Until this moment, he assumed this area existed as an imagined scene conjured by his slumbering mind. The landscape resembled the precise image he saw in his recurring nightmares. Only the absence of the apparition prevented the scene from matching the terrifying experience.

During each of their meetings, the hollow armor's actions contradicted themselves. It provided assistance yet caused him great pain. It showed him the path to his greatest desire yet withheld the required information to achieve his goal. Elendor tried desperately to find a clue to the strange being's source through books and scrolls, but no text mentioned its existence. Very little information existed about the Exiled Forest itself. He rarely faced any situation without prior research, but this instance required him to face the forest's mysteries alone and unprepared.

Cautiously, he began the painful walk into the clearing. After the first few steps, he learned to gently push the grass aside with the outside of his feet before allowing it to support his full weight, but this method only reduced the number of stabbings. Arriving at the center, he squatted down and ripped out a small section of grass to allow him to stand on the soft dirt beneath. As he did, the surrounding trees shook as if his actions angered them. Not wanting to disturb the forest further, he stopped pulling the grass.

The trees in front of him rumbled as they shifted

their position to form an opening in the surrounding timber walls. At the center of the newly created path, the apparition stood in the exact visage of Elendor's nightmares. Jangling steps brought the ghoulish specter into the clearing, its invisible head turning from side to side as it observed the area. The moment the terrifying wraith stepped onto the bladed grass, the trees returned to their previous spot like a door shutting behind it.

Gilded full-plate black armor gave the ghostly manifestation a humanoid shape. Smoldering wisps rose from its breastplate, only to dissipate into its cloaked hood. Glowing red eyes, serving as its only facial features, pulsated in intensity, matching the throbbing rhythm of Elendor's rapid heartbeat.

Elendor covered his ears in anticipation of its deafening wail. During the previous encounters, the screech threatened to destroy his ears and drive his mind into madness. Even though their meetings occurred in the realm of dreams, the aftermath of the scream left ear-ringing that took days to deafen. Now face-to-face, no awakening could save him.

Elendor searched for a route of escape in hopes of finding a slightly larger crack between the trees, a low branch he could climb, or any opportunity that increased the distance between himself and the mysterious apparition. Seeing no reprieve, he began to run toward the tree-line. He intended to use his magical arm to hack at the trees, but the moment he took a step, the grass at his feet spiked to the height of his knees, preventing him from moving any further.

Panicked, he spun in a circle. His most cherished memories replayed in his mind—each recollection displayed in vivid imagery and intense detail. The smells of his forest home flooded his nose. The melodic tunes of Parvus Arbor's indigenous birds filled his ears. Recollections of the joyful time spent with his mother flashed in his mind. Images of the many ceremonies and celebrations performed by his people replayed as though they occurred just yesterday. His final vision saw his dearly departed friend Vaylon smiling at him with welcoming, open arms. He took the scene as an ominous foretelling of his destiny.

In the distance, the unmistakable dissonance of armored steps approached. Tears flowed like rivers down his cheeks. Dropping to the ground and curling into a ball, he prayed to Matera as he awaited his inescapable fate.

Clarissa

Clarissa awoke. With a startled gasp, she shot to a seated position. Everything that preceded her fall into unconsciousness surged into her mind. She recalled coming to Villam with a desire to marry the first-born son of Francisco Alcaldo in a desperate attempt to regain her lost title as High Priestess of Sanctum. Unfortunately, she didn't account for the arrogant and abusive personality Antonio Alcaldo possessed.

During their first meeting, the immoral heir of the Villam province assaulted her. Placing his hands on her body, he attempted to despoil her.

She fought wildly against the assult. She kicked, scratched, spat, and shoved, but found herself overpowered. Through seething teeth, she released a primal grunt as he twisted her arm behind her back. The despicable nobleman leaned in to steal a kiss as he ran his hand down her side. In response, she tried to take a chunck of flesh with her teeth, but his reflexes allowed her to only bite the air.

The commotion of the struggle caught the attention of her personal paladin guard, Sir Gabriel. Bursting into the room, he found Antonio in the midst of the violating attack. Clarissa tried to de-escalate the situation by informing the honorable paladin he misunderstood the situation and that she and Antonio merely played a flirtatious game. Sir Gabriel failed to fall for the ruse and reacted by lopping off the nobleman's arm at the elbow. A chivalrous act that led to his arrest and subsequent imprisonment.

Antonio's father, and his contingent of soldiers, barged into the room. Seeing his son grasping at his bleeding stump, he shot a cruel eye of blame upon Clarissa. At that moment, she knew her well-laid marital plan slipped through her fingers like sand. Her mind and body collapsed, and in her panicked state, a horrifying hallucination emerged.

Recalling the events produced various affects on her well-being. Antonio's pawing behavior roiled her stomach. Sir Gabriel's protective reaction pained her head. The event's repercussions sent her heart to beat at the pace of a hummingbird's wings. Lord Alcaldo's response brought the sensation of knives being twisted in her side. However, none of her thoughts disturbed her as much as the scene that transpired next.

Amidst the chaos, a ghostly figure manifested. It stood amongst a crowd of people, yet no one but she noticed its presence. Clad in an ancient style of black armor, the phantom seemed to lack a physical body beneath the plating. Smoke served as the only semblance of a head's presence, and glowing red eyes, like embers beneath a raging fire, served as its only facial feature.

Pointing a finger at Clarissa, it released a wail that pierced her ears in deafening pain. The suffering lasted until the world faded away as she drifted into the abyss of unconsciousness.

She wanted to share her experience with a sympathetic ear but knew no one would believe her. Rumors of her making up fantastical stories to alleviate the repercussions of her involvement in the encounter would rapidly spread. Questions would arise about her moral conduct and sanity. People would add monikers of "mad" and "mental" to her already humiliating title as the disgraced priestess. Everyone, even herself, if the situation were reversed, would call her a liar, a deceiver, a jezebel. In truth, she doubted her own memory of the event. Chalking it up to the fear of the moment, she convinced herself that she imagined the vision.

"I am glad you are awake." A feminine voice startled Clarissa.

In her delirious state, she failed to notice the woman sitting beside her bed. Something seemed not quite right about the woman. No cosmetics adorned her ordinary facial features, yet the sequins across the chest, cuffs, and waist of her dress signaled great wealth. Her silky, brunette hair hung to the center of her back, lacking the elaborate stylings of the noble women she met in the past.

"Who are you? Where am I?" Clarissa pulled the bed sheets up to her chin as she examined her surroundings.

"You are in the castle guest room, and I am Catalina Alcaldo."

"My lady!" Clarissa's heart jumped into her throat. Of all the nobles she met during the elaborate balls, celebrations, and tournaments, she never met Lord Alcaldo's wife. Along with the rest of the nobles, Clarissa assumed the lady chose to live as a recluse. She had even heard rumors that Lord Alcaldo insisted on leaving his wife home due to her homely appearance. Although most people likely did not consider Catalina a great beauty, any hearsay of her revolting appearance proved greatly exaggerated.

"Shush, child. You have had quite an experience and need to recover. Try not to get yourself too worked up." An unexpected kindness exuded in Catalina's soft voice.

"B-but, m-m-my lady, I-I…" Clarissa couldn't form the words.

Shortly after the arrival of the disgraced priestess, Catalina's son received a grave injury. Of all the people in Villam, she expected no one to hate her as much as the mother of the child she bore responsibility for maiming. She wanted to beg for forgiveness. She wanted to explain the situation and that she never meant for her son to get hurt, but only a stuttering rabble escaped her lips.

"Do not worry. I am not angry with you, dear." Catalina responded as if reading Clarissa's mind. "I do not know the details of what happened, but I do know my son. He is very much like his father...perhaps worse. He is intelligent, arrogant, and full of rage. By the knot on the back of your skull, finger-shaped bruises on your wrist, and red marks across your face, I can guess the situation grew well out of your control. I pray to the gods he didn't do anything...inappropriate."

Clarissa cast a wide-eyed look. In her experience, nobles defended their children, even when any fool could see the child's fault in the situation. Yet, this noble woman chose reason over instinct. She knew her son for the monster he became and refused to allow her motherly emotions to paint him as anything else.

The mention of Antonio's similarity to his father gave Clarissa pause. If Antonio inherited his father's ruthless personality, how long and how much suffering had Catalina endured? How many times did she shy away from the rest of the kingdom to hide her own bumps and bruises?

"N-no, my lady," Clarissa responded sheepishly. Although Antonio did attempt a tasteless act, he did not succeed. She thought to inform Catalina of this but decided against burdening her with any more weight than she already bore. "How is Antonio?" She asked, feigning concern for the despicable son.

"Luckily, Doctor Gaviel is one of the most gifted magic doctors in all of Preclarium. He was able to re-attach Antonio's arm, but he will suffer a loss of feeling and mobility. I'm afraid the arm will never be quite the same."

"That is unfortunate." Clarissa lied again. "What of Sir Gabriel? Where is he?"

"He awaits trial in the dungeon."

"May I see him?"

"I believe that can be arranged, but there is more."

"What is it? Has my guard been harmed?" Clarissa clasped her hands at her heart.

"No, but the trial is likely to take place here in Villam, not in Sanctum."

"What? Why?" Clarissa furrowed her brow with concern. She knew Sanctum traditionally handled the kingdom's judicial system. Until recently, she served as the high priestess and made these decisions herself. A mistake in her judgment served as the reason for her lost title, leading to her brother Aaron becoming the first male to inherit the position.

"The paladin attacked a noble. In cases like this, a lord may submit a request to the king to conduct the trial to seek justice for their family members. I am certain you are aware of this."

"Of course, but the request must go through Sanctum first. I doubt my brother…"

"He has already approved the request." Catalina interrupted.

"He what?" Clarissa asked with disbelief. Approving such a request when the incident involved a paladin of Sanctum seemed ludicrous. She couldn't imagine why her brother accepted the request so quickly. "How long have I been asleep?"

"Two days."

"Two days? Th-that's not possible!"

"Unfortunately, it is my dear. I am sorry to pile all of this upon you at once, but Sanctum is sending a contingent of paladins to Villam to question Sir Kenneth as well. Sir Gabriel's attack falls far outside the paladin's teachings. They want to ensure Sir Kenneth has not been corrupted. They said they refuse to allow anyone to besmirch the paladin's name further. They should arrive in a few days."

"None of this makes sense." Clarissa stood from the bed. Her quick movement caused her to stagger with dizziness. Catalina rushed to her side and grabbed her arms to ensure she didn't fall. "Thank you, my lady."

"You haven't eaten in days. You need sustenance before you move around like that."

"I appreciate your concern, but I must speak with your husband. I cannot allow this to happen. If Lord Alcaldo executes Sir Gabriel, it will be my fault. He only wished to defend my honor." Clarissa's eyes welled with tears.

"That would not be wise. My husband is not the type with which one can reason. Besides, he has not rescinded your betrothal to Antonio yet. If you want to try to return to Sanctum, you should not anger him further."

"You know?" Clarissa asked

"Of course, dear. Why else would you ask to marry my hot-headed son? You wish to have a daughter with a noble. You can then return to Sanctum, train her to inherit the high priestess title, and spend the rest of your days in the city of your birth. I only wish my second son, Ramon, hadn't joined the king's guard. He is a kind and gentle soul. I believe you could have learned to love him.

However, we women are allowed few options. We endure what we have to. At least you can escape this family someday."

"No."

"No, what dear?"

"No, I refuse to believe that. Just because we are women doesn't mean we have to endure a life forced upon us. Our sexuality does not determine our fate; we do."

"When I was young, I believed that as well. I had plans, dreams, and aspirations of my own. I wanted to travel, paint the kingdom's beautiful landscapes and meet new and interesting people, but the real world had other plans for me. None of the lords had daughters of appropriate marrying age, so Lord Salvador Alcaldo went to his marshals to find a suitable bride for his son Francisco. Marshal Hector Torres was more than happy to farm out his daughter to gain favor with his lord. It wasn't all bad, though. Antonio is a mirror image of his father, but Ramon and Carlos fill my heart with love. They are both such good boys."

Clarissa dwelled on Catalina's words. Before her excommunication, she would have believed Catalina's statement. Outside the Bright family, the family she was born into, the kingdom's political system heavily favored men. Being born a noble's son provided many more advantages than being born a daughter.

Shortly after she left her home, she learned a different way of existence. She and her guards stumbled upon a secret organization near the Hygard Mountains that showed her a world where women are treated equally to the physically superior men. In this particular guild, women possessed the same respect, credibility, and social standing. They weren't treated as delicate flowers, nor were they forced to submit to a man's will. This experience sparked a change in Clarissa, and she intended to let that spark grow into a raging inferno.

"No! I refuse to allow this to happen. First, I will speak with Sir Gabriel, and then I plan to speak with Lord Alcaldo. If he thinks I will just sit back and allow him to execute my paladin guard, he is sorely mistaken."

Dorian

With each passing day, the burden of traveling eased. The muscles in his legs no longer ached when they stopped for rest. His lungs no longer burned from the relentless pace of trying to keep up with his human and wild elf companions. His new boots fit much better than his old ones, and his new, looser-fitting pants didn't chafe his inner thighs. On a nightly basis, he trained with Razuul and discovered his skill with a sword increase dramatically with the practice. A kinship grew between him and his travel partners, and he enjoyed their company more each day. Nevertheless, a darkness crept into his heart.

He found himself short-tempered. In their last stay in a small town along their path to Prasillo, a man refused service to a half-blooded mongrel such as himself.

Typically, he ignored the discriminatory words of fools who didn't understand the tribulations of someone born of half-dwarven blood, but this man sparked fury in Dorian. For reasons beyond his understandings, he lashed out at the man, nearly drawing his sword. Luckily, Brett remained level-headed and grabbed Dorian's arm, blocking him from revealing a sword that would have brought more attention to the group than they wanted.

Shadowflame, a sword of Dorian's creation, possessed the combined power of a fire and a darkness runestone. With the sword solely in Dorian's hand, the blade lit with black flames as dark as the midnight sky. In all of his reading, Dorian never found an instance of anyone successfully combining two runestones' power. The drawn sword instantly grabbed the attention of anyone who caught a glimpse of it. With events that unfolded in Dorian's past, allowing anyone to recognize him served as the opposite of a wise decision.

Some time ago, Dorian met a group of friends, the first friends in his life. The group secretly learned and practiced magic at the risk of defying the king's command, a law that meant certain death for those who broke it. Looking for a safe place to study, they stumbled upon the wooded area surrounding Dorian's secluded home.

Besides his father, Dorian had never met another person. His father raised him away from the civilization to avoid the discrimination he would face due to his half-dwarven heritage. Dorian made fast friends with the group, and for a time, he lamented in the pleasure of their friendship. His happiness lasted until the day he met a man that would change his life forever.

Jonas Werner, the king's guard's high commander, hunted the magic-practicing friends down to serve justice to those that broke the law. Accompanied by the elite group known as the Three Heads of Cerberus, the confrontation ended with only Dorian and his friend Elijah surviving the encounter.

On that fateful night, the five inexperienced outlaws battled the four finest warriors in the kingdom. Although Dorian managed to kill one of the Heads, they found themselves wholly outmatched. Two of his friends perished, and another sustained a life-threatening injury. Just as the high commander intended to remove the half-dwarf's head, Dorian's father returned home in time to finish the battle alone. His interference allowed Dorian and Elijah to escape; however, his heroic actions resulted in the dwarven warrior paying the ultimate price. The only family Dorian had ever known died in battle that day, sending his life into a whirlwind of change and uncertainty.

Perhaps the loss of his father left a growing stain on his heart. Maybe his life of seclusion failed to prepare him for the harshness of outside world. Whatever the reason, Dorian found his roiling anger grow with each passing day. Revenge consumed his mind. He couldn't understand how someone as kind, loving, and joyful as his father could die while a despicable man like Jonas Werner walked amongst the living. For the most part, he kept his rage in check, but he feared the consequences of his bursting temper with the most powerful sword ever created gripped in his hand.

The sun peeked through scattered clouds, the rays highlighting the red, orange, and yellow leaves that left behind the vibrant green hues of summer. No bugs swarmed their heads, and the birds sang a sullen song as winter approached. They bought warmer clothing in a previous town, but the crisp air still sent shivers across Dorian's body.

Brett leered at the map in his hands. Looking up from time to time, he pointed in a direction, mumbled something beneath his breath, and returned to scouring the parchment. At the start of the journey, Brett, a career thief, boasted about his vast knowledge of the kingdom's lay of the land. To his credit, he had gotten them far without incident, but now he seemed utterly lost.

"Have you figured it out yet?" Elijah dropped his arms and cocked his head to the side. Since the start, Elijah whined a lot. His upbringing as the child of a well-off family granted him a life of ease and comfort, but it left him ill-prepared for the kingdom's harsh realities of life.

"Do you want to try?" Brett grunted a frustrated tone, shoving the map at Elijah.

"We could just ask the people in that cottage." Razuul pointed to the north.

"What cottage?" Brett and Elijah asked in accord. Following the wild elf's gesture, they spotted the small home.

"Perfect!" Brett exclaimed. "Maybe we can get directions and steal any gold they have hidden."

"You don't have to steal everywhere we go!"

Elijah called out as he chased after Brett.

Dorian hung back, looking up at the smirk on Razuul's face. "How long ago did you notice that cottage?"

"A while back." Razuul chuckled as he watched Brett and Elijah jog down the overgrown path.

Dorian found that he wasn't the only one who changed since the start of their journey. Razuul's harsh, spiteful attitude seemed to lighten. He still snapped at strangers that angered him, but his swords remained sheathed more often. A smirk cracked his face from time to time, and he delighted in teasing his companions...especially Brett. He still bore a great deal of hatred in his heart, but tranquility seemed to grace his attitude.

When the two met, Razuul had just earned his freedom from the fighting arena in Regiis. After decades of living in the arena's dreadful cells, the wild elf fulfilled the requirement of winning fifty straight battles to the death. The final match, a barehanded fight against a dragon, unlocked a power in Razuul that magnified his strength and speed. Using this new-found ability, he ripped the heart from the dragon's chest, earning him the moniker, 'Dragon Fist.' Now, he chased his ambition to find the tribe that slavers stole him at a young age.

"Can you see anyone around the cabin with your elven eyes?" Dorian asked as the two meandered to catch up with Brett and Elijah.

"In the field just beyond the cottage, I see four humans. It looks like they are arguing."

As they drew closer, Dorian saw three men shouting at an old woman as they defensively held their pitchforks, shovels, and hoes. The woman stood with her arms outstretched between the men and a barn as they threw rocks at the closed doors. Elijah and Brett waited for Dorian and Razuul to catch up to them before approaching the heated debate. Before long, the squabble reached Dorian's ears.

"Get out of the way, hag!" The first man jabbed his pitchfork at the air.

"That thing must die!" The second man wound up and threw a rock that bounced harmlessly off the barn doors.

The third man drove his shovel into the ground. "The king's guard will hear of this!"

Strands of gray hair escaped the bun at the nape of

the elderly woman's neck. Dirt and holes riddled her clothes. The hunch of her back, leathery skin, and gnarled fingers showed signs of many years of farm work. Worn, rust-covered tools littered the ground behind her, providing evidence that her financial situation matched the state of her equipment. "Just leave us alone! He's never hurt anyone, and he never will!"

"I see an opportunity here," Brett said with raised eyebrows and a gleam in his eye.

"Here we go again." Elijah rolled his eyes as he followed Brett.

"Gentlemen! What seems to be the problem here?" Brett asked with arms stretched as wide as his smile.

"Who are you?" One of the men demanded.

"Me? I'm just a traveler, roaming the kingdom to help those in need. My compatriots and I heard your quarrel and merely wish to see if we can provide help to settle this disagreement." Brett put his arm around the man's shoulders. Using his other hand, Dorian saw him pick something from the man's pocket.

"You best leave here, stranger." The woman snarked. "You have no idea what you're getting yourself into."

"That woman keeps a beast! If we don't kill it, it's going to kill us all!"

"Beast? Where could she possibly keep a beast?" Brett released the first man to address the second.

"Right there, in that barn." The man pointed at the barn with the handle of the hoe, allowing Brett the opportunity to snatch something from his pocket as well.

"He'd never hurt a fly, and you all know it!" The woman shouted.

"You don't know that!" The third man bent over to pick up a rock.

"Now, now," Brett grabbed the man's hand to pretend he wanted to stop the man from throwing the rock while slipping something from his pocket as well, "let's not get carried away."

The first man picked up a stone and whipped it at the woman, bouncing it off her head. Covering an open wound with her hands, she collapsed to her knees.

A deep-voiced shout burst from the barn. "Mama!" Within an instant, a twenty-stone-tall cyclops burst through the barn doors, splintering them from the hinges.

The beast rushed at the men. Each stomp of the goliath's foot rattled the ground. The men froze in place, shivering in fear. Raising its fists in the air, the cyclops quickly, yet gently, brought them down and hunched over his apparent mother to protect her from further harm.

The cyclops's sudden appearance startled Dorian. Grasping Shadowflame, he started to draw the blade, but Razuul stopped his hand by grabbing his wrist while keeping his eyes fixated on the beast.

Dorian instantly knew why Razuul stopped him. During the wild elf's final match in the arena, he unlocked a power that included the ability to see a person's essence. When he used this skill, no living being could hide their true nature from him.

The men scattered like cockroaches. Elijah ran back to the cottage while Brett stared slack-jawed. Dorian just watched. He felt neither fear nor instinct to run and hide, just an overwhelming indifference to the situation. Whether Razuul's calm reaction or his own self-loathing caused his lack of concern, he did not know.

Razuul strolled toward the colossal monster. Placing his hand on its hulking shoulder, he looked less than a toddler compared to the mountainous cyclops. "They're gone. You don't have to protect her anymore."

The cyclops lifted his head. A single horn protruded above the lone eye that seeped tears. "Gone?" The cyclops repeated.

"I'm alright, Njal!" the woman's voice muffled beneath the monster's immense frame.

The cyclops stood. The woman looked up at Razuul, squinting her eyes from the blinding sun. "You're still here. I expected everyone to run off once they caught sight of Njal."

"It's as you said," Razuul folded his arms. "He wouldn't hurt a fly."

"Well," the elderly farmhand brushed dirt from her clothes, "I doubt too many people would take my word for it, but I thank you." The woman looked around at the group of visitors. "I see I'm not the only one that keeps strange company. Might even be even stranger than an old woman caring for a cyclops. Wild elves never travel without their tribe."

"You find that stranger?" Dorian asked as he approached and stood next to Razuul.

"Well, maybe not stranger." The woman released a raspy laugh. "So, are you lot hungry? I have stew cooking. You're more than welcome to have some if you'd like."

"Yes!" Brett broke from his bewilderment as soon as

he heard someone offering something for free.

"The name's Thyra. Looks like we both have an interesting story to tell. Come on, Njal; let's fix these nice men some supper."

"Mama." The cyclops uttered as he followed his mother home.

Marius

Marius hung from shackles inside a cell. His body, weakened from lack of food and rest, no longer held the energy to fight against his restraints or call out in demand for answers. None of the beast races that took over his home city of Baxis visited the prison. This surprised him as he expected interrogation about how he snuck into the city's castle while avoiding detection. His eyes and head repeatedly drooped, only to snap back as his mind dwelled on the rest of the citizens' fate. During his infiltration, he saw no clues to their whereabouts and no signs that they either fled or fell victim to the invading force. Licking his dry, cracked lips with his parched tongue, he prayed to the gods that they had escaped, especially the love of his life, Richard.

In his capacity as the high commander of the Baxis guard, Marius saw many criminals thrown into the dungeon, but he never experienced prison in such a state. No lanterns lit the pitch room, and no cries for attention bounced off the thick, musty stone walls. Aside from the occasional rat or random insect, he remained the only living being to occupy one of the fifty cells that snaked across the area.

A light emerged from the top of the stairs, followed by the clip-clop of hooves. Soon, a centaur holding a lantern appeared before the iron bars. "Are you the one named Marius Vybian?"

The horse half of his body twitched as his tail whipped at his hindquarters. In the style of the common Baxis citizen, a tunic covered his human half, signaling his recent theft of a nearby clothier in the city he attacked. His brown hair hung in waves below his shoulders, and his thick beard spread like the outstretched wings of a bird, resting just below his neckline.

"Where is everyone? What have you done with my people?" Marius refused to answer any questions until he got answers to his own.

"I should have expected such a response. Allow

me to introduce myself first. My name is Thomanthus. I am second-in-command and younger brother to the centaur leader, Poseas."

"Where are my people?" Marius knew the centaur expected an introduction in return, but he refused to allow any pleasantries.

"I understand. You were not here when my brethren and I arrived, so this all must be very confusing to you. I assure you, though, if we can have a polite conversation…"

"Stop trying to be my friend!" Marius spat. "Your interrogation method won't work on me. I'm not going to tell you anything until I know where my people are!"

"Interrogation? You are misunderstanding. You hold no information that I desire." Thomanthus smiled at Marius.

"Then why come down here? Why talk to me at all?"

"Because I have a request, two requests, actually."

"Why would I oblige any requests from the beasts that stole my home?"

Thomanthus cringed. "There's that word again, beast. I will never understand why you humans assigned us this name. We are just as capable of thought and speech as any elf, dwarf, or human. And I assure you, I know exactly how it feels to lose your home."

"We call you beasts because that is how you act! Look at this. The city is in shambles! The hopes, dreams, and desires of thousands are crushed because of your actions. How many can never return home? How many became separated from loved ones they will never see again? This is the way of the beasts! Take, hurt, maim and destroy everything that does not belong to them, all for their own fulfillment. The realm has enjoyed twenty-five years of peace since the lot of you were removed, and now you return just to show how right the king was in excommunicating all of you!"

Thomanthus looked at the floor with narrowed eyes. Beneath his beard, Marius saw his lips purse between deep breaths. "I can see this conversation will get us nowhere. I believe we can compromise about your people, though."

"Where are they?"

"That I cannot tell you, but what I can tell you is they are safe. Food, water, and shelter are provided for them, and no one has been harmed."

"Liar!" Marius shouted. "There is no way you could have gotten into the city without harming anyone. Where were the guards? How did you get into the port without ships? None of this makes sense!"

"That is where the first of my requests comes into play. I simply wish for you to hear my story."

"What of the second request?"

"You will only understand that after you have heard what I have to say."

"Fine. Get on with it. It's not like I could have stopped you anyway." Marius shook his chain restraints.

"True, but in order for you to understand, I need you to have your ears open, as well as your mind." Thomanthus opened the cell door and poured water from a leather skin into Marius's mouth.

Marius guzzled the cool liquid, choking from drinking too fast. "You talk way too much. Do you know that?"

"I have been told." Thomanthus grinned. "My story begins shortly after what you humans call the Beast Wars."

Marius rolled his eyes with an audible sigh. "Great. This should be a short story."

Ignoring the comment, Thomanthus began. "After being exiled to the Allium continent, my people found true desolation of the land there. Sand replaced the once-fertile soil. The few plants that existed were either poisonous, covered in thorns, or inedible. Tornadoes ripped across the horizon during the day while raging thunderstorms poured upon us at night. The only option for us was to escape west in hopes of finding refuge from the inhabitable conditions, and so we did.

"I was but a young foal at the time, barely past the age of ten, but I remember it like it was yesterday. Both my parents died during the war, leaving my older brother to inherit the chief's title before he came of age. With few options, he banded together with the leaders of the other races. Centaurs, orcs, trolls, cyclops, minotaurs, and knolls all marched across the desert together. We hunted together, leaning on each of the races' strengths, and gathered what little we could find. However, with each passing day, the conditions worsened, and the alliance weakened.

"The elderly, no longer stable enough to make the harrowing journey, died at an alarming rate. Children, lacking the constitution and resistance to disease, fell ill

51

and perished. Even healthy adults fell prey to the unpredictable weather and deadly creatures that hunted the desolate lands. All the death shook the foundation of the alliance, and soon, certain members began to question how much the other races actually contributed to their survival.

"The centaurs, with their natural muscular physique, pulled the carts that housed our sick and the dwindling food supply, which eventually became one in the same. The knolls found large insects in crevices and caves that served as food for the weary. The orcs, trolls, minotaurs, and cyclops fought off the predators with their superior might and prowess. Each race contributed to our survival, yet arguments erupted about how much more work one race contributed than the other.

"All the while, I watched as my brother gallantly kept the peace, brokering agreements, dividing supplies, and settling disagreements like a leader well beyond his years, but even he couldn't keep up the façade.

"At night, he spoke to me. I saw the man I admired more than anyone turn into someone I barely recognized. The problems he faced, the adversities he overcame, and the blockades he trampled wore on his soul. His mind twisted into hatred for those that forced us into this situation. He screamed his repulsions for the humans, dwarves, and elves. He swore vengeance upon all those in Preclarium, and soon the focus he devoted to keeping his people alive shifted to the intense hatred he bore.

"Instead of settling disagreements, he instigated fights. Instead of comforting those in need, he lashed out, threatening to leave the decrepit behind. I attempted to mend what relationships I could, but I lacked the charismatic charm and confident demeanor of my brother. I knew that soon the shaky alliance would shatter, and none of us would survive the battle that would surely ensue.

"One day, everything changed. As we crossed into the northwestern section of the continent, we stumbled upon something extraordinary. A group of four-armed beings covered in fur guarded an oasis at the foot of a mountain. We attempted to contact the strange beings in hopes of attaining food and shelter, but each time we approached, they attacked us, repeating a single word...*guard.*

"The night after finding these creatures, the

leaders of the races met. As our chief's brother, they allowed me to sit and listen to their meeting, but I was forbidden from contributing. Together, they planned to eliminate the four-armed beings and take the land as their own. The four-armed creatures seemed like mighty, capable warriors but didn't appear to have the numbers to stop us. It seemed wrong, and I wanted to voice my opinion of trying another way, but I knew that my brother would not even try to save me if I spoke out of turn.

"Luckily, it never came to pass. Before the meeting concluded, a female group of the peculiar creatures approached our encampment. Their appearance significantly differed from those of the guardians we met. They stood upright instead of hunched over like their male counterparts. Their eyes lacked the soulless gaze, and elaborate clothing adorned their bodies instead of a single shard of cloth.

"We soon discovered the nature of the beings known as the quarm, as they communicated with us using their minds. The quarm's society differed greatly from any that ever lived here in Preclarium. The males of their species were born mindless, only capable of a single thought that a female must psychically place. If a female implanted a thought to walk, the male would walk to the end of the land and into the ocean without a single instinct to preserve its life. If a female implanted the thought to guard, the male would guard without any consideration as to the intentions of visitors.

"Their leader told us their story using words and pictures she painted in our minds. She informed us of their own plight after explaining why the males refused us entry. Even though they inhabited the only section of land left that could sustain life, their species were dying.

"The quarm reproduce by laying eggs like a bird. Unlike their avian counterparts, quarm eggs did not require heat to incubate and hatch. Quite the opposite, actually. Quarm eggs hatch by placing them in the snow and ice. With the ever-changing climate of Allium, very little snow and ice remained, even at the top of the lone mountain that remained standing after the devastating incident turned the continent desolate.

"That is how we befriended the quarm. They had never heard of the runestones. The centaurs and a few elder orcs possessed the power of the runestones, and luckily, a few mages remained with water runestones. Thus, a deal was made: our mages would freeze their caves with ice spells while they shared their land and resources."

"I met them, the males at least," Marius added.

"So you are paying attention. Good! The story nears its end."

"I cut one of them with my dagger. The dagger has the Decay spell imbued on it. It should have instantly killed the thing, but it seemed immune to the magic."

"We discovered the same thing. It was unlike anything we ever experienced. The cyclops, minotaurs, and trolls lack the intelligence to trace out a runic symbol properly. The orcs prefer to test their bodies' strength and consider using runestones dishonorable except for the elderly shaman that live to reach an advanced age. The knolls despise all things magic and avoid anyone using runestones. However, all of them hold a connection to the magical ability. Only culture and lack of higher brain function keep them from performing magic, but the quarm seemed to lack even the power's basic connection. We couldn't get a runestone to connect to their skin, and healing magic couldn't heal the shallowest of wounds. Luckily, freezing an enclosed space still allowed the eggs to incubate, but none of our limited magic seemed useful to them otherwise."

"How did you get them to come along with you?"

"I'm getting there. I know it is a long tale, but be patient for a bit longer." Thomanthus scratched at his beard.

"For years, we lived in harmony. The orcs loved sparring with the quarm. Their hardy constitution provided a worthy outlet for the tusked warriors to release their pent-up aggression. The trolls bore holes into the mountain, creating new homes for themselves. The knolls and minotaurs who thrive in darkness settled in uninhabited caves. The knolls explored the mountain's cracks and crevices with their compressible bodies, discovering an underground river that provided fresh water to all. The centaurs taught farming techniques that provided fresh fruits and vegetables. The cyclops moved heavy boulders to create a defensive wall that protected us if anyone ever found our haven. We came to know our new home as Paradise, and our new civilization prospered.

"Then a single man changed everything. I'll never forget the day Karl Richter showed up in Paradise. I was teaching the pan flute to a small group of centaurs, female quarm, and even a few orc children, as I always did in the afternoon. Surrounded by a small army of skeletons, he passed through our makeshift defenses with ease. I gathered the children behind me, trying to keep them protected, but he summoned cages of bone around each child. I charged at him, demanding he set the children free, but I proved no match for the necromancer. I soon found myself in the same predicament as the children in my care."

"Richter? I know this name, although not Karl. The Richters have served as lord of province in Tenebris for centuries, but I have never heard of him."

"Yes, he is the son of a previous lord in Tenebris that was executed for treason during the war."

"Walter Richter? I didn't know he had any children." Marius racked his brain. Walter Richter's execution barely registered in his memory. Tenebris held little significance in his life, so he mostly ignored any news or rumors that the province provided.

"I do not know his family history. I only know the things he told my brother. It is of little consequence. Allow me to get back to my story." Thomanthus peered up the staircase, leaning his ear to ensure no one eavesdropped on the conversation.

"He told me he intended no harm to any of my people and that he only wished to speak with our leaders. He promised that no harm would come to the children, as long as no harm came to him.

"I saw no other option. We walked into our Paradise, surrounded on all sides by skeletons holding knives to the children's throats. The looks of the horrified denizens still haunt my nightmares to this day. All the while, Karl Richter smiled, as if he were proud of his loathsome plan to infiltrate our beloved new home.

"When we found my brother, he demanded the children be set free, but Karl Richter refused. He insisted he be granted an audience with every race's leader, promising to release the children once they heard his words.

"Poseas found himself in the same predicament as me. Despite his rage and frustration, my brother cares for his people. And although he sometimes makes poor decisions through his anger, his heart always burns with the love of his brethren. So, he granted Karl Richter's request.

"I wasn't allowed in the meeting. They adjourned

into the over-sized tent, leaving me outside to attempt to dampen the fears of the terrified children. I don't know exactly what happened in that tent. I could hear the screams of the infuriated orc leader Burrmogg. The yips and yelps of Inhurk, the knoll leader, the grunts of Durbur, the minotaur leader, flowed together. The desperate pleas of Hanthua, the leader of the quarm, accidentally leaped into the minds of all the surrounding citizens."

"What of the trolls and cyclops? Did they not care enough to attend?" Marius decided to use this opportunity. He cared little for Thomanthus's story, but every bit of intelligence he gathered on his enemy could prove useful in the future.

"The trolls and cyclops's limited intelligence leaves them with little care or understanding for our tribe's doings. We provide them with food and shelter; in return, they are more than happy to assist with their absurd strength."

"Tribe?" Marius raised a brow.

"Hmm, yes, I suppose it is. Although, until now, I have never referred to the other races as part of my people, I do care for them as much as my centaur brethren." Thomanthus paused for a moment to consider his words before continuing. "After a while, the shouting ceased. They couldn't have been in the tent for more than fifteen minutes when they emerged, all bearing smiles.

"Instantly, Karl Richter released the children, allowing them to run to their parents. I expected my brother to announce an execution. How could a human dare to enter our home and expect to live? Instead, my brother announced that we would return to Preclarium under the shadow of war. I couldn't understand it. The war in Preclarium ended years ago, and the horror still lingered in every mind of those old enough to remember.

"That night, I spoke to my brother. I asked him how he could have allowed a human to brainwash him into fighting another war. In return, he lashed out at me. He said he knew better than I did. He insisted that in our present home, food supplies ran thin. He lamented about unpredictable weather plaguing our people and the lack of space needed to ensure our population grew. He shouted, berated, and threatened me with each opposing word I returned, insisting he knew the best course of action for the centaur race, but I knew the truth. Hatred once again swayed his decisions.

"Karl Richter presented a method to return and re-take our old home. He told my brother and the other leaders that he procured several ships to carry us and discovered a means of safe passage onto the continent. He promised that other lords would side with us as they felt displeased with the rule of the current king."

Marius scoffed. "And your foolish leaders believed that? Since the war, Preclarium has known only peace and prosperity. Only a buffoon would fall for such drivel."

"I agree. The notion that any human would side with us seemed idiotic and arrogant, but the wounds of battle and loss run deep. The war wounded our leaders' pride, and the loss of loved ones planted deep-rooted hatred that no shovel could dig out. Such rage can blind a person to common sense, allowing one to accept the unacceptable. However, some truth existed in Karl Richter's words. We were able to take over your city without raising a single sword or firing a single arrow."

"Yes, this is the part of the story that holds my interest. How did you manage to occupy this city, and where are the citizens?" Marius rose to his feet. He listened to this entire story, but only this part truly mattered to him.

"I do not know how Karl Richter accomplished such a feat. All I know is that when we got here, the only human remaining in the city was Eric Hardwood. He greeted us at the edge of the city with smiles and open arms."

"Lord Hardwood let you in?" Things began to make sense to Marius. Lord Hardwood insisted that Marius go to the Shattered Islands for his mother's funeral. The despicable lord even paid for the trip. He knew that he couldn't have allowed this invasion with Marius in the city. He still didn't know how the citizens disappeared, and he couldn't imagine the people voluntarily leaving if they knew the beast races would soon occupy their homes.

Marius pushed these thoughts to the back of his mind. While he visited his mother's final resting place, an assassin tried to take his life. Marius already assumed his own lord hired the killer. With his mother's death conveniently occurring during a time when Hardwood needed him out of the city, the Baxis High Commander could only conclude that Hardwood hired an assassin to kill his mother.

"That treasonous bastard! I'll kill him!" Marius growled through gritted teeth. "Why would he do this? Where is he? Where are my people?"

"Lord Hardwood dwells with his family in his chambers. Why he would do this is a mystery to me. I am told he expects some sort of compensation after we win the war. As for the rest of your people, I do know where they are; however, I will hold that secret for now."

"Why tell me any of this? I am your prisoner. I imagine someone will be along to execute me once they have starved me enough to ensure I can't fight back."

"Because I intend to set you free."

Marius stood slack-jawed. "Why would you do that?"

"My brother's judgment may be clouded by rage, but mine is not. We must stop this war before it begins, or thousands, possibly more, will die. I will return your weapon and escort you out of the city. All I ask in return is that you report the situation to your king. Surround this city with a force that we would have no chance of defeating. If my brother and the other leaders see an undefeatable army, perhaps they will see reason and return to Paradise. I've seen enough death and destruction. If I can prevent any further bloodshed from occurring, I must take the chance."

"If your deception is discovered, they'll certainly kill you. You know this, don't you?"

"I am willing to pay that price. If my life prevents the loss of thousands more, it is more than acceptable."

Thomanthus reached into a bag hanging from his horse-half, pulled out a loaf of bread and a canteen, and tossed them to Marius's feet. "That is to ensure you have the strength to at least make it out of the city. I should be able to keep anyone from visiting you, but for safety's sake, eat and drink as fast as you can. Make sure to sit on the canteen to hide its presence when you are finished. I will return tonight."

Jonas

Jonas sat atop his galleon. His home city of Regiis sprawled out before him as he approached the gate. He could hear the prince's amplified voice through the drawn portcullis, although he couldn't make out the words. The dull roar of a crowd hummed through the autumn air, and the gate guards focused their attention on the commotion ensuing within the city. This would typically infuriate him as the city's high commander, but even his soldiers' negligence could not release him from his dwelling thoughts.

He left the city to investigate the ancient kymarian ruins in the south to fulfill a dying wish for his friend,

Simon Oxbridge. While there, he found evidence that the crown prince of Preclarium discovered plans to create a powerful weapon. A weapon with the potential to send the kingdom to ruin, or at least that's what he assumed. Written in the dead language of the kymarians, he could not decipher the device's plans. Although the diagrams gave him clues about the weapon's capabilities, he couldn't go to the king with conjecture. He needed solid evidence, and only decoding the text could produce the proof he needed. He knew one person who could translate the text, but speaking with him without detection would prove a difficult task.

The death of Simon Oxbridge weighed heavily on the high commander. The man served as a surrogate father of sorts to Jonas, and the last person remaining he called 'friend.' During the Beast Wars, he and a group of friends fought countless battles together. It was the most difficult time in his life, yet produced some of his fondest memories. The group built a prestigious reputation through many victories, but glory played no part in his endearment to their time together. He cherished the bond they formed. Back then, he thought nothing could ever drive them apart, but life's twists and turns proved him wrong.

Jonas thought of his old friends far more often than he would ever admit. At the beginning of their time together, every group member possessed years of battle experience, except Jonas. He'd only recently completed his death knight training. Prior to their meeting, Jonas's life consisted of little more than study and training. Even though the others already earned glory and accolations for their battle prowess, they treated Jonas as an equal. Over the years they spent together, their camaraderie grew. He felt nothing could separate the group, yet everything changed the day he accepted the high commander position in Regiis.

His friends abandoned him. Everyone, including himself, expected the king to select the leader of their group for the position. To everyone's surprise, King Thomas chose Jonas instead. He tried to explain the circumstances that led to him accepting the king's offer to his friends, but none of them listened. Each one looked at him with disappointed eyes and soon ended contact with him. Only Simon remained loyal, and the pain of his loss left a void in his heart, an emptiness that threatened to drive him to the madness that often consumed the death knight. Luckily, the love he felt for his wife and child kept him grounded.

"Soldiers!" Jonas shouted, startling and grabbing their attention.

"High Commander!" One of the men returned with the customary fist-to-chest salute, while the other fumbled to secure his helmet before showing the same respect.

"What is going on here? Why are you negligent in your duties?" Jonas's interrogation shook the trembling guards.

"Our apologies, High Commander." One of the guards began. "The prince is holding a public execution in the square."

"What? That isn't…" Jonas stopped himself for fear of sounding disrespectful to the prince. Dismounting from his horse, he jutted the reigns forward. "Here! Take my horse to the stables."

The man saluted his acknowledgment of orders. Jonas didn't bother returning the gesture. Marching to the square, he found the packed onlookers standing on their toes to catch a glimpse. "Move!" He shouted as he barreled through the gathering.

Normally, his mere presence parted any crowd

like a ship cutting through the sea, but without wearing his usual skull-covered black armor, the citizens failed to recognize him. Above the crowd, he saw the prince standing atop a newly constructed stage at the center of the square, flanked on either side by two men in torturous positions. The prince spoke into a wind-runestone-powered amplification device as the citizens watched the spectacle.

"That is why I must do this." The prince announced. "I take no joy in executing our own people, but they have disobeyed our laws, and in doing so, betrayed the crown."

The display on stage sickened Jonas. The first man sat in a chair with nails driven through each of his hands and into the armrests. Next to him, a stout man stood hunched over in stocks with wooden reeds pounded beneath his fingernails. On the other side of the prince, two wooden planks pressed against the temples of a man strapped to a vertical standing table, squeezing his head with metal screws. Jonas didn't recognize the tortured citizens, except for the last man.

Ballard Grey, a local drunkard, attempted to scream through his sewn-shut lips. His chained arms and legs dangled outside a suspended cage, and iron spikes pierced the space between his ribs. Jonas never directly dealt with Ballard, but he knew the stories. Many nights, Ballard slept off his drunken stupor in the cells. He routinely caused a ruckus late at night, shouting and screaming as he stumbled down the streets. While his foul mouth earned him many beatings from other tavern patrons, he never actually hurt anyone other than himself, to Jonas's knowledge.

"Today," the prince continued his announcement, "we set an important example. As your future king, I must show you all that your safety is my prime concern. These men here have threatened the basic desire to live a peaceful existence. They will pay the ultimate price, but their sacrifice shall not go in vain. They will serve as a reminder to any of those who are tempted to cause harm to my citizens. I deplore you to see this as an opportunity," Prince Godwin turned to the tortured men, "an opportunity to transform your wretched lives and serve your kingdom in a way no other could match. Your death shall hinder the temptation of many criminals and save countless lives!"

The crowd erupted. Jonas couldn't believe the

people fell for such nonsense. He couldn't understand how no one could see this act as anything other than a demented man flexing his authority. The sight of blood and gore never bothered the high commander, but Price Godwin's vain and unnecessary declaration of control turned his stomach.

Every fiber of Jonas' being screamed for him to go to the king. He wanted an explanation. For twenty-five years Jonas served under Thomas Magicent, and during that tenure, he never saw the king allow such atrocities aimed at his people. King Thomas ruled with a firm hand but never an iron fist.

Jonas knew that addressing the prince's treatment of the citizens would have to wait. He couldn't afford to waste any more time, ensuring that the information about the ancient kymarian weapon took precedence. He knew no one should have the kind of power that could destroy a kingdom, especially a vindictive demon like the prince.

So far, the king turned a blind eye to the prince's actions, choosing instead to allow him to conduct savage tortures and cruel executions. Jonas could see only one option before him. He must provide a situation the king could not ignore, or his son would rule over a kingdom of corpses and ash.

Jonas continued pushing through the crowd until a hand grabbed his shoulder from behind. Gripping his sword, he twirled around to see a familiar face. Paul Cormac, a member of the elite guard under his command, named the Three Heads of Cerberus, stood with a concerned look upon his face. His bald scalp gleamed in the mid-day sun nearly as much as the fire runestone in his eye socket. "High Commander, I am so glad you've returned." His pointed beard twitched with each spoken word.

"Cormac, I'm glad to see you. Is this the first execution the prince has committed since my departure?"

"Yes, but he said he intends to execute criminals every day until the cells are empty."

"This is madness. The cells only hold those who commit petty thefts and minor infractions. The arena takes care of the murderers and rapists."

"He said he intends to eliminate all crime within the kingdom, and anyone who defies the laws of the kingdom has therefore committed treason against the crown, but that's not why I wanted to talk to you." Cormac leaned in so Jonas could hear him above the roar of the surrounding crowd. "Did you hear about his new law?"

"New law? No, what is it?"

"He said when he inherits the crown, he intends to outlaw the use of runestones for anyone outside the royal family."

"What?" Jonas indignantly shouted, grabbing the attention of the citizens surrounding them. Finding a nearby empty alleyway for privacy, he looked back at Cormac. "Follow me."

Storming into the alleyway, several feral cats scurried away before he turned to face the trailing Head of Cerberus. "Outlaw the runestones? Are you sure that's what you heard?"

"Yes. He even intends to take them away from the nobles."

"The nobles will never accept that. They will undoubtedly go to war before giving up their source of magic." Jonas stroked the darkness runestone embedded on his chest.

"My thoughts exactly."

"What of the king? Surely his council has attempted to speak with him about this."

"The king has locked himself in his chambers. He refuses to allow anyone to enter. You must speak to him. You must convince him to stop this insanity!"

"The king has never listened to me before, I doubt he will take parental advice from me now, but I will try. There is someone I need to speak to first, and I could use your help."

Cormac cocked an eyebrow at Jonas. "Help how?"

"I need to speak with a prisoner in the cells, and I'd rather the guards not know who it is. I need you to distract the guard so I can sneak in."

"Who do you need to speak to in the cells?"

"The less you know, the better. Right now, I ask you to trust me. This is not an order; it's a request."

Cormac paused. Of the two remaining members of the Three Heads of Cerberus, Jonas only trusted the runestone-eyed warrior. Cormac served under Jonas for over a decade and never once failed to follow orders during that time. The two men weren't close, but they shared mutual respect as brothers-in-arms.

Cormac took a quick glance over each shoulder. "Alright, I trust you. I hope you know what you're doing."

"One more thing. I'll need the keys to the cells."

"That might be asking a bit much."

"I know, but I cannot understate the importance of this mission. I must speak with this prisoner."

Cormac ran his hand over his sweaty dome as he pursed his lips. "Fine, but remember, you owe me one."

"Thank you, Cormac."

The two snaked through the city streets until they arrived at the dungeon entrance. Standing in front of the wooden door, Cormac turned to Jonas. "Which direction do you need to go?"

"Left."

"Ah, that's who you need to speak with." Cormac gave Jonas a knowing smile.

"You know nothing." Jonas glared at Cormac.

"Yes, of course. Stay hidden. You'll know when it's safe."

Jonas put his back to the wall. Cormac opened the door and entered the dungeon. Immediately, the pleas and cries of the prisoners poured out the open portal. Each voice begged for freedom or mercy. The news of the prince's intention to execute all criminals reached their ears, and all of them feared their inevitable fate.

"Guard!" Cormac's voice rang out. "What is going on in here? These prisoners are disturbing the prince's announcements! Why aren't you keeping them under control? Perhaps you need to join them!"

"C-Cormac, s-s-sir! I-I..."

"Shut up! Come with me! I'll teach you how to keep prisoners quiet!" The rattle of keys rang. "What are you doing? What if one of the prisoners grabs those keys and escapes? Did no one teach you how to guard prisoners? Leave them on the hook, and follow me. Now!"

Jonas took that as Cormac's sign. He waited for a moment, then peered into the dungeon. Seeing no signs of any other guards, he crept into the dank corridor.

As expected, the dungeon keys remained on the hook behind the guard's table. Grabbing them, Jonas proceeded to his destination.

Prisoners reached through the bars as he passed, each hand wildly grasping at the air. Every captive begged for mercy, telling their sob stories. Some cried out of concern for their family; others lamented their innocence after their mistaken identity for their charged crimes. Jonas ignored each plea. Searching every prisoner, he soon found one with the body and stature he required.

Opening the cell, Jonas stepped in and grabbed the young man by the throat. "It's your lucky day. You're coming with me." Releasing the young man, he drew his sword and placed the tip at his stomach. "Move."

"H-high c-c-commander! W-what's going on?" The young man stammered.

Jonas struck the prisoner hard across his face with an open hand. "I didn't give you permission to speak." He threw the young man from his cell and placed the tip of his sword at his back. "Move!"

At the end of the hall, Jonas guided the young man down the stairs. The lower level of the dungeon held the worst criminals in the kingdom. The prisoners here only stayed until torture forced them to relinquish desired information or until their wounds healed enough to be transferred to the arena. Each prisoner resided in their own windowless cell. This blocked the prisoners from seeing the torture the others received, thus leaving their imagination to run wild as they listened to pained screams. Only criminals with injuries too severe to provide an entertaining fight stayed here permanently.

However, the starvation and beatings they received from the guards persuaded them to wish for an end as quick as an arena death.

Arriving at his intended cell, Jonas opened the door and shoved the young man inside, knocking him onto the damp stone floor. Locking the door behind him, he turned to the cell's inhabitant and pulled several folded parchment pieces from the pouch on his belt. The papers contained recreations of the diagram he saw in the kymarian ruins. His depictions didn't match the mural perfectly as he lacked the original artist's skill. Still, he knew his drawings would allow a person familiar with the kymarian dialect to decipher the code.

Jonas knew the person inside the cell possessed such knowledge. Months ago, he arrested this young man for illegally learning magic with a group of four friends in the woods outside the city. Runestones of differing elements imbued to each of them, except for the fifth member who possessed a sword that proved the extent of the group's intensive research into magic. The blade belonged to a young mul named Dorian Kinsman, the son of his former friend Thane who died at Jonas' hand. With two runestones imbued, it combined the power of a darkness and a fire runestone, a feat previously thought of as impossible. The group resisted, but in the end, they proved no match for Jonas and the Three Heads of Cerberus. After dispatching two of the criminals, the mul escaped with an insignificant group member in tow, leaving their severely injured leader behind. Jonas searched the wreckage of the battle and discovered several books written in kymarian with writing in common tongue along the borders used to interpret the ancient language.

Tossing the parchment to the prisoner's feet, Jonas pointed his sword at the cell's occupant. "Nathaniel Liber, I need your help."

Razuul

Razuul awoke with a startle. Sweat covered his body from the nightmares of his past flashing in his mind. No matter how many times the visions haunted him, he couldn't grow accustomed to the horrors. At night, his mind forced him to relive the sorrow, death, and torture. One night, he nearly snapped Brett's neck after being awoken during a particularly disturbing dream. The others asked him about the terrors he saw while he slept, but Razuul refused to allow anyone to know the turmoil that boiled beneath the surface of his tough exterior.

Running his fingers through his long, black hair,

Razuul let loose a deep sigh. He looked around the room of the small cabin to ensure he hadn't disturbed his sleeping companions. Dorian slept peacefully. Elijah hadn't returned yet from getting supplies from the nearby town. He searched for Brett but found no sign of the thief. Assuming the ruffian wandered out to find a place to relieve himself, he wrapped his blanket around his shoulders and exited the cabin to sit in the cool night air.

Razuul sat upon the cabin's porch and stared into the starless sky. The songs of thousands of crickets filled his ears, and the random snap of a twig signaled the presence of nocturnal animals searching for their nightly meal.

He thought about their current host, Thyra. Apparently, during the Beast Wars, the old woman lost her husband and both of her young sons. A raid by the king's army drove a pack of cyclopes from their cavernous dwelling, leaving them desperate to find food and shelter. At the time, the elderly lady lived in a small town near the Cientia mountains. The monstrous beasts ran through their town, destroying and eating everything in their path, including the villagers. During the attack, Thyra's home collapsed on top of her, knocking her unconscious. By the time she woke and clawed out from the rubble, the cyclops moved on to find their next prey. Few of the town's inhabitants survived the raid, and she never found her family's bodies.

Near the end of her desperate search, she discovered a juvenile cyclops left behind. The child cowered inside a dilapidated barn outside the small town with its legs folded to its chest. Thyra immediately raised the kitchen knife she'd found during her search but stopped her vengeful blow upon peering into the child's weeping eye.

Compared to the savagery of the other cyclops, something seemed different about the child. The distant gaze of his eye conveyed a lack of understanding of his situation. Looking around the barn, he barely noticed the threat before him. Even for the simple-minded cyclops race, the child appeared to have a feeble intellect.

At that realization, Thyra dropped her knife and decided to raise the cyclops child as her own. She knew she used the child as a distraction from the grief of losing her family, but she didn't care. Moving away from civilization, she raised her child in a home far away from judgmental eyes.

Thyra's story further fueled Razuul's hatred toward the king's guard. Although the cyclops destroyed the old woman's family, the human soldiers' actions resulted in the attack.

Razuul closed his eyes, slipping into his enhanced state. The nearby insects sparked with life-energy as they drank droplets of water from blades of grass. He sensed an owl as it sat in a tree, searching for a mouse to devour. Woodland creatures radiated from every direction, but the presence of one animal caught his attention in a different way.

The small presence felt odd, like a flame amongst a field of ice. Its non-threatening aura felt strange, as though it didn't belong in the natural order of life. With each passing moment, the presence grew brighter until it's the little flame burned with radiating heat. Opening his eyes, he found an unexpected creature standing before him.

The raccoon cocked its head to the side. Razuul habitually rested his hands on the handles of his swords, but he knew he wouldn't need them. The raccoon's life-energy gave off a similar presence as Dorian's sword, but without the ominous essence of death that permeated from the magical blade. Heat didn't describe the raccoon's presence accurately. It resembled heat without warmth, light without glow. The small animal kept Razuul's curiosity fixed upon it until the door opening behind him grabbed his attention. Razuul turned to see Dorian exiting the cabin.

"Does this raccoon look strange to you?" Razuul pointed to the small animal.

"What raccoon?" Dorian yawned, stretching his arms out with his blanket gripped in each hand.

Razuul returned his gaze to where he last saw the raccoon to find no trace of the woodland creature.

"Are you alright? You were talking in your sleep again." Dorian sat next to Razuul, clasping his blanket around his shoulders.

"Oh, that. Yes, I'm fine."

"You want to talk about it?"

"No."

The two sat in silence. Razuul appreciated Dorian not pressing him to explain. Anger, rage, and hatred served as the only feelings he felt comfortable expressing. Even happiness and joy left him feeling a bit awkward, let alone fear and anxiety.

"You know," Dorian began, "sometimes I have trouble sleeping. Most nights, when I close my eyes, I see my father. Sometimes he is smiling or laughing as he drinks his ale. Sometimes he's yelling at me for some mistake I made working away in the forge, but every dream ends the same. A sword stabs him, and I have to watch him die all over again. Sometimes it's in his back, sometimes it's in his belly, but it's always Jonas Werner holding the blade.

"It hurts, you know? My father was a grumpy old dwarf, but he was also kind and loving. Sometimes I'll think I heard him laugh or heard him groan the way he always did when he stood. Every time I turn, expecting to see him standing there, but I'm always disappointed. That's when it hits me the worst. That's when I realize that he'll never tell me I need to put down the book and pick up the hammer. I'll never hear one of his terrible jokes or see him stumble around in a drunken stupor. Worst of all, I'll never tell him I love him or that I think he was the best father I could have asked for." Dorian wiped the tears from his face with his blanket.

"I didn't know him well, but he seemed like a good man," Razuul responded in an even tone.

"Aye, sometimes I forget that you met him. Oh, gods! Listen to me prattle on. After everything you've been through, I must sound like a whining child."

"No, I think it's good. I don't remember my parents, so hearing how you talk about your father lets me think about what it could have been like. Sometimes I'll wonder, did they love me that way? Were they proud of me? If they saw me now, would they be pleased with who I've become?

"I'll never know the answers for sure, but a part of me knows. Somewhere, beneath all the anger, I can still feel their love. I can still feel how much they cared for me. I don't feel it often. The only time I do is when I hear you talk about your father."

The two sat in silence, looking into the empty sky. Razuul's chest grew warm. The tips of his ears burned, and his scalp tingled. He began to wonder if he contracted some illness from sitting in the cold.

"After the slavers caught me, I didn't go straight to the arena." The words burst from Razuul like a caged animal finally set free. He couldn't stop the words from pouring out, and in truth, he wouldn't have stopped them even if he could. "After I was hauled away from my tribe,

I was brought to some marshal to serve as a field hand alongside several other slaves. Apparently, wild elves are sold for a lot of gold. Our natural resistance to the harsh sun and muscular physique make us perfect for working in the field. Moreover, our long life allows us to work for a family for several generations.

"The man that bought me turned out to be a special kind of evil, even for a human. If I spoke when I wasn't spoken to, I was punished. If I stopped working to wipe the sweat from my brow, I was punished. Even if I needed to relieve myself when it wasn't time for our three-minute break, I was punished.

"The only time we weren't in misery was at night. There were twenty of us, all crammed into a tiny shack that served as our home. We cared for each other's wounds, washed the filth from each other's backs, and made sure everyone ate when our master provided us the scraps from his table. It was the closest thing I can remember to having a family."

"By the gods," Dorian shivered. "That sounds awful. Were any of the others human?"

"Yes, most were, but even they turned out to be the worst of the bunch."

"How long were you there?"

"Twenty years."

"Twenty Years? I'm so sorry this happened to you."

"It wasn't all bad. There was one person I bonded with more than anyone else. Her name was Hedditryd, but we all called her Heddy. She was a half-dwarf like yourself. She told me her human mother was a slave. Her owners forced her to bear a half-dwarven child so they could raise it to become a fighter in underground fighting pits. Unfortunately for them, Heddy came out female, so they sold her as a slave instead."

"I'm sure they were very disappointed." Dorian's face turned red with anger.

"Yes, I'm sure they were. A half-dwarven female sells for very little money. They're no stronger than a human male, and as a half-dwarf, she could never have children of her own to be sold like a mule."

Razuul saw Dorian hold a sullen look. The term mul came from the word mule because of what they had in common, infertility. Saying it aloud reminded Dorian that he could never become the same kind of father that raised him.

"She worked in the marshal's kitchen." Razuul continued. "You might think that sounds better than working in the fields, but in actuality, it was much worse. Working inside the manor meant she was under constant surveillance. I don't remember her ever not having fresh bruises when I saw her at night. Yet, she always wore a smile. She would have blackened eyes and cracked ribs, but she would always pull the thorns from my hands instead of caring for her own injuries."

"She sounds wonderful. Did you love her?"

"Yes. She felt like a sister to me. That's why I reacted the way I did the day she died."

"What happened?"

"One day, our master hosted a party for the other marshals of the province. During the time leading up to the party, I saw Heddy's face without bruises for the first time. That's not to say they stopped beating her. They just didn't want the other marshals to see the abuse that we endured. Instead, they made sure to strike her in places easily covered by clothes."

"Monsters!" Dorian furrowed his hairless brow.

"They weren't monsters. That would be an insult to actual monsters. I don't believe there is a word for the vile pit of humanity our masters represented."

"Good point."

"Anyway, a few days before the party, our owner received word that the lord of the province would be in attendance. The news shifted our master's attitude completely. Now the preparation needed to be perfect, and the marshal needed to do everything he could to impress the lord. One of the best ways he could do that was to present a servant of a rare breed...like a wild elf. So they hired a clothier to dress me up in fancy clothing and forced me to serve food on a silver platter to the humans. They trained me on how to stand and how to speak to my betters. They bathed me, combed my hair, clipped my nails, and took me out of the fields to allow the callouses on my hands to heal. During my training, I got to spend a lot of time with Heddy. She tried to give me pointers so to save me from the beatings she frequently endured. I hated working in the manor, but she made the time tolerable. When the day of the party arrived, an incident occurred that changed my life forever.

"I was bringing a tray full of the marshal's most refined dinnerware, passed from one generation to the next, into the kitchen where Heddy continued slaving to cook the meals. I bumped into a counter and dropped the tray, breaking every single hand-painted plate. The sound echoed throughout the manor, and soon our master burst into the kitchen to find the source of the ruckus. He found both Heddy and me on our hands and knees, trying to pick up the pieces of porcelain. His face was red as a beet. He asked which one of us caused this, and Heddy shot to her feet, claiming responsibility before I could speak a word.

"I tried to argue, saying I dropped the plates, but the marshal had already made up his mind. He began beating her so bad, and all I did was stand there." Razuul wiped tears from his face. "I was so afraid of what would happen if I interfered. I just stood frozen and watched. She fell to the ground, and the marshal got on top of her to continue the thrashing. I can still hear the sounds of his fists slamming against her face. Then he began bashing her head against the floor, and I knew she wouldn't be able to take the punishment much longer. That's where my memory gets a bit hazy.

"I remember everything looking like it turned a tinge of red. I remember grabbing a knife, slashing it against the marshal's cheek, and blood spurting from the wound. I remember a group of men rushing in to prevent me from killing my master, but I don't recall how I put most of them on the floor. It took five full-grown men to subdue me, pinning me on my belly. I fought, squirmed, screamed, and cursed, but I couldn't get free. One of the men yanked my head off the floor by my hair and held a knife to my throat, and that's when Lord Harken entered the room.

"He commanded the man to stop once he saw the damage I had done to my attackers. He told them that I should be put in the arena since I was such a good fighter. He insisted that my punishment there would be much worse than the quick death they had planned."

"What about Heddy?" Dorian's eyes looked ready to well with tears over hearing Razuul's tragic story.

"I saw her once more, but I wish I hadn't. The next day, they placed me in a cage to ship me off to the arena. While there, I saw two of the other slaves carrying her out of the manor by the arms and legs. Another slave followed alongside them with a shovel in hand. Her face was so battered and bloody that I barely recognized her."

"By the gods. I have read many tragedies, but none compare to that. I don't know how you were able to live on after that."

"It fueled me. Every time I got into that arena, I thought about Heddy. I thought about my deep hatred for my former masters and pictured their faces upon each of my opponents. I used every moment in my cell to train my body and allowed my rage to grow."

"Do you still have it? Your hatred?"

Razuul looked to his open hands, then back to the black sky while he contemplated Dorian's question. "I still hate humans, but it's not the same. I don't picture my former masters, and I no longer desire to hunt them down and rip their throats out. I only wish to find my people and live away from humans for the rest of my life."

"When? When does the rage dampen?"

Razuul knew Dorian asked this question for his own sake. Better than anyone, he understood his plight. Rage and hatred are a heavy burden to carry; it weighs on you. It burns your joints and aches your back. The weight never fully leaves your body, but it does lighten with time. "I'd say the anger began lessening when I met the three of you."

"Really?" Dorian's eyes lit.

"Don't look at me like that. I don't like it."

The two sat in silence until Brett came strolling up

from somewhere in the darkness, scratching at a bracelet he always wore on his wrist.

"What are you two lovers doing out here?" Brett asked sarcastically.

"Shut up before I kill you," Razuul responded before getting up to return to the cabin. Grabbing the door's handle, he stopped short when an unfamiliar voice called from the opposite side of the old woman's home.

"Come out here, now! I know you're in there!"

Razuul, Dorian, and Brett crept into the house. Peering out the home's front window, they saw an armored man standing in front of a contingent of soldiers. Each man stood with a drawn weapon, and the leader's breath exhaled in plumes of fog as if he stood in much colder weather than the rest.

"They must be here for Njal. Those men from yesterday must have reported him to the king's guard." Brett whispered. "This has nothing to do with us. We should leave out the back before anyone notices."

"Thyra gave us food and shelter!" Dorian returned in a harsh whisper of his own. "We can't just leave! They'll kill Njal for sure! Besides, Elijah hasn't returned yet."

"The thief is right." Thyra's voice startled the trio

from behind them. "I knew this day would come someday. You three retreat out the back."

"Do not test my patience...Kinsman!" The leading soldier called out.

"Kinsman?" Brett whispered in a shocked voice. "They're here for you, Dorian?"

The color drained from Dorian's face.

"If you don't come out here now, I'm going to decorate the ground with your friend's innards!"

The trio returned to peeking out the window. One of the soldiers pushed through the crowd with Elijah in his grasp. The leader snatched their portly companion and placed his blade at his throat.

"That's how they found us." Brett clenched his fists. "That fool led them here. What do we do now?"

"Only one thing to do." Razuul returned, drawing his swords. "I haven't had a good fight in a while. This should be fun."

Elendor

No scream came from the specter. Apprehension filled Elendor as he lifted his head to find the ominous figure standing statue-still. The flat air felt stale. No birds sang, and no insects buzzed. Only the hollow sounds of the cool autumn breeze disrupted the silence. The surrounding trees stood staunch against the wind, not allowing a single creak to interfere with the ghostly meeting.

"What do you want with me?" Elendor demanded.

The apparition responded wordlessly by raising a single finger to indicate to Elendor to remain patient.

He observed the ghostly figure. Its armor appeared thin as parchment, yet thick enough to hide what dwelled beneath. It stood taller and thinner than the average human, and its gauntlets formed around three fingers and two thumbs on each hand. Gray smoke tendrils drifted from its chest plate and danced against the faceless head.

The apparition pointed to its left. Elendor followed its gesture to see the trees open another path. A moment later, Jocia emerged with a bewildered look upon her face.

"Jocia!" Elendor called, grabbing her attention.

"Elendor! What is happening?" Jocia stepped forward, but the razor grass shot erect to warn her to go no further.

"I do not know, but be wary of that grass."

"Is that...?" Jocia asked, pointing to the armored figure.

"Yes. It is the same thing I saw in my vision. I have only been here for a short time, and it has not done anything but stand there."

The mysterious being pointed to its right. The trees parted again, allowing Galain to step into the clearing.

Galain spotted the apparition. Without hesitation, he drew back an arrow and fired it at the ghost. The perfectly aimed arrow whizzed at the figure's chest but flew right through its body as if unhindered by its presence.

"Galain!" Elendor called.

"Elendor! Jocia! What is happening? Is that...?"

"Yes." Elendor responded, "I feel as though it has purposefully guided us here."

Galain narrowed his eyes at the strange being. "What is it you want from us?"

The wraith turned, spreading its arms wide. As it did, the trees behind the hollow armor parted, opening a new path that revealed a mesmerizing sight.

A city stood with buildings unlike any other in Preclarium. Every structure gleamed of white marble. Towers pierced the sky, waterless fountains etched in aquatic animals' shape awaited admiration of their beauty—intricately carved statues of tall, thin figures stood in precise formation. A single rail snaked its way around the city's perimeter, sometimes disappearing into buildings. Atop the rail, a train of carts sat with windows that revealed bench seats inside.

Elendor recognized the city belonged to the ancient kymarians. In all his research, he had never seen a city so large and in such pristine condition. No vines crawled up the building's sides. No moss obscured the statue's faces. It seemed as though time forgot to wear on the empty city, leaving it to remain in its original splendor.

The haunting figure faced the elven friends. Pointing to each one, the razor grass sunk into the ground, forming a path in the clearing that led to the unblemished city. The ghostly figure gestured to the three to follow it before entering the city. As it walked, the hallow armor eerily chimed with each step.

Elendor looked at his friends, who shared the same frightened, confused look. With no other choice, the three marched down the path and into the city.

Elendor walked side-by-side with his friends, and he could sense they felt the same uncertainty as he did.

A cold aura, conveying an array of emotions, emitted from the apparition, sending a rippling wave of chills across his skin. Feelings of anger, sadness, loss, depression, fear, and terror radiated from the being as if several entities resided within the armor.

The mysterious effigy stopped before an over-sized fountain. Four back-to-back marble dolphins rose at the center, surrounded by delicately carved porcelain sprays of water. Inside the seashell-shaped base, several marble fish species sat at the bottom as if frozen in time.

The apparition silently faced the trio. Jocia grabbed Elendor's arm in fear while Galain reached for the handle of his sheathed dagger. With its eyes pulsating a haunting red glow, Elendor anticipated its high-pitched attack.

"Galain, Jocia, help me take Vaylon off my back."

Jocia and Galain took their dead friend by the arms and gently laid the body on the marble street.

Elendor rose and readied himself for an attack of his own. He doubted he could cause the figure any harm, but he refused to allow it to release its sonic scream without resistance.

Cocking back his prosthetic arm, Elendor shot his wooden appendage toward the apparition. The arm stretched, wrapping around the ghostly figure like a snake, ensnaring its armored body. To the grief-stricken elf's surprise, his arm did not pass through its intangible body like Galain's arrow. The trapped spirit wriggled against the wooden restraints, trying to free itself from the bonds. Lifting his arm, Elendor stretched the ghost into the sky and slammed it into the marble road. A mushroom cloud of dust, dirt, and marble debris rose from the impacted ground.

"How did you do that?" Jocia asked.

"It appears his body is susceptible to magic, but I doubt that was enough to stop it." Elendor snapped his arm back and readied himself to continue the battle.

The armor pieces floated into the air and rushed past them like leaves carried by a fall breeze. Retaking its natural form, the apparition raised its hand as if readying to cast a spell of its own.

"Jocia!" Galain called out.

Understanding Galain's urgency, Jocia swiftly drew out a runic symbol. Two rock spikes burst from the ground, piercing its body from opposite directions. The wraith grabbed hold of the stone, trying to free itself.

"Jocia, try encasing it so it cannot break apart like last time," Galain suggested.

Jocia drew out another runic symbol. Three triangle-shaped stones shot from the ground to form a pyramid around the hollow armor.

The rapid casting took effect on Jocia as her breathing deepened. "I do not know if that will hold it. We should escape while we have the chance."

Elendor rushed to her side. "Are you alright? You look too exhausted for casting only two spells."

"I am fine. We have not eaten in a while. I just..."

The apparition burst through the ground behind the trio. Rocks, chunks of marble, and dirt sprayed the friends, forcing them to duck and cover.

Elendor prepared to attack, but before he could, the phantom raised its arms, summoning gray tree roots from the dirt. The roots wrapped around the arms and legs of the elves, pinning them to the ground.

Elendor struggled to break free. The memory of this identical situation from a dream recalled in his mind. With the might of his magical arm, he tore a root off his body, but four more roots sprung up to keep him in place.

"What do you want from me?" Elendor screamed. "Why can you not just leave me alone?"

"I..." Several voices echoed in his mind. Some spoke in high feminine tones; others spoke in a deep baritone. Each voice blended collectively with the sound of tortured pain. "Need...you...to...listen."

Clarissa

Clarissa approached the dungeon entrance. Sweat trickled from her temples, rolling down her face to drip from her chin. Chills reverberated throughout her body, and shallow breathing left her light-headed. Grabbing the door, her moist palms slipped from the handle. After finishing the appeal she sent to King Thomas, she knew she needed to visit Sir Gabriel in his cell, but the thought of seeing him in chains threatened to cause another breakdown. The last time her nerves fractured, she hallucinated a terrifying scene of a specter that released an ear-splitting scream, nearly rupturing her ears. She wanted to tell someone about the horrifying image she witnessed but no longer had anyone with whom she could confide. Even if she found someone she could talk to, she doubted anyone would believe her traumatic story.

Upon entering, the guard stood, shooting her a look of disgust. Typically, a member of any city's guard would address her with proper due respect. Even without her former title, she still belonged to a noble family, and therefore customs dictated he follow proper protocol. Nonetheless, she lost the regard even her name demanded. Word of her involvement in the amputation of their lord's heir's arm spread throughout the city, and rumors about her traveled on the wings of gossip. Refusing to speak to Clarissa, the guard permitted entrance with a dismissive wave of his hand.

Walking down the dark hallway, prisoners whistled and cat-called, shouted profanely, and posed rude gestures as she passed. Ensuring to avoid eye contact with them, she approached the door at the end of the hall that restrained her paladin guard.

The unlocked door creaked open with a gentle push. Peering inside the room, Clarissa understood the reason for the lax security. Sir Gabriel sat in burlap clothing with wrists and ankles shackled to the stone wall. The thick, rusty chains, long enough to allow him to sit or lay, could hold back a troll. Rats scurried across the dirt-covered floor. Piles of filthy, matted straw gathered into each corner. The humid air filled her lungs and covered the walls in a film of moisture. The low ceiling, barely high enough for Clarissa's short stature to stand erect, dripped water into puddles on the floor.

"My Lady, what are you doing here?" Sir Gabriel stood, bumping his head on the ceiling.

"I've come to tell you that I plan on refuting your imprisonment. Please don't despair. I will…"

"It doesn't matter." Sir Gabriel sat, folding his legs.

"Sir Gabriel, please, I will resolve this. Lord Alcaldo cannot…"

"He can do whatever he pleases. It's his province. I am just a paladin, and I assaulted a nobleman's son. There is no chance for me."

"Please allow me to finish!" Clarissa adjusted her throat and took a calming breath. "When a death sentence is handed down, it does not mean that the king will allow the execution. If anyone knows that, it is me. If the king pardoned Marshal Bartram, I see no reason he wouldn't grant you the same pardon. I have sent an appeal to King Thomas. All we must do is wait. I feel certain that he will reverse this decision."

"Do you not see the difference here? When you sentenced Marshal Bartram, Lord Bentley claimed innocence. Then, when you executed him anyway, I'm sure Lord Bentley went straight to the king and whispered in his ear about your disrespect and treason. King Thomas felt insulted. You wounded the pride of the most powerful person in Preclarium. This is different. I do not hold a title even as prestigious as marshal, and you no longer hold the sway of a lord. Besides, Lord Alcaldo is awaiting the necessary time before my execution. There is no chance for me."

The door opened. Sir Kenneth ducked into the dungeon room and glared disgust at the former noblewoman. "What are you doing here?"

"I am here to speak with Sir Gabriel. I believe we can stay his execution and perhaps find a way to release him from imprisonment."

Sir Kenneth clicked his tongue. "Since when do you care?" He pulled up a nearby stool and took a seat to prevent his skull from colliding with the ceiling.

"H-How dare you!" Clarissa put her hand over her heart, insulted by Sir Kenneth's insinuation. "Of course I care! I even sent a letter to the king! I will do anything to make sure this execution does not take place!"

"Anything? Tell me, have you tried telling Lord Alcaldo what his son tried doing to you?" Sir Kenneth folded his arms.

Clarissa shot her attention back to Sir Gabriel. "You told him?"

"What does it matter?" Sir Kenneth spoke before Sir Gabriel could answer. "It's not like we are your guards any longer."

"I…" Clarissa couldn't continue, consumed with shame. Through her selfish desires, she allowed Lord Alcaldo to control the paladin guards, betraying the men who staunchly vowed to protect her.

"Sir Kenneth," Sir Gabriel interjected, "you are too hard on her. I am sure she had her reasons for volunteering us into the Villam army."

"You are too kind to her, Sir Gabriel. And you, my lady, have you ever cared for anyone other than yourself? Have you ever stayed loyal to anyone when it didn't align with your own goals? If you have, I have not seen it. You are just a spoiled brat, fumbling through life and throwing childish fits when things do not go your way. Sir Gabriel saved you, and how do you repay him? You send a letter. What do you think that will accomplish? If you possessed any honor or courage, you would approach Lord Alcaldo and tell him that his son is a monster."

"I-I-I cannot." Tears spilled from Clarissa's eyes. Hearing Sir Kenneth's true feelings about her shattered her heart. "You do not understand. If I tell Lord Alcaldo what truly happened, it will accomplish nothing."

"Do you even know why Sir Gabriel did what he did?"

"Sir Kenneth! Please...don't." Sir Gabriel begged.

"I must. She needs to hear this." Sir Kenneth approached Clarissa. "Why do you think he volunteered to accompany you after your excommunication? Did you really believe his devotion laid only in his vow to protect you?"

"Well, yes. Why else would he…"

"Because he loves you! He's admired you from afar for the past three years, but you have never noticed. You've been so self-consumed with position and power. You failed to see the man in front of you."

"I-I didn't know." Clarissa turned her tearful eyes to her chained protector.

"What fool would assault a lord's son due to a sense of loyalty?" Sir Kenneth continued his tirade. "He knew the consequences. All he needed to do was take you by the hand and guide you out of the room, but he couldn't. The thought of that repugnant man defiling you caused him to make a foolish decision. His caring for you put him in a position that will end his life. And how do you repay him? With a letter."

"You must understand, I…"

"Please leave." Sir Kenneth interrupted, turning his back. "Please leave and do not return."

"Is that how you feel as well, Sir Gabriel?"

Sir Gabriel remained silent, unwilling to relay his true feelings.

Clarissa ran from the cell. As she passed the cells, the prisoner's depraved comments returned. The guard added a disrespectful comment of his own, but she paid none of their remarks any mind. She wanted to run to her room and bury her head in the soft down bedding, but not the bed lent to her in this castle. She wanted the bedding she still thought of as her own in Sanctum. She wanted her usual servants to bathe her in the warm waters of her tub, allowing her worries to drown in the water. Instead, she leaned against the wall of the nearest unoccupied hallway, gathering herself while wiping the tears from her reddened face.

Finding a nearby mirror, she took a moment to check her appearance. She adjusted her hair, smoothed her dress, and blinked rapidly to clear her bloodshot eyes. Taking a deep breath, she lifted her chin and confidently walked down the dimly lit path.

Clarissa walked down each hall, displaying a poised demeanor. Servants and soldiers bowed as she passed, and she returned each courtesy in kind with a smile. Arriving at her destination, she knocked on the door and waited for a reply.

"Enter!" Francisco Alcaldo called from within his office.

Marius

The journey neared its end. The capital city of Regiis sat in the distance, and Marius couldn't imagine a sweeter sight. His stomach rumbled, the muscles in his legs ached, and his jaw vibrated as the chilly autumn air whipped against his bare skin. Sitting atop his mare, he wanted to spur the horse into a gallop to end the trip, but he knew his horse couldn't handle the extra strain.

After Thomanthus helped him escape Baxis, the

centaur provided Marius with saddlebags containing food, oats, and water. Though adequately stocked, the supplies did not last long. He passed a few towns along the way where he could have resupplied himself, but he knew better. His mission required expedience. He knew it wouldn't be long before the beasts discovered his absence. This left the beasts with two options. They could send a party to trail him, but that would reveal their presence to the rest of the kingdom. Or they could remain in Baxis, waiting until the rest of their troops arrived, but that would risk Marius getting to the capital and returning with an army to counter-attack. Either way, he needed to move along quickly, and he needed to remain as hidden as possible.

Few people wouldn't recognize Marius. His position, notoriety, and islander appearance made him identifiable anywhere within the kingdom. Rumors spread quickly in Preclarium, and seeing the High Commander of Baxis traveling alone with a haggard appearance would raise suspicion amongst the citizens. Even if he told no one the pretext for his situation, the people would devise their own explanations. They would gossip that he lost his position or concoct any number of reasons. Whatever speculations they formed, Marius did not need the hearsay to arrive in the capital before him, making it even less likely that the king would hear and believe his story.

Marius never cursed his fame before this expedition. He commonly met his notoriety with a smile and friendly gesture. He didn't bask in the glory of prestige, nor did he turn up his nose at the acclaim. He felt honored that many people admired him and graciously accepted their praise.

He dwelled upon the reasons for his celebrity status. The odd occurrence of an islander being appointed as high commander spread his name across the kingdom, but participating in his first king's tournament, cemented his renown. He never learned to joust, and he didn't have a runestone to perform a magical display, but his melee skills allowed him to make a name for himself. He participated in twelve melee tournaments, winning his first and six of the eleven proceeding contests. The lone year the king allowed Jonas Werner to participate, he lost handily to the death knight and everyone else. He defeated and lost to Heece, the elven counterpart in Parvus Arbor, three times, and he lost to the upstart knight Isaac Bentley of Regiis. His final loss came at the hands of High Commander Calder Heskin of the Villam province in his final tournament before retiring from the contests.

His combat skills earned him the moniker 'Marius the Swift,' a name he despised as he thought it sounded silly. While the other tournament entrants donned heavy armor and utilized swords and shields, Marius wore loose leather clothing and fought with a small dagger. At first, the crowd laughed at his audacity for showing up so ill-prepared, but he quickly changed their tune. His propensity for performing acrobatic feats and unpredictable movements allowed him to get past the other's defenses. Soon, most of the fighters prayed not to have to fight the Baxis High Commander, and no one guffawed at the sight of his small weapon.

Marius's horse quivered between his legs. Like himself, the mare hadn't eaten for nearly two days, and the lack of food wore on its constitution.

"Hang in there, girl." Marius gently patted the equine's neck. "We're almost there. I'll get you the finest bag of oats the kingdom has to offer once we arrive."

As if responding to his words, the horse crumbled to its side. Marius's reaction, slowed in his weakened state, allowed the horse's body to pin his leg beneath it.

Marius pushed, pulled, and tugged to free himself to no avail. The pressure of the horse's frame hurt, but not as much as the loss of circulation. Pins and needles traveled up and down his leg, and his toes grew numb. He cursed himself for leaving his dagger in the saddlebag he could not reach. If he hadn't, he could cut the horse, allowing the embedded Decay spell to take effect. With the horse's body a husk of its previous state, he could slip his leg out as easily as crawling out of bedsheets. Screaming for help proved as fruitless as praying to the gods, but he tried both many times.

Laying on his back, he gazed at the coral sky as the sun dipped on the horizon. Several vultures circled, waiting for Jonas to release his final breath. The thought of the scavengers feeding off his corpse sickened him. As time passed, the winged carnivores grew bold, landing near him to peck pieces from the lifeless horse.

"Get out of here!" He screamed at the birds, swinging his arms in a failed attempt to strike the avian predators. He picked stones from the dirt, whipping them at the vultures in hopes to discourage them, but an unexpected ally appeared to scatter the birds before he threw a single stone.

A black blur streaked from the sky, landing in a cloud of dirt. Marius covered his eyes to protect him from the swirling debris. Once the air cleared, he found a beast he'd never seen in all his travels.

The animal possessed a Doberman dog's size and shape with pointed ears, long snout, and thin hind section, but the similarities ended there. The rest of the creature resembled a dragon. Red-tinged black scales covered its body. The two spiral-shaped horns jutting from the top of its head pointed toward its hindquarters. A pair of veiny wings folded tightly against its hide, and a row of curved spikes passed between them from the base of its neck to the tip of its long, whipping tail. A forked tongue hung between its pointed teeth as it panted with green saliva dripping from its jowls.

The vultures scattered. The strange creature stared at Marius as it sat on the dirt.

"What the hell are you?" Marius tried pushing himself free again in a wasted effort.

The unusual beast closed its mouth and cocked its head to the side as if it contemplated Marius's words. "Do you understand me?"

The beast looked away from Marius as if it heard something nearby. After seeing nothing, it turned back to Marius, panting with its tongue hanging once again.

"Apparently not."

The scaled animal approached the dead horse, cautiously sniffing its hide.

"I don't know what you're planning, but you better not…"

Before Marius finished, the miniature dragon opened its fanged maw, clamped down on the horse's stomach, and whipped the carcass off Marius in a feat of unnatural strength for its diminutive size. Flapping its wings, it hovered in the air and released a blue stream of fire that roasted the dead horse in a matter of seconds. Once the flames extinguished, it swooped down and began devouring its meal. The dog-like dragon quickly ravaged the charred flesh, leaving only scraps for the other scavengers.

Marius gathered himself to his feet. Pins and needles traveled down his leg as the circulation returned.

Cautiously, he approached the beast with his hand extended, shaking his leg to return circulation and slowly craning the kinks from his neck.

The creature spun around, startled as if it forgot about Marius's presence. Raising its lip in a snarl, it quickly dropped its aggressive posture and sat next to the ruined horse's remains.

"Easy, boy," Marius spoke in a calm voice to avoid startling the creature further. "I just want to thank you."

Placing his hand on the dragon-dog's head, he brushed back the scales between its ears. In return, it closed its eyes and released a grumble that communicated its pleasure of being petted. Popping up on its hind legs, it placed its clawed paws on Marius's shoulders and licked his face with its forked tongue.

"Alright, alright." Marius laughed as he gently pushed the creature back to all fours. The dragon crouched on its forelegs in the playful manner of a dog with its pointed tail wagging.

"You want to play?" Marius grabbed a nearby stick from the ground.

The dragon hopped as it spun in circles.

"I think you need a name. What should I call you? You look like a tiny dragon, but you act like a dog. Dragog?"

The dragon growled in a deep rumble.

"No? You don't like that one, huh? How about Dogon?"

The dragon jumped up and licked Marius's face. "You like that one?" Marius scratched behind the excited Dogon's pointed ears. "Alright, your name is Dogon."

Jonas

Jonas glared at Nathaniel. His dirty-blond, disheveled hair hung to the tip of his nose, hiding his eyes from view. His prison rags hung loosely from his skeletal frame, and the stench of his unwashed body filled the interior of his cell. A ruddy scar spanned across his chest, resulting from a runestone being forcibly removed from his skin, and his crooked leg served as a reminder of their previous encounter.

"What's going on? Who is this?" Nathaniel pointed at the prisoner Jonas brought with him.

"Don't worry about him. The papers at your feet contain kymarian writing. I need you to decipher it for me."

Nathaniel scoffed at Jonas. "Why would I do anything for you?"

"Because I can get you out of here."

"Ha! Like I would believe you."

"You don't have much choice. Word probably hasn't gotten to you down here. The prince is currently torturing and executing criminals in front of the entire city. He plans on emptying all the cells."

"That cannot be true." Nathaniel struggled to his feet, his mangled leg cracking and popping as he stood.

"It's true!" The young man Jonas brought along shivered with fear.

"That's why you brought him in here?" Nathaniel spat with disdain. "You wanted a fellow prisoner to reinforce your story. How stupid do you think I am?"

"That's not why he is here." Jonas grabbed the young man by the back of the neck. Forcing him to his feet, he shoved him to the nearby wall. "Sorry about this."

Jonas smashed the young man's face into the stone wall. The unmistakable sound of crunching bones blended with grunts and gags. The young man flailed his arms in a desperate attempt to escape, but Jonas kept ramming his face into the wall until his body fell limp. Laying the boy on his back, the death knight checked his neck for a pulse. Blood poured from his shattered nose, his eyes swelled shut, and shards of shattered teeth lay like islands in a sea of gruesome viscera. Even the boy's mother wouldn't have recognized his destroyed face. Satisfied that the young man no longer breathed, he turned to Nathaniel.

"There," Jonas began, "I'd say no one will know that this is not you."

Nathaniel gagged. "You're even more of a monster than I thought."

"Do we have a deal or not?"

"How do I know you're not lying?"

"You don't." Jonas gave a cocky smile. "But what choice do you have? Help me, and you have a chance. Don't help me, and you have none. Your choice."

Nathaniel sat and reached out a shaky hand to retrieve the folded parchment. "I hate you so much."

The crippled boy's eyes darted across the diagram. After aligning the hand-drawn pictures together, his eyes widened for an instant. The momentary reaction served as a signal that he understood the strange device's purpose.

"I don't know what this is." Nathaniel folded his arms and leaned back. "I can't help you."

"Don't lie to me! I know you can decipher this!"

"Sorry. I don't know who drew this, but it's terrible. The symbols aren't drawn correctly, and the diagram makes no sense."

"Do you really think...?" Jonas halted his shout. He knew Nathaniel successfully interpreted the drawing, but he didn't want to give his enemy the means to create a powerful weapon.

Jonas stroked the hair on his chin. He knew that threats wouldn't sway Nathaniel's answer. Adjusting his throat, he continued to press the young man to reveal the truth.

"Listen, I already have an idea of what this thing does. I just need to confirm it before I make my next move. I know you hate me. I can do nothing to change that. However, I will tell you this: I am not the only one who has this diagram. I have a strong suspicion that the prince also has it. If you think I am a monster, you have no idea what kind of atrocities the prince commits. He delights in the agony of others. He tortures those that show the slightest disrespect. Does that seem like the kind of person who should have such a device? Tell me what you know about this thing, and I will do what I can to stop him."

Nathaniel stared at the bloodied corpse. "I don't care about the weapon."

The prisoner's gaze shifted, signaling to Jonas that he guessed right…the diagram depicted a weapon.

"I have a family myself: a mother, a wife, and a daughter. I only wish to protect them as well as every man, woman, and child in this kingdom. I'm sure there are still people you care about outside. The mul perhaps?"

"Dorian? He is alive?" Nathaniel's face lit.

"For now. One of my best men is hunting him, but he has alluded us thus far. I doubt he has a chance of escaping Isaac the 'Frost Blade' Bentley for much longer, but at least he has a chance. Tell me, if the prince creates this weapon, knowing that finding the mul is one of his highest priorities, would he still stand a chance?"

Nathaniel bit his lip as his eyes shot from corner to corner. "You're certain the prince has these diagrams?"

"Yes."

"Then we are all doomed."

"Tell me! What does it do?"

Nathanial began to interpret the diagram. "Some letterings are missing. The way the symbols are drawn makes it hard to decipher, but the best I can tell, it's a weapon that drains a person of their magical energy. It transfers the power to the wielder. The person who utilized this would have an infinite magical supply and the ability to utilize all of the runestones at once."

"By the gods!"

"I can't be sure, but it doesn't seem to have a range of distance. This weapon could likely reach the furthest corners of the kingdom. No one would be safe."

"What's worse is the repercussions of the kingdom discovering its existence. Every fool marshal and lord would do anything within their power to obtain such a device. If one of them did, a war would ensue that would make the Beast Wars look like a schoolyard scuffle." Jonas voiced his thoughts aloud.

"If the prince didn't kill them all off first."

"Give the papers back." Jonas wished he could kill Nathaniel to keep the device's existence secret, but his ability to read kymarian could still prove invaluable.

"Get up. We need to get out of here."

"Where could you possibly take me?" Nathaniel stood, stumbling on his weak leg.

"The cabin where you were arrested."

"Dorian's home? Won't that be the first place people would look for me?"

"If anyone looks for you in your cell, they'll find a mangled body and assume you committed suicide. Besides, Thane Kinsman built that cabin. I knew that dwarf better than most. He intended to keep that son of his a secret from the world. I am certain he built secret areas where his son could hide if anyone unexpectedly found his home. We just need to find them."

"How do you plan on getting me out of the city?"

"Luckily, the entire city is watching the prince torture citizens at the moment. If we go through the castle, we should be able to find you a place to hide. Once night falls, I'll come back for you and get you out of the city."

"What about..."

"Enough questions." Jonas interrupted. "Let's go before the prince finishes his executions, and the castle floods with people."

The death knight led the way while Nathaniel hobbled behind. At the end of the hall, the stairway curled upward. Heading up the stairs, Nathaniel struggled to keep pace. Jonas groaned as he impatiently waited for the struggling young man to climb. Reaching the top, the high commander pushed the wooden door open to find a man standing in his path at the upper platform.

Adam Garrison, the other Head of Cerberus, greeted Jonas. "Hello, High Commander. What do we have here?"

Dorian

Dorian gazed out the window at the contingent of armored men surrounding Thyra's cottage. Each held weapons at the ready for battle. Some held spears or swords; others prepared to fire crossbows with notched arrows. Among the men, the leader stood out like a lion in a crowd of domesticated cats. His silver armor gleamed in the torchlight, unlike the dull gray plating of his compatriots. His snow-white hair defied his youthful appearance, making it difficult to determine his age. In the cold night air, the breath of all the men fogged, but the leader's breath escaped from his blue lips in dense plumes.

"Do not test my patience, Kinsman!" The leader shouted. "And Razuul, I know you're in there as well. We have no qualms with you. We just want the mul. We have some information on a wild elf tribe that traveled near here recently. As long as you stay out of this, we will tell you what we learned and be on our way."

"Gods!" Brett exclaimed. "Did that idiot tell them everything?"

"I don't want anything from the king's guard," Razuul snarled. "I think I'll go tell him exactly where he can stick his information." Drawing his swords, he began to approach the door, but Dorian grabbed his shirt, halting his progress.

"Stop! There's no need for you to go out there. They aren't here for you. You two get out of here. When I go outside, the soldiers out back will come to surround me. Once they do, you two can sneak out."

"Sounds good to me!" Brett chimed in.

"Shut up, Shaw!" Razuul replied in a harsh whisper. "If he goes out there alone, he will die!"

"It's alright, Razuul," Dorian interjected. "This group was never about friendship. I can't allow you to risk your lives for me. You allowed me to follow you and taught me how to use a sword. I can't thank you enough for that, but the deal was that I would not hinder the search for your people. I'm sorry I didn't hold up my end of the deal."

Razuul stared daggers at Dorian. He had only seen such rage in his eyes after they were captured in the Villam province.

"He's right." Brett placed his hand on Razuul's shoulder, which the wild elf immediately slapped away.

"Even if we did go out there, I'm not sure we'd make much of a difference. There must be fifty men out there. Even you can't overcome those odds."

"Don't underestimate me, Shaw!" Razuul grabbed Brett by the shirt, twisting it in his fist to yank him close. "Fifty men or a hundred, I'll kill them all!"

"No!" Dorian blurted. "The last time someone finished a battle I couldn't, I lost my father. You spent seventy years inside a cell you did not deserve. If something were to happen, and someone else lost their life because of me, I don't think I could go on. Please don't put extra weight like that on my shoulders. Go, find your people."

"Dorian, I…" Razuul's rage-fueled expression deadened. The half-dwarf recognized the wild elf's look of frustrated confusion. He'd seen it many times during the sessions he spent teaching him how to read.

"Again, thank you for everything." Dorian smiled, placing his hand on his mentor's shoulder before turning to exit the cabin.

Outside, Dorian approached the white-haired man, surrendering with hands held high. On his hip, he could feel Shadowflame hum in excitement, as if it lusted for battle. He wanted to satisfy his blade's hunger for action, but he knew drawing his weapon meant instant death for Elijah. The soldiers pointed their arrows, spears, and swords at him. As predicted, the men from the back of the house encircled him, leaving a clear path for Razuul and Brett to escape.

"Wise choice," The leading soldier began. "Now, take off that belt and throw your sword here. Make sure to leave it in its scabbard. If you attempt to draw it," the man lifted Elijah's chin with the flat of his blade, causing a scared whimper to escape his lips, "I'll slit his throat."

"Alright, just don't hurt him." Dorian began unbuckling his belt. "Are you alright, Elijah?"

"I-I'm fine." Elijah stammered, looking away.

The moment Dorian threw his sword at the leader's feet, a pair of soldiers grabbed Dorian's arms and began tying his wrists behind his back.

The white-haired man bent to retrieve Shadowflame. Pulling the sword from the scabbard, he examined the blade before turning to Elijah. "You are certain this is the sword that ignites with black flame?"

"Y-yes. The black flames only appear when Dorian holds the sword." Elijah returned in a meek voice.

"You better be telling the truth. If you're lying, the deal is off."

"Deal?" Dorian's heart raced as he began to piece together the reality of the situation. "What deal? Elijah, what did you do?"

"I-I…"

"Don't be ashamed," The leader interrupted. "You served your king well." Turning to Dorian, his blue lips curled in a cocky smile. "I lost track of how long we've been trying to find you. Your traveling pattern was so unpredictable. We began to wonder if we would ever track you down. Imagine our surprise when your friend here approached us in the last town and told us exactly where to find you."

"He came to you? Elijah, you betrayed me? Why? How could you?" Dorian's chest ached, and every breath felt like he inhaled flames. Tears spilled from his eyes as he tried to make sense of what he heard.

"I-I…I just want to go home!" Elijah shouted. "I can't do this anymore. I am not like you. I can't survive out here, and you know it. I miss my parents. I miss my bed. This was the only way I could get my life back!"

"You idiot! Do you think they're taking you home? They are taking you to the dungeon! What makes you think…

The leading soldier smacked Dorian's face with the back of his gloved hand. "Now, now, don't go filling the poor boy's head with lies. We are the king's guard. Of course, we'll hold our end of the bargain."

"What's going on out here?" Thyra asked, emerging from her home.

"Go back in your house, old woman. This has nothing to do with you."

"You have no right to be here! This is my land, and these are my guests. You can't just barge onto my property and do as you please."

"Ma'am, I am Captain Isaac Bentley of the king's guard. Our jurisdiction encompasses the entirety of the kingdom. Please, go back inside your home, and all this will all be over soon."

"Bentley, huh? As in a member of the Harken family? I heard the Bentleys were once Harkens, but your family got stripped of their last name because they weren't good enough to be called Harkens." Thyra slowly pushed past the other soldiers to confront Isaac.

"That is not…"

"Oh yes, I heard all about it." The feisty elder quickly cut off the white-haired soldier's rebuttal. "After being stripped of your name, your family decided to name yourselves after Bentley the 'Sea Snake' Harken to kiss his noble butt."

Isaac's face twisted in frustration. "Ma'am, you know nothing about my family."

"Oh, but I do! Your family is nothing but a bunch of watered-down nobles, trying to cling to what little royal blood you have left in your veins. That's why you joined the king's guard. You thought you could…"

Isaac backhanded Thyra. The moment she struck the ground, the nearby barn exploded as Njal thundered across the yard. "Mama!"

Njal rushed to his mother. Each step covered the ground of twenty paces for a normal man and sent vibrations in the dirt like a herd of stampeding beasts.

The frightened soldiers attempted to block his path, but he swatted them aside as easily as swatting at a swarm of flies. The soldier's armor clanged together as they flew through the air, and their frightened screams ended as they crashed onto the ground. The remaining soldiers prepared to attack the enraged cyclops, but Njal ignored them. Raising his wagon-wheel-sized fists, he slammed them down, intending to flatten Isaac.

Isaac dove, narrowly avoiding the deadly attack. The strike's impact encompassed the area with dust and debris, leaving a crater in the ground large enough to swallow a mule.

Seeing his opportunity, Dorian searched for a means of freeing himself from his bonds. Before he could find a discarded weapon to cut the binds that tied him, he felt the ropes cut, releasing his arms.

Dorian turned to see Brett standing with a dagger in hand.

"Hurry up and find your sword. We need to get out of here now!" Brett instructed.

"Thanks, Brett." Dorian didn't need to search for his blade. He could feel Shadowflame calling for him. Running to its location through the dust cloud, he scooped up his weapon and drew it from the sheath. The lightless black flames instantly consumed the Hygard steel.

A quiver of excitement traveled through Dorian's body like a million tiny needles lightly pricking his skin. All fear of his fate at the hands of the king's guard washed away. Escape no longer felt like an option, nor did allowing Isaac Bentley to retreat. Peering through the settling dust, he searched for his prey but found a familiar sight instead.

The same pair of wooden doors he'd seen several times before loomed amidst the dust cloud. With no building attached, a soft glow emitted from the outer frame. He nearly touched the doors once, but they vanished before he made contact. Since that day, their appearance lasted no more than a fleeting moment, yet the frequency of visions of doors looming at the edge of his vision increased as of late.

Njal's guttural roar muffled the screams of the soldiers. Arrows released from bows and crossbows twanged their one-note song and the clash of steel resounded from every direction. The sounds of battle snapped Dorian from his momentary bewilderment, allowing him to re-focus his rage.

"Kinsman!" Isaac called from behind Dorian. As the dust veil settled, Dorian found the captain standing with his sword at the ready as a cloud of exhaled mist obscured his face. "Bringing you in alive is not part of my mission. I only intended to allow you to live out of respect for your father. Put the sword down, and come with me."

"My father?" Dorian's fury grew hotter than a smelting pit as his blood boiled with rage. "Don't pretend like you know anything about my father!"

Dorian rushed at Isaac, bringing Shadowflame down with all his might. Isaac easily parried the strike and stepped away from the half-dwarf's follow-up swing.

Razuul's lesson of keeping calm during battle rang in his head like a bell, but smithing a blade without a hammer seemed an easier task. His skin tingled, his breath deepened, and his hairless brow tightened in knots. His rose-tinted vision focused solely on his adversary, dismissing the surrounding chaos. A copper taste lingered in his mouth as if he could taste his enemy's blood. The beating of his pulse pounded throughout his body, releasing waves of heat with every heartbeat.

Dorian sliced a wild upswing at Isaac, followed by a series of vertical and horizontal strokes. Each attempt clashed against the captain's blade as the enraged half-dwarf kept his opponent on the defensive.

"This is what the son of Thane Kinsman is capable of?" Isaac spoke over the shrill. "I am disappointed."

"Do not speak my father's name!"

Dorian decided to use a move he recently learned. Coming down with a vertical strike, he would leave the blade loose in his hands. Once Isaac brought up his inevitable block, he would tighten his grip a moment after the blades met. This would alter the angle of his sword. A swift thrust forward would aim the tip of the blade at his opponent's unprotected face.

Isaac already proved himself a capable fighter. Dorian assumed the technique wouldn't land a direct hit, but with Shadowflame, any cut would prove deadly. With a single scratch, an enemy turned to ash once the black flames finished consuming flesh.

Dorian brought Shadowflame down. The moment the blades touched, he tried to squeeze his hands, but the attempt failed. The muscles in his hands froze solid, allowing Isaac to knock the sword out of Dorian's hands and send it spinning across the yard.

Narrowly escaping the follow-up strike, Dorian dove to the side and rolled on the ground. Without Shadowflame, panic consumed him. The dust cloud no longer lingered in the air, but it didn't matter. Even blinded, Dorian could find his sword. The connection he felt to the blade resembled a magnet being drawn to iron, an invisible force demanding that he and his sword remain together.

Dorian dashed to his sword. Ducking beneath Isaac's horizontal swing, he scooped up Shadowflame, instantly igniting the blade's flames and his passion for battle.

Looking at his hands, he found why his plan failed. Tiny crystals of ice scattered across his blue-tinted skin. His fingers barely responded to his commands, and every movement hurt.

"Took you long enough to notice." Isaac mocked. "You were so angry, swinging your blade like a mad-man that you failed to notice. Every time your blade crossed mine, I sent freezing energies down your sword and into your hands. Lucky for me, those flames of yours don't actually produce heat. This wouldn't work on a normal fire-sword. Face it, boy, you are an amateur; you don't stand a chance against my magic. This is why I will be the next Head of Cerberus and why you will be coming with me one way or the other."

"You call that magic?" Dorian mocked. "Pathetic! I'll show you magic!"

Dorian focused his energies on Shadowflame, silently praying for the successful casting of a spell. Not long after he and his friends discovered how to activate the sword's black flames, they encountered a surprise attack by the Three Heads of Cerberus. During that ambush, Dorian released a devastating spell that reduced one of the members to ash. Since that day, he had not attempted to cast magic, but he always felt its draw. Shadowflame beckoned for him to release the blade's destructive capabilities, but the need never arose. Other than his mentor, Razuul, none of his combatants required the use of magic. Thieves and ordinary soldiers posed no threat to his sword skills. Isaac posed a danger that finally justified releasing the true potential of his blade.

Dorian cocked his sword, allowing his energies to flow into the weapon like a swirling vortex. Black flames shot from the blade in a jetting blaze. Swinging Shadowflame in a horizontal arc, the other-worldly fire shot forth in a pattern that echoed his motion. The flame spelled certain doom for his opponent, but Isaac Bentley's reflexes served him well. Dropping to his stomach, he planted his hands onto the ground and waited for the spell to pass overhead harmlessly. Dorian released another torrent, this time in a vertical swing, but Isaac sprung to his feet and side-stepped the attack.

Dorian's vision blurred. His chest heaved, and muscles ached as if he just finished climbing a mountain. Sweat poured from his brow, and chills ran down his spine, leaving his skin cold and clammy. Crumbling to his knees, he thrust the tip of his sword into the ground to use as a crutch, steadying him to prevent collapsing face-first into the dirt.

"Your inexperience is astounding," Isaac taunted. "Do you think I can't cast spells? I only use magic to freeze my opponent's blades because it requires so little energy. We are warriors, not wizards. Our energy is vital to fighting. Casting major spells like that leaves us vulnerable if we miss."

Isaac kicked Shadowflame from Dorian's hands, sending the infuriated young Kinsman crashing to the ground like a felled tree. The world spun as the half-dwarven warrior struggled to rise. He cursed himself for allowing such a simple strategy to affect him. He knew his opponent goaded him into using his magic, yet he ignored reason and allowed arrogance and rage to dictate his actions.

Looking up, he saw Isaac with his blade overhead, readying himself to cleave Dorian's head from his shoulders. He squeezed his eyes shut, awaiting his inevitable demise, but the final blow did not come. Instead of the blade rending his flesh, he heard the clang of metal striking a solid object along with the sound of Isaac spewing curses in confusion.

Dorian opened his eyes to find a wall of bone stretching higher than the oldest trees surrounding the farmland. The marrow blockade saved him from certain doom and trapped his aggressor like a caged animal. On the other side, the ring of steel clashing against bone reverberated as his foe hacked and slashed at the summoned wall. He searched the area for the savior that cast the spell but found only soldiers scrambling to deal with the enraged cyclops.

Dorian scurried on all fours to retrieve his sword, knowing the undead barrier would not last. Shards of bone fell as the wall cracked and splintered from the onslaught of attacks coming from the inside.

Struggling to his feet, Dorian took a deep breath to calm his nerves. He knew he stood no chance against the more experienced soldier in his current state. Drawing focus to settle his all-consuming rage, his shallow breathing deepened, strained muscles loosened, and his hazy mind cleared. He could feel his body's magical energy returning. He knew his foe would be upon him before he could fully recuperate, but no choice remained but to face the Frost Blade. Raising his sword, he took a defensive posture in hopes that he could repel Isaac's attacks long enough for his body to fully reclaim his expended energy.

Isaac burst through the wall, raining shards of bone to the ground. His face twisted in fury as he pointed the tip of the sword at Dorian. "I don't know who just saved you, but whoever it was will soon meet the same fate as you."

Isaac unleashed a flurry of strikes. Each blow aimed at a vital area, signaling his desire to end the feud quickly. Dorian blocked each strike, keeping his blade close to expend as little energy as possible. He had witnessed this defensive method many times, as his father used this tactic to wear down a certain younger and more versatile fighter. Against any other fighter, this strategy may have bought him enough time to launch a counter-attack; however, Isaac's magic countered the plan.

Invisible daggers of ice stabbed at Dorian's hands as they turned a shade of blue.

In desperation, Dorian threw a counter. Swinging his sword in a horizontal swipe toward Isaac's head, he knew the attack went against all his swordsmanship training. Both Razuul and his father drilled that such a reckless strike should only be thrown when there is a clear opening. He wished he could apply his mentors' teachings, but his frozen hands would soon force him to drop his only means of defense.

As expected, Isaac ducked beneath the swing and landed an open-palm strike into Dorian's chin. The blow slammed his jaw shut, crushing his tongue between his teeth, and sent him sprawling onto his back.

Dorian swiftly raised his sword in anticipation of a follow-up attack, but none came. Lifting to an elbow, he peered at his enemy to see his sword tucked beneath his arm as he frantically struggled to remove the glove from his left hand. Whipping the glove to the ground, he saw the reason for Isaac's panicked state. At the center of his palm, a tiny cut bled, but the minuscule drop of blood failed to represent the wound's life-threatening condition. Embers slowly spread across his hand from the laceration.

Dorian, aware he would rise as the victor, deduced what happened after the strike to his chin. As he fell, his sword-arm whipped upwards and the tip of Shadowflame caught the open hand of his aggressor with just enough force to cut through the leather gauntlet and pierce his flesh.

A sour look twisted on Isaac's face as he grabbed the hilt of his sword. Without hesitation, he swung his sword and hacked his hand off at the wrist. A spray of blood shot out from the wound as Isaac growled in pain. On the ground, his dismembered hand turned to ash and drifted away in the night breeze. Pressing the flat of his sword against the stump, he froze the wound and released a torturous wail.

Dorian rose and shifted his stance to defend.

"No," Isaac began. "You can put your sword down for now. Even if I killed you, your friend would just end me here and now."

Dorian looked over his shoulder and saw Razuul standing amongst a pile of corpses. With his focus fixed on the battle, he hadn't realized that the wild elf joined the fray against his wishes.

"Next time we meet, you will not be so lucky."

Isaac ran to his horse and retreated into the night.

Lena

She followed him for days. Dorian looked beautiful to her. Keeping herself hidden, she listened to every word he and his friends said. She couldn't remember any of the other's names, but his sounded like music in her ears. His rounded nose, defined cheekbones, and square jaw gave him a majestic look that stood out from the oval, expressionless faces of everyone else. Everything about him fascinated her, but none of his distinct features entranced her more than his eyes. Gray as a storm cloud, reflective as a mirror, and burning with life, she felt she could gaze into them for an eternity.

The day she left her home, she dressed in her finest non-formal clothing. She could scarcely remember the last time she wore an outfit bereft of holes and dirt. Wearing clean leather pants, a belted tunic that hung to her knees, and polished boots that actually matched, she dressed herself in a manner that the rest of society considered appropriate. She even brushed the knots from her long, black hair. It hurt much more than when her uncle instructed the chambermaids to style her hair, but she felt that she needed to make a good first impression.

Of course, none of this mattered if she couldn't muster the courage to meet him. Every time she tried to approach him, her heart raced, breathing grew rapid, and it felt as though a thousand insects skittered in circles inside her stomach.

She tried to call out to the group once to introduce herself, feeling that she could keep her composure if she remained at a distance. Instead, a squeak escaped her mouth, and she quickly ducked behind the brush to stay hidden. Dorian and his friends dismissed the sound as some woodland animal.

On this particular night, she couldn't keep her distance. It felt as though she'd stuffed her mouth with cotton, and the insects in her stomach no longer crawled, likely a result of not feeding them in over a day. She hoped she could still save the bugs, but even if she couldn't, the prospect of summoning undead insects from her mouth left her giddy.

She waited until the tall, bald one left. She noticed that this one separated himself from Dorian and the black-haired one at roughly the same time every night. She trailed him to see where he went a few nights ago, only to find him mumbling quietly at his wrist. She tried talking at her own wrist, but it never talked back.

Silently, she approached the duo. "Hello." Lena spurted in an awkward high pitch that took even her for surprise.

Dorian and his friend shot to their feet, drawing their weapons in the process. Seeing him up close, Lena felt the stomach bugs spring to life and attempt to jump out of her mouth. She swallowed hard to keep them in place. His magnificence glowed even brighter from this distance, and staring into his ashen eyes intensified the beating in her chest.

"Who are you?" Dorian demanded.

"My name is Lena. I'm sorry for bothering you, but the stomach bugs are dying, and the head swimmies won't go away."

Dorian glanced at his friend with a look she interpreted as confusion.

"Faces are so wonderful! They tell such amazing

stories." Lena thought aloud.

"I…what?" Dorian returned.

"Okay, well, I have been following you for the past few days, and I couldn't see faces, but your face, I can see your face, but the stomach bugs started crawling, so I hid and…"

"Whoa, wait, wait, wait." The black-haired one interrupted Lena's ramblings. "Did you say you have been following us for days?"

"Yes, I wanted to talk to a face, but I got cold, my heart started playing music, and my legs didn't want to go where my brain was telling them to go."

"I have no idea what you are saying. Do you?" The black-haired one asked Dorian, who shrugged his shoulders in return.

"Okay, let me start over. I left home because all the other faces were the same. So I…"

"I don't think this is going to help." Dorian seemed exasperated. "How about you tell us what you want instead."

Lena twisted the tip of her boot in the dirt. "Well, I think I killed the stomach bugs because I haven't fed them."

"Are you saying you're hungry?" Dorian asked.

"Yes! Weren't you listening?"

The black-haired one sheathed his swords. "That runestone on your forehead, does that mean you're a necromancer?"

"That's right! Everyone in my family is a necromancer. I like to make cute zombies and chimeras. It's a lot of fun."

"Are you the one that made the bone wall that saved Dorian's life?"

"Oh, that. I'm sorry, it's just that the cold man looked so mean, and I didn't know if I'd ever see another face."

"You did that?" Dorian approached Lena. "You saved my life. Thank you."

"Y-your welcome." Lena's face warmed, and the stomach insects skittered faster than ever. "Oh good! The bugs aren't dead."

"Aye, you must be starving. We caught some rabbits earlier, but they aren't done cooking. You can keep warm by the fire until they are ready."

"Dorian? What are you doing? We don't know anything about her." The black-haired one's voice seemed upset.

"She saved my life, Razuul. The least I can do is offer some food."

"Black hair, Razuul, black hair, Razuul, black hair, Razuul," Lena repeated to commit the name to memory.

"She's a human." Razuul folded his arms. "I don't trust her. She probably saved you so she could catch and sell you later."

"She said she has been following us for days, and she hasn't done anything yet." Dorian returned. "Besides, if she's been following us for that long, aren't you curious? I know you use your ability to make sure no one is following us, yet you never sensed her once. Don't you want to know why?"

"I admit, that is strange, but this is still a terrible idea. I…"

Razuul rambled on, but Lena stopped paying attention. Throughout her life, people consistently talked about her as if she wasn't there. For a time it bothered her as she found it quite rude, but she grew accustomed it over the years. Taking a seat in front of the fire, she extended her arms to warm her hands.

"You two arguing over who is going to cuddle who tonight?" The wrist-whisperer returned from the woods. "What the…"

The taller bald one drew a knife and prepared to throw it at Lena. Quickly standing, she drew out a runic symbol and summoned a bone wall to protect herself from the projectile.

"Brett, put that stupid toothpick away!" Lena heard Dorian say from behind her protective blockade.

"Brett is the tall, bald one; Brett is the tall, bald one," Lena repeated.

Peering from behind the barrier, she saw Dorian approaching her. Ducking back, she flailed her arms to try to find the invisible man that lightly choked her.

"Are you alright?" Dorian asked.

Lena stopped waving her arms as the invisible man seemed to go away. However, a new symptom of her strange sickness manifested as she stared into Dorian's sparkling eyes. Her heart grew wings and tried to fly right out of her mouth. Gulping hard to keep the organ where it belonged, she looked away and tucked her hair behind her ear. "Y-yes. I'm fine. I just wish the invisible man would leave me alone and my insides would stay where they're supposed to be."

"I still have no idea what you are talking about, but I felt I needed to thank you again." Dorian took her hand. "If you hadn't interfered, I definitely wouldn't be here right now."

Lena looked at Dorian's hands holding hers. They felt rough and callous, yet gentle and tender. Their warmth traveled up her arms and to the pit of her stomach. Without warning, her stomach bugs dashed to exit through her mouth. Leaning over, she gagged and released a small pool of yellowish liquid. To her surprise, she saw no insects in the excretion.

Dorian released her hand and took a step back. "Are you sure you're alright?"

"I thought the bugs wanted to leave, but I guess they really like me! Although the hot-cold keeps coming and going, and the no-see clouds keep raining on me."

"Are you trying to say you're sick?" Dorian took another step back, covering his mouth and nose with his hand.

"She's saying she's hungry." Razuul approached.

"You understand her?" Brett asked.

"Nonsense was a common language used in the

arena. After seventy years, you learn to interpret drunken guards and insane prisoners." Razuul turned to Lena and continued. "I still don't trust you, but Dorian brought up a good point. I want to know why I couldn't sense you. Even standing in front of me, I can't feel any life-energy emitting from you."

"I don't know. Maybe it's because when I was born..."

"Wait!" Brett interrupted. "What is your name?"

"Lena. It's nice to meet you." Lena proudly stuck out her hand, performing the greeting ingrained in her since childhood.

"Your name is Lena, and you are a necromancer? Is your full name Lena Richter?"

"Why, yes! Do we know each other?"

Brett turned away and began walking with his hands in the air. "I just wanted to find some wild elves, but no. We have to fight the king's guard, run into a cyclops, and meet a runaway noble. I'm not meant for this magic sword stuff and super-elves. I'm just a thief, trying to find some elves..." He rambled on as he walked out of earshot.

Lena looked at Dorian and Razuul. "He doesn't make much sense when he talks, does he?"

Elendor

The deafening silence befit the overwhelming sense of dread storming in Elendor's mind. No birds sang, no insects buzzed, and none of the young elves spoke a word. The rays of the new day's sun struggled to break through the canopy of Nigereous Forest's ashen branches, and the windless atmosphere left the air stagnant and stale. The trees shifted in the dirt to form a trail, but an easy path to follow did little to brighten the spirits of three mentally, emotionally, and physically drained grieving friends.

Vaylon's lifeless body hung limp in the wooden harness affixed to Elendor's back. Before their journey began, they all agreed that their departed friend deserved the elven rite of passage. The rites could not be performed within the cursed forest, not that it mattered. None of them would have allowed the body of someone they loved to become one with that grim place.

The apparition's tale repeated in Elendor's mind. None of it made sense, yet the specter provided too much evidence of the truth in its message to cast doubt. He knew they would need to discuss the disastrous information they learned, but only saying a proper farewell to their friend mattered for now.

The trees opened to a field, pouring the blinding sunlight onto the group. Upon exiting, the three looked in the direction of their conquered elven home.

"Jocia, please prepare the site. I will find the seed." Galain solemnly requested before wandering off into the nearby trees.

Jocia drew out a runic symbol, opening a shallow pit in the earth. Shortly after, Galain returned, holding a single acorn in his hand.

"Not that it is any solace, but look what I have found." Galain presented the seed to Jocia and Elendor.

"A golden acorn. Vaylon would…would be…" Jocia attempted to convey her thoughts, but sorrowful tears overtook her ability to speak.

Elendor placed his arm around his grieving friend. "You are correct, Jocia. A golden acorn is rare, and when planted, never fails to grow a magnificent oak tree.

Vaylon would be proud."

Elendor placed Vaylon's body in the pit while Galain placed the acorn on his chest. After three tries to steady her hand, Jocia drew another runic symbol that moved the earth and buried their deceased friend.

"Do you mind if I say the prayer?" Elendor asked.

"I think it is only right that you do. Vaylon was closest with you." Galain replied.

"Thank you. Vaylon..." Elendor took a moment to gather himself and fight back the tears. "We return you to the Mother. Although your spirit has departed from this world, your body shall live on. May this seed inherit your will, rising through the dirt and into the skies above. May it inherit your strength and grow to resist the harsh weather. May it inherit your beauty and bloom in the same fashion that yours warmed our hearts. In death, you bring life, and while you have made your final departure, your memory shall live on the hearts and minds of those you held dear."

"Can you imagine how angry Morace would be if he discovered that a half-elf received the elven rites?" Galain solemnly asked, keeping his gaze fixed on Vaylon's grave.

"I wish he did know. I would like nothing more than to shove it in his smug face." Elendor returned with spite.

"Elendor, your words are too harsh. He is still the elder of Parvus Arbor." Jocia replied.

Elendor wanted to unleash his true feelings about the elven chief. Any mention of the elder elf that intended to execute a disabled member of his own race for no other reason than his birth circumstance always boiled his temper. However, throwing insults at the memorial service of a friend felt disrespectful and inappropriate.

"What should we do now?" Galain purposely changed the subject. "The other provinces must be informed of the apparition's warnings. Perhaps we should venture to Baxis."

"Baxis is closest, but we do not know anyone in that city. In Tenebris, we know the lord regent. I think it best to journey back there." Jocia replied.

"Our horses are gone. The path to Tenebris is long and hard, and we do not have the supplies to make the trip." Galain argued.

"What about our own city?" Elendor interjected.

"Elendor, you know as well as I that Parvus Arbor

fell to the orcs." The look on Galain's face conveyed his frustration.

"Yes, of course, but what of the elves?"

"Please do not tell me you still think you can defeat an army of orcs by yourself. Besides, we do not even know if the elves were spared."

"No, those delusions have passed, but think on it. The elves must be alive. If what the phantom conveyed to us is true, would it not benefit from leaving as many elves alive as possible?"

"That is true," Jocia agreed. "But what difference does that make? It does not change the number of orcs roaming the city. Plus, we do not know where the elves are being kept."

"As far as the orcs are concerned, I believe we can circumvent that issue. We are elves. We are born with night vision and are naturally light on our feet. Besides that, we know these woods far better than any orc. If we wait until nightfall, we can sneak into the city undetected."

"Even if we could enter the city undetected, we still do not know where our people are being kept." Galain pinched his chin in thought.

"There is only one place they could be hidden."

"The Vincula cells?" Jocia blurted. "Those have not been used since the Elven-Dwarven Wars a millennia ago. Surely they are decrepit."

"Not true. Once a year, Morace ensured that I used my arbormancy to prevent them from decaying. I never understood why, but I could not be more grateful for the stubborn fool's insistence."

"The cells are on the forest floor." Galain fidgeted with the dagger on his belt. "Getting to the cells undetected should be simple."

"True, but there will certainly be several orcs guarding the cells," Jocia added.

"Nothing an elven warrior and two mages cannot handle." Elendor gave a confident smile.

Seeing his friend's smile felt foreign. Elendor knew the grins' superficiality, but it warmed his heart to see them after spending days without seeing any joyful expressions. Having a goal to accomplish distracted them from the misery of losing their close friend and allowed them to focus on a mission instead of the ominous tale of the apparition.

The rest of the afternoon, the friends spent

planning their route, discussing strategies, and ensuring their bellies were full. Once the night reached its darkest hour, the mission began.

The three darted through their woodland home. Galain lead the way, followed close behind by Jocia, while Elendor trailed from a distance. With Elendor still utilizing new legs, the trio thought it best for him to remain separated as he posed the largest threat to alarm the orcs of their presence.

High above their heads, Parvus Arbor burned with activity. Lantern light beamed faint rays through the branches and walkways. The foreign smell of burning timber drifted in the air, blotting out the familiar aroma of nature that Elendor adored. The murmur of deep voices filled the night in a strange mixture of hostility and merriment. Footsteps boomed on the wooden paths as he passed underneath, wafting the stench of their unwashed bodies from above.

Elendor found the treacherous trek far easier than he expected. He took his first steps only a short time ago, yet silently speeding through the wooded area felt natural. Not a single twig snapped, and not once did he lose his footing. Only an elf could traverse an area filled with obstacles that threatened to reveal their location with such grace and ease. Elendor never felt more one with his heritage.

Strangely, his nerves remained calm. He expected his stomach to quiver, yet he felt uncharacteristically confident. No sweat covered his brow. His hands remained steady as he darted between the shadows of the trees. Not once did he worry that his lack of coordination would jeopardize the mission.

Elendor silently approached his friends as they peered behind trees with the Vincula cells in sight to assess the situation.

"What do you see, Galain?" Elendor whispered

"You were correct, Elendor. All of our people are held within the cells. Three guards roam the front of the cells, but I want to get an aerial view to make sure there are none out of sight."

Galain climbed the tree with the speed of a squirrel fleeing a predator. Elendor wondered if his new-found eleven abilities would allow him to do the same or if Galain's years of tutelage to become a warrior allowed him to climb with such speed. Before long, Galain returned to the forest floor.

"It is only the three. Each one holds a spear and shield, and one possesses an alarm horn. He will be our first target. Also, Heece is being held separate from the rest. They have him bound to a tree to the east, and he does not look well."

Elendor saw the pain in Galain's eyes. Throughout the years, Galain gushed about Heece, the Parvus Arbor Guard captain and Galain's mentor and hero. Elendor could not imagine the torment he felt from seeing him in such a state.

"How bad is his condition?" Elendor asked. "Does it appear that he could still fight?"

"Of course! It is Heece. Only death could prevent him from swinging a blade."

"Then we should free him first. He would be a big help in getting the rest of the elves out of here."

"Should we take out the guards first?" Jocia asked.

"He is pretty far removed from the others, and the orcs do not seem to patrol that area."

"Then it is settled. With Heece's military mind, we will assuredly come up with the best strategy to liberate our people." Elendor gave a sly smile.

The trio crept through the forest, with Galain

leading the way. After taking another scan to ensure no orcs roamed the area, they quietly approached Heece.

A rope, tied on one end to a high branch, bound his wrists overhead and served as the only means of keeping him upon his feet. His head hung, drooping his stringy hair across his face. No clothes adorned his body, save for a single strip of cloth that preserved the humiliation of exposure. Small wounds throughout his battered body crusted with blood, and one of his fingers bent unnaturally to the side. One of his wounds stood out far more than the others. A bruise in deep colors of black, blue, and purple covered his side from the pit of his arm to his waist.

Galain approached first. "Heece!" He said in a whisper. "Do not worry. I will get you down."

In a single swift motion, Galain jumped and cut the rope. Heece collapsed to his knees, looked up, and rapidly blinked his eyes to clear the haze. A trickle of dried blood ran from his nose, and a bump formed on his swollen lower lip, but his face remained otherwise unmarred.

"Galain? Jocia? And is that you, Elendor?" Heece asked in a dry, cracked voice.

"Yes, it is us." Elendor smiled.

"By the mother, you have legs!" A joyous tone emitted through the strain of pain in his voice. "And look at that arm! I am so happy for you."

"Thank you, Heece. However, there is no time for that right now. What has happened here?"

"Where is Vaylon?"

The three friends dropped their heads. "He…he did not make it." Elendor struggled to reply.

"I see. I am so sorry. How did it happen?"

"Let us talk about that later. Please tell us what happened." Galain knelt to be eye-to-eye with his mentor.

"Morace happened."

"What? What do you mean?" Jocia asked.

"Not long after you three left, the Chieftain Ceremony commenced for Morace. Shortly thereafter, he left for the capital to swear allegiance to King Magicent. When he returned, I saw a change in him. He seemed on edge…nervous, jumpy, and unnaturally indecisive. I tried confronting him about his behavior, but he dismissed me, insisting that he was merely settling into his new role as chief."

"That makes little sense." Elendor rolled the cloth

of his tunic between his finger and thumb. "That man has thought of nothing more than the day he would become chief for over a century."

"I thought the same thing." Heece attempted to rise to his feet, but the pain in his side crumbled him back to his knees. Gently, Jocia and Galain helped him to stand. "However, his intentions soon became clear." Heece stared off for a moment. "Gods! I should have seen it. This situation is my fault."

"Please, Heece, remain calm." Jocia placed a gentle hand on his shoulder.

"One night, Morace gathered the entire city in the Grand Hall. He insisted that every citizen attend and even pulled all guards from their posts. I protested, but Morace stood firm. He said that his announcement was of vital importance and that every elf needed to hear his words. He stood before the congregation and began announcing his intentions as chief. He spouted about returning the elves to the old ways and maintaining the purity of the race. I thought it odd, as he recited these same declarations during the Chieftain Ceremony, but his words were not the only peculiar thing about this gathering. He seemed anxious. Sweat dotted his brow, and his eyes constantly peered at the Hall's windows. He gave me the impression of a man stalling for time. He stammered his words, repeated himself, and asked inconsequential questions. All the signs were there. I curse myself for not realizing it sooner."

"I am sure you are not to blame," Galain reassured. "Please, continue."

"Just as I drew my sword, intent on confronting Morace, a battalion of orcs burst through the Hall's doors. We stood no chance. They corralled us like sheep. Many of my guardsmen attempted to fight back, but between the surprise of the attack, the orcs' overwhelming size, and Morace screaming for us to lay down our arms, we were quickly defeated. Before long, only I fought back. I fell one of the savages, but before I could continue the fight, a club stuck me from my blind side and threw me into the wall. I woke here."

"By the way you tell the story, it seems as though Morace conspired with the orcs," Elendor interjected.

"That is exactly what happened. He told me himself."

"What?" Elendor, Jocia, and Galain whispered at once, louder than expected. Instantly, the three slapped their hands over their mouths.

"Shortly after I woke, Morace visited me. He walked up, still dressed in his finest robes, and completely free to roam our ancestral home, boasting he was doing this for our people. He insisted that our people's imprisonment was temporary and that once the beast races overthrow the king, we will be freed and allowed to secede from the kingdom. Morace says our union with the humans is unnatural, and he wants us to return to independence, the way it always should have been."

"That makes no sense." Elendor began his rant. "The union of the kingdom ended the Dwarven-Elven War that lasted over a hundred years. We depend on trade with the other provinces, and the realm has celebrated peace ever since the Beast Wars ended. Besides, what guarantee does he have that the orcs will keep their word? For all he knows, they will leave our people to rot in their cells and..."

"Elendor." Jocia took his hand. "Allow Heece to finish his tale."

"I understand, Elendor." Heece continued, "I thought the same. He only told me that he has certain guarantees that the orcs cannot disregard. Tell me, did you see our people before you came here?"

"Yes," Galain confirmed.

"Are they unharmed? Morace promised that our people are being treated well and are fed regularly. Did you see anything to the contrary?"

"They did not seem harmed or mistreated. Although, I could only see them from a distance."

Heece gave a relieved smile. "That is good news."

"Let us continue this conversation after we leave this area." Elendor insisted. "We must establish a plan to get our people out of here. Heece, what do you suggest?"

"I suggest we do no such thing."

"What do you mean?"

"Morace is a monster, not a fool. He knew that these ropes could not keep me bound forever. So, he devised a method of imprisonment with a threat. He told me that if I were to escape, he would kill one elf for every day I spent away from Parvus Arbor."

Jocia gasped. "Monster is not a strong enough word for that despicable elf."

"Agreed. However, we now an advantage… you three. Morace does not know that you returned and know what is happening here. If the three of you can get to the capital and warn the king of this invasion, he can send forces to liberate the city."

"Why not at least release our people from the cells?" Elendor asked.

"It would be impossible to get all of our people out of the forest without suffering massive casualties. Even if we could get them out, if our people were to disappear suddenly, the orcs would know an army would soon be on their doorstep. They would prepare traps and an ambush. It would put the king's army at a disadvantage. Besides, what would we do with hundreds of elves? Where would we go? And if we had a place to go, could the elderly and young ones make the journey?"

"What about you?" Jocia inquired.

"You will have to return me to my bindings. We cannot let the orcs know that anything is amiss."

"No, we cannot return you to that miserable state! Besides, we…we have reason to believe that the king will not help us." Galain replied in a harsh whisper.

Heece gave a single chuckle. "How could you possibly know such a thing? The peace treaty clearly…"

"It is a very long story that would require much more time than we presently possess." Elendor soured his face, looking away from the elven guard. "Please trust us for now."

Heece raised an eyebrow at each of the friends. "Alright, I do trust you. There is another way: Marius Vybian, the commander of Baxis. He is a good man and a friend. Tell him about what has happened. He will want to gather his soldiers and come to help. I am certain. Remember, his lord, Eric Hardwood, is a degenerate. You will have to appeal to his selfish nature to persuade him to allow such a venture, but I believe it can be done. If that does not work, you must make the treacherous journey to Villam. Seek out High Commander Calder Heskin. He is stubborn and old for a human, but he is noble and just. If all else fails, journey to Prasillo. Lord Bently will assuredly not stand for this."

"What of the dwarves in Durrum?" Jocia asked.

"The dwarves still harbor hatred of the elves. I am afraid it is unlikely they will allow you even to enter their province, let alone their city."

"Why are we talking as if this is happening? I refuse to leave you here like this, Heece." Galain's eyes reddened and lips quivered as he fought to prevent his emotions from spilling forth.

"Galain, my apprentice, have faith that what I tell you is our best course of action. You must put your feelings for me aside and do what is best for our people." Heece looked at each of the young elves. "This journey will be long and hard, but I am certain the Miracle Three can handle it. Stay with each other, trust each other, and most importantly, believe in each other. Galain, please return me to my restraints."

Galain gave his mentor a hug, which caused him to wince in pain. Jocia re-tied the ropes around Heece's wrists while Galain ran the other end of the rope back up the tree. Once he returned, he could no longer hold back the tears.

"Before you leave, take the ring from my finger. It has the emblem of the High Commander of Parvus Arbor etched into it. I use it to press wax seals on official communications. Perhaps it will help you convince the other provinces."

Galain took the ring. "You must stay alive. Please, Heece, do not tempt Morace. I promise we will return."

"Be strong young ones."

With heavy hearts, Elendor and his friends began their journey north.

Ramon

It happened again. The future leader of Tenebris, Lena Richter, disappeared. For days, they searched in vain to locate the young heir. Some of Ramon's men sustained injuries or fell ill as they waded through the treacherous surrounding swamp. Leeches attached to their skin, swarms of insects buzzed at their heads, and aquatic creatures attacked from beneath the murky waters. The search spread to include the surrounding towns, recruiting hundreds more to help, yet they found no clue to her whereabouts.

This disappearance felt very different from the last. She did not leave a note, she did not experience a traumatic event, and she did not have a confrontation with her Uncle Stefan. Ramon felt certain that Lena left the province, but he couldn't put his finger on why he possessed this premonition.

With his second-in-command, Diana Torres, at his side and his soldiers bringing up the rear, Ramon entered through the gates of Tenebris. They barely made it past the city's portcullis when Stefan Richter, the lord regent, Lena's currently-distressed uncle, approached them.

"Any luck today, Commander Alcaldo?" Stefan's eyes glistened with worry.

"I'm sorry, Lord Regent."

Ramon knew the next step. A noble vanished, meaning a search that covered the entire kingdom would ensue. Messenger birds would be sent to every province with a royal decree that all armies should conduct a thorough search of their respective province. Trackers would be sent from the capital, and bounty hunters would scour the landscape. The addition of thousands of people searching would help everyone, except Stefan Richter.

Lena Richter's ascension to lordship loomed in just a few short months. All eyes would shift to Stefan, who stood the most to gain by her sudden vanishing. With Stefan being the only other Richter remaining, the king would have no choice but to promote him to lord. However, rumors and accusations would spread like wildfire. Whispers of his involvement in Lena's disappearance would follow him like a shadow. Eventually, he could even face a revolt that would throw the entire province into chaos.

Ramon knew better. He only met the Richter family a short time ago, but their relationship's nature became immediately apparent. Stefan raised Lena since early childhood, and even though the girl's eccentricities produced many difficulties, he loved her. Ever since Lena disappeared, Stefan abandoned all of his duties to focus on finding her. He paced around the city. He prayed to his god for assistance. He prepared fresh clothing and gathered ingredients for her favorite meals for her eventual return. Not a single doubt lingered in Ramon's mind that Stefan could ever involve himself in anything that could cause his adoptive daughter harm.

"Oh, I nearly forgot. A message arrived from the capital." Stefan handed a rolled parchment to Ramon. Diana's face lit upon seeing the paper.

"Ram…Commander Alcaldo, look at the seal." Ramon turned the parchment to see the king's stamp pressed into the wax. Messages and orders for members of the king's guard like himself always came from the High Commander's proxy. Messages from the king were traditionally reserved for nobility. Although Ramon possessed noble blood, being the son of the lord of Prasillo, he gave up his noble rights the day he joined the king's guard.

Ramon immediately unfurled and read the message. "It seems we have been recalled to the capital, but this is very strange."

"What is it?" Diana insisted.

"The message is signed by the prince."

"The prince? Why would he use the king's seal? Do you think something has happened to the king?"

"Seems unlikely. The king has yet to reach seventy, and last I saw, he was healthy as a horse."

"This is beyond unfortunate," Stefan interjected. "I don't know how we can possibly continue the search without you."

"I apologize, Lord Regent. I wish that…"

"Don't worry. I'll find her." The baritone voice appeared suddenly behind Ramon, scaring him nearly out of his skin.

Ramon turned to find the source of the voice. "Alexander! Where have you been?"

"None of your business."

"You are Lord Regent's bodyguard. What kind of bodyguard disappears for days on end?" Ramon turned to Stefan. "Why do you allow this behavior?"

A look of embarrassment spread across Stefan's face. "Alexander and I have a...special arrangement."

Ramon approached Alexander, stopping when their noses were a finger's length apart. "What kind of arrangement exists that allows a bodyguard to be bereft of his responsibilities?"

"R-Ramon, I mean Commander Alcaldo, I don't think..."

"I don't care." Ramon cut off Diana's protest. "I have been told that Alexander here is the best tracker in the kingdom. Yet, when his talents are needed most, he vanishes without a word."

"You need to back off...right now" Alexander's last words rumbled in his throat like a beast's growl. His eyes changed shape, with the iris widening until white no longer remained.

Ramon jumped back and drew his sword. "What are you?"

Ramon's soldiers drew their weapons and formed a circle around their commander. The citizens tip-toed to see the skirmish taking place at their city's gate.

"Please, please, put your weapons away." Stefan placed a hand on Ramon's shoulder. "I promise, Alexander is not a threat."

"It's not just that, Lord Regent." Diana began. "Duty means everything to Ramon. He cannot turn a blind eye to those who neglect their responsibilities."

"If it will sheath your swords, I will tell you everything."

"Fine." Ramon sheathed his sword and ordered his men to begin preparation for their journey home.

Stefan released a deep sigh. "This tale brings shame upon my family, so I feel no joy in telling it. Shortly after the Holy Wars between Tenebris and Sanctum, the Tenebris forces were left vulnerable. A clan from a nearby settlement saw this as an opportunity. They attacked the city, intending to conquer it for themselves. Their forces outnumbered our own by five to one, but they failed to realize that a talented necromancer can easily equal twenty through summonings. The battle did not last long. Hordes of zombies, skeletons, and chimeras surrounded their army and left them with no choice but surrender.

"My ancestor, Heinrich Richter, did not take kindly to the attack. The clan begged for their lives, vowing to serve the Richter family if they were allowed to live. However, servitude would not satisfy Heinrich's anger. He wanted to ensure that not only the clan's current members would suffer, but their children and their children's children as well. History tells us of Heinrich's ineptitude as a leader but also praises his talent for casting curses. In his anger, he devised a new curse for the attackers, a curse named lycanthropy."

"Lycanthropy?" Ramon could not believe his ears. "You mean werewolves?"

"That's correct. Curses of such magnitude require the person on which the spell is cast to accept the hex willingly. In order to escape death, the clan accepted the curse, with the term of serving the Richter family for three generations."

"However," Alexander interjected, "Heinrich lied. I am the seventh generation of the clan, and I am still compelled to serve."

"I don't understand." Ramon looked between Stefan and Alexander. "You routinely venture off on your own. How is that servitude?"

"As the current ruling leader of the Richter family, I can allow him to leave the city for seven days. After that, the curse compels him to return. If he resists, the curse will permanently transform him into a mindless beast."

"If Alexander's family has already fulfilled the terms they agreed to, why don't you lift the curse?" Diana asked.

"Curses don't work like that. There is always a tether to a curse. If I tether a curse to myself, the moment I die, the curse is lifted."

"Which means," Alexander continued, "the curse is tethered to an object."

"My grandfather was able to loosen, or rather twist the centuries-old curse. Alexander's entire clan is no longer required to serve the Richters. Only one needs to serve, but if no one in his clan volunteers, the entire clan will lose their humanity."

"That doesn't sound so bad," Diana replied. "I mean, servitude is certainly undesirable, but you're a clan of lycanthropes. I imagine you are one of the fiercest fighters in all of Preclarium. Even the death knight himself would likely fall to you."

Frustration filled Alexander's voice. "Being a lycanthrope causes one's blood to run hot. None of my clan survives past the age of forty. This has drastically reduced our numbers. I am one of only twenty of us left. I recently reached my thirty-eighth year, and I will soon leave my daughter fatherless."

"Where is the object now?" Ramon asked.

"No one knows," Stefan replied. "However, Alexander can feel its presence. That is why he leaves. When he feels its presence, he asks to leave to try to locate it."

"If Alexander can feel its presence," Ramon raised a brow, "why not send a search party? A group would have a much easier time finding a stationary object."

"It is not stationary," Alexander replied. "I feel its presence from time to time, but as soon as I get close, it vanishes. Recently, the object has been far more active, though. During my last trip, the sensation led me to a farm to the northwest, where a battle had taken place. Bodies of the king's guard scatted across the field, patches of scorched grass and trees spread in every direction. I found imprints in the ground in the shape of feet far too large to belong to any human, elf, or dwarf.

The prior time, I traced the object to a ravine in the far north. There, I found the bodies of a couple of scoundrels with their throats cut."

"So is someone roaming the kingdom, fiercely guarding the object?" Diana speculated.

"No. If that were the case, my lycanthrope senses would easily be able to track and catch them. With the way the object vanishes, I have a different theory. I believe the object resides in Sapientae, the library of Doleum."

"Library? Doleum? As in the father of the gods, Doleum?" Diana looked at Ramon to see if the proclamation confused him as much as she.

"I have heard of Sapientae," Ramon recalled.

"According to legend, Doleum built a temple at the beginning of time. Its purpose was to store all of the world's knowledge for all of its inhabitants to share. However, people misused the information. They used the library to gain advantage over others in conflict and war. It culminated the day a human stole ancient texts from the library and used the spells within to wipe out the kymarian race. In response, Doleum hid the library, placing a guard of infinite power at its doors to prevent anyone from entering it ever again. Nevertheless, this is all just legend. There is no historical account of the library's existence, nor any record of how the kymarian's disappeared."

"That is because the library moves," Intensity flashed in Alexander's eyes. "Think of every tale told of the heroes of the past. They appear seemingly from nowhere with a new ability or spell that saves the kingdom from ruin in every account. Euroch the Storm appeared on the Dwarven-Elven War battlefield to summon a lightning bolt with more power than anyone had previously seen. No one knew where Garrett the Bold vanished to before the Battle of the Rivers, yet he suddenly appeared in the center of the orc army, utilizing spells that should be too powerful to cast through a sword. In almost every account of these legendary figures, they disappear for a time and reappear with immeasurable power. I believe it is happening again. The library is appearing to someone of vital importance to the kingdom, but for some reason, this person has not entered yet. Instead, others are finding the library, and the guardian is leaving the bodies of those who dare to enter without permission in its wake."

"This all seems pretty unbelievable, doesn't it?"

"Diana, the other day, we saw the soul of a young girl jump into the body of a demon. At this point, my propensity for disbelief has greatly diminished."

Diana confessed, "Ever since we came here, nothing makes sense anymore. Just wait until Luis hears all of this."

"Speaking of Luis, is he well enough to travel?" Ramon asked.

"The doctor's magic should keep him well enough, yes."

"Alright, go make sure the men are ready for the journey back to the capital." Ramon turned to Stefan and Alexander.

"Thank you for telling me your tale. I am sorry for giving you such a hard time, Alexander. I wish you luck in finding Lena. I pray to the gods she is healthy and safe."

"Thank you for everything, Commander. I wish you safe travels."

Marius

Marius lifted the hatch to a tunnel that led to the king's castle. Only the king and the high commanders of the provinces knew of this secret entrance. It served as a means of escape for the royal family if a situation arose that demanded a confidential and expedient retreat. He considered entering through the main gates, but he knew the protocol for gaining an audience with the king.

Policy required that those from the other provinces first meet with their province's representative, serving as a member of the king's council. This way, citizens could not bother the king with trivial matters. If the council member thought the citizen's complaint required the king's attention, he or she could introduce the issue to the king during the weekly council meeting. If the representative determined the citizen possessed dire information that required the king's immediate attention, the council member could arrange for the meeting with haste. Outside the lords of province and the king's high commander, no one could circumvent the system. Marius wouldn't have dreamed of bypassing these procedures until this day, but he faced a peculiar situation.

Normally, he would meet with his representative without pause, but his lord's brother, Felix Hardwood, served as his province's representative. Eric Hardwood allowed the beast races to invade Baxis, meaning Felix was likely involved in whatever nefarious plot Eric hatched. He assumed Felix must have been controlling any reports and sightings by dismissing them as hearsay and rumors.

He expected to be chastised for utilizing the tunnel for an unintended purpose. He brought a significant risk of someone discovering the secret entrance, but since he held information vital to the kingdom's survival, he assumed the king would grant forgiveness.

"I guess this is where we part ways, Dogon," Marius said to the strange creature as it spun in circles, chasing its tail. "I hope we meet again." Marius found he really meant his words.

Marius entered the tunnel. With the hatch shut

behind him, no source of light remained to guide his way. Keeping his hand against the wall, he cautiously moved forward. Centuries of slippery mildew covered the stone. The squeaks of wandering rats reverberated as they ran from the human intruder. Waving his free hand in front of himself, he cleared away countless spider webs, hoping that none of the silken weavers decided to hitch a ride somewhere on his body. More than once, he nearly lost his footing on the slick path, but he managed to arrive at the end of the tunnel without sustaining injury.

The path ended at a wooden door that acted as the back of a wardrobe on the other side. Stepping into the cabinet, he pushed aside the hanging clothes to peer into the room through the crack between the wardrobe's double-doors. Aside from some lavish furnishings meant for castle guests, Marius saw an empty room three times his own chambers' size. Feeling it safe to step out, he quietly closed the doors behind him.

"Alright, now what?" He asked himself aloud.

Marius began mapping the castle in his mind. His visits to the capital were few and brief, but the extravagance of the king's home left an unforgettable impression. Each visit left him in awe over the castle's immaculate condition, especially when compared to his home's dilapidated state in Baxis.

He preferred to meet with High Commander Werner, but he knew the odds of finding him would be slim. Like Marius, the death knight took great pride in his position. He frequently roamed the city, overlooking every aspect of the army's condition. Training procedures, siege weapon's condition, watch routines, the state of the battlements, no facet of the city's defense escaped Jonas Werner's watchful eye.

King Thomas Magicent rarely broke routine. Outside of special events, the man lived his life within three rooms: the Throne Room, the War Room, and his chambers. No one in the kingdom knew much about the enigma who held the title of king. He cared little for being seen by his subjects and held no desire for social interaction. Even during events such as jousts and balls, he only spoke when social standards required him to do so. Although his repute served him as an honorable and just man, his ominous aura and threatening posture kept most of his subjects at bay. Marius had seen the king a dozen times and never once saw him smile.

Marius crept to the only other door in the room.

On the other side, he heard the sounds of a bustling castle. Running back to the wardrobe, he searched for any clothes that would allow him to traverse the castle undetected. He inspected each garment but found only women's clothing. For a moment, he considered posing as the opposite gender, but without a wig or a means to shave the stubble from his face, no dress could hide his identity.

Marius devised a new plan. Keeping his ear to the door, he waited patiently. Before long, he heard the unmistakable clang of metal greaves striking the stone floor. As soon as the footsteps rang in front of the door, Marius pulled the door open with force. The action startled the unsuspecting knight, but not as much as what he turned and saw.

"Hello there," Marius said with a smile and open arms.

"H-High Comm…" The knight stammered as he entered the room, but before he could finish his words, Marius grabbed him and threw him to the ground. Marius struck the knight's chin with a swift kick, sending his helmet rattling on the floor. The downed knight panicked, trying to get to his feet, but the Baxis High

Commander mounted him before he could rise. Pulling the dagger from his belt, Marius struck the knight in the temple with the handle, knocking him unconscious.

"Sorry about that pal but I really need your armor."

Marius began to unbuckle the knight's armor, but before he could release the first binding, a high-pitched screech grabbed his attention.

Marius turned to see a trembling handmaid standing in the hall.

"Wait. It's not…" Before Marius could finish, the handmaid screamed and ran away. "Ugh. Of course!"

With Marius's plan blown, he knew only one option remained. He needed to find the king at any cost. He dashed out of the room and down the hall. As he ran, servants hugged the wall to give him a wide berth. Marius tried to circumvent the workers with a slower reaction speed but accidentally toppled a young servant and an unaware old man carrying a tray of scrapped food.

"Halt!" Two knights ran up the staircase that led down to the Throne Room.

Marius spun and ran toward the opposite staircase. Before he could reach them, two more knights came running, brandishing spears.

With both paths blocked, Marius decided to push forward. The first knight thrust his spear at Marius, but Marius quickly ducked beneath the strike. Without breaking stride, he drove the tip of his dagger into the crook of the knight's arm. The second knight thrust his spear at Marius, but the Baxis High Commander twirled to evade. Using the spin's momentum, he brought his dagger up and slashed a shallow wound in the opening at the jawline below the knight's helmet.

Marius ran down the stairs. Guilt flashed in his mind. He knew the men he cut suffered behind him as the Decay spell imbued on his dagger took effect. Soon they would both be nothing more than the husk of a decayed corpse. He thought about how the men did not deserve it. They merely performed their duty, trying to stop an invader. For all Marius knew, they both had children that would never see their fathers again.

Pushing down the remorse, Marius reached the bottom of the stairs and burst into the Throne Room. Scanning the room, he found the throne empty. Only two rooms remained to check.

Armored men flooded the room. Marius dashed to

the door that led to the War Room. Three men blocked his path, but none could compete with his skill. He sidestepped the first swing, pushed the man's shield arm inside, and stabbed at his armpit. He kicked the next man in the chest to knock him back and slashed the third man's uncovered nose. Returning to the second man, he dodged a sword swing and slid his blade into the back of his skull.

Several men chased him as he burst into the unoccupied War Room. Only one room remained to inspect. He began to leave, but a dozen men poured into the room. Marius postured himself to prepare for an onslaught, but instead, the men surrounded him with their weapons at the ready.

"Marius the Swift." An unfamiliar voice shouted from the Throne Room.

A man entered the room with an arrogant swagger. Marius recognized him as Adam Garrison, one of the Three Heads of Cerberus. His wide eyes seemed to smile as much as his mouth. The moon's light pouring through the nearby windows danced on his red-trimmed black armor. A blue hue reflected off the blade in his hand, identifying the scarce Hygard steel.

"I have waited a long time to meet you. You could say you're a hero of sorts to me." A high-pitched, maniacal laugh erupted from Adam.

"Listen, I know this is all crazy, but I have…"

"Vital information that you need to present to the king?" Adam finished Marius's sentence. "We are all aware of your important message. You want to tell the king that the beast races have infiltrated Baxis. Lord Hardwood sent a messenger bird ahead of you."

"What? Why would he…"

"He also told us of the real reason you are here. You plan to tell the king your lies so you can get close and cut him with that little cursed blade of yours."

Marius's jaw dropped. He didn't know if he felt more shocked about the lie or that he did not see it coming. "You can't possibly believe that."

"He's lying. You're lying. To be honest, I really don't care."

"But if I am telling the truth, the entire kingdom is in peril!"

"I'm sorry, you must not have heard what I just said. I. Don't. Care. I just want to fight you. Our orders are to capture you alive, but you know…accidents happen." Adam gripped his sword in both hands but kept his distance.

"I thought I was your hero."

"Of sorts. You see, I admire your skill, but you also stole something from me."

"Stole? I've never even met you."

"It's your name! They say Marius the Swift is the fastest man in the kingdom. They're wrong! I am the fastest man in the kingdom!" Red-faced, Adam screamed at the top of his lungs, veins in his neck corded.

"That's what you're upset about? That is the dumbest thing I have ever heard."

With lightning speed, Adam dashed at Marius. He leaned back to avoid the sword swipe, but his instincts proved a bit too slow. The tip of Adam's sword caught Marius's chest, opening a shallow wound from shoulder-to-shoulder.

Marius dropped to a knee, clutching the wound. Blood ran down his abdomen, but he knew the injury merely cut his flesh. His muscles remained in tact. As long as he could ignore the pain, he could continue the fight.

Adam skidded across the floor to stop his

momentum, knocking over two of the surrounding guards. From behind, a pair of soldiers approached Marius to capture him.

"Don't you dare!" Adam shouted. "Don't lay a finger on him! This is my fight!"

Marius rose to his feet. "You're mad."

Garrison's face twisted in rage. Seeing this, Marius discovered the key to winning the duel. His apparent mental instability served as his greatest weakness.

Adam dashed again. This time Marius expected the attack. Kicking off the nearby wall, Adam launched himself with another speedy attack, but Marius ducked once again.

"This isn't possible! No one can see me when I use my speed. How are you doing this?"

"I'm not seeing your attacks. They are just predictable. Do you think you're the first opponent I've faced with a Haste spell inscribed on the wind runestones in his legs?"

Adam gritted his teeth. "Predictable? I'll show you predictable!"

Adam streaked across the room, repeatedly

bouncing off the walls in every direction. Without care, he rammed into the other guards, sending each one flying. Marius tracked the mad speedster with his eyes, waiting for the right opportunity. More than once, Adam swiped his sword at Marius's head, but each attempt failed.

Finally, the moment came. Garrison dashed at Marius's back, expecting to run him through. Instead, Marius dropped to his hands and knees. Unable to stop, Adam tripped over the prone fighter and rolled across the floor.

Adam screamed, pounding his fist on the granite. Marius stood holding his side where his opponent's legs struck. His body ached, but he knew Garrison's condition fared worse than his own. Aside from the high-speed collision with the floor, the mad soldier just expended a vast amount of magical energy. One way or another, Marius knew the battle's end approached.

Adam began reciting a chant under his breath. Marius couldn't make out the words, but he deduced its purpose as the Head of Cerberus's breathing shallowed and the blood withdrew from his face. Only a maniac with a history of violence would have training to calm his madness, and Marius saw his opening.

"I thought you were fast. Is that really the best you have?"

"I am no fool. I know what you are doing." Adam rose to his feet and calmly walked to Marius while repeating his inaudible chant.

Adam swung his sword in a vertical stroke. Using the edge of his dagger, Marius redirected the strike while side-stepping. He followed by thrusting his weapon at his opponent's face, but Garrison leaned back to avoid the attack.

The two clashed their weapons. Marius ducked, swayed, spun, thrust, and slashed. Adam stabbed, swiped, blocked, and parried. Marius knew his choice of weapon put him at a disadvantage and that if the battle continued with his calm opponent, Garrison would eventually emerge victoriously. Even if he could land a killing blow, little time remained before dozens of more guards flooded the room. He needed to make his move now.

Marius thrust his foot into Adam's chest. The kick against his armor did no damage to his opponent, but it created the distance he needed. "Your name is Adam Garrison. I've heard of you too."

"I'm honored." The mad knight slashed at Marius,

but Marius jumped back to avoid.

"Your father, he's the head of the Galley Trading Company, isn't he? Burgess Garrison, I believe."

Adam's eye twitched. "You know nothing about my family. Keep your filthy mouth shut."

Marius found his point of attack. "Of course he is your father. How else could you have gotten into the Heads of Cerberus? It certainly wasn't your skill that earned you the position."

"Shut up!" Adam wildly swung his sword. With one hurled insult, all of the unstable warrior's form and technique diminished into amateurish desperation. His blade clanged against the stone floor and walls. Screaming and grunting with each attack, he discarded any concern for his rapid loss of endurance.

"Tell me, how much money did your father have to pay? Five hundred gold? No, that's far too low a price for the king to throw away his pride and allow someone with little skill to joining his elite force."

"I'll kill you!" Gripping his sword with both hands, Adam hacked at his opponent like a lumberjack chopping wood. The telegraphed strikes, Marius thought, even a child could avoid.

Veins bulged from Adam's neck as he screamed and threw a vertical strike. Marius dodged and stomped on the sword, ripping the blade from Garrison's hands. Seeing his opening, he raised his knee into the mad-man's chin, sending him sprawling to his back. Following up, Marius mounted him before Adam could rise and brought his dagger overhead to end the battle, but a glint from the corner of his eye halted his progress.

Marius turned to see a young soldier readying to slice him in two with a strange weapon. His staff, with a bladed sickle on each end, tore through the air. Marius ducked to avoid the strike, but the clever boy didn't aim for the head. The curved blade clashed against Marius's dagger, sending it sliding on the floor. Diving off Adam, he barely avoided the young man's follow-up strike.

"Yates! I told you and everyone else that he is mine! Do not interfere!" Adam shoved the young Yates before picking up his sword.

Yates seemed to barely notice Garrison. His stone-cold expression remained fixed on Marius. The blank look in his eyes reminded Marius of the gaze of the dead, yet he knew no necromancer summoned the transfixed young warrior.

Adam resumed his wild attacks. Marius ducked and dodged until the mad-man backed him into a corner. "I've got you now. Die!" Adam thrust the tip of his sword at Marius's abdomen.

Garrison's maddened and exhausted state resulted in a slow and sloppy attempt. Marius spun on the ball of his foot and avoided the strike. Mid-spin, he grabbed the back of Adam's skull and used the twirl's momentum to smash Adam's face into the wall.

The insane Head of Cerberus collapsed to the floor. Marius scanned the area for his dagger but found nothing. Looking back to Yates, he found him standing statuesque, glaring with a deadened look on his face.

"This way! Over here!" Marius heard echoing from deep inside the castle.

Marius bolted for the door. Looking back, he saw that Yates remained motionless. In the Throne Room, he could hear a legion of footsteps approaching from the far stairway. He dashed to the nearby stairwell, down the hallway, and into the room from which he first entered the castle. He sprinted into the secret path, shutting the doors behind him. Blindly, he ran the length of the passage, slipping, tripping, and falling along his way. Emerging through the hidden trap door, he collapsed onto his back to catch his breath. As he drew in gulps of air, a wet, rough hunk of flesh dragged across his face. Jolting up, he saw Dogon standing next to him with his pointed tail wagging in excitement.

"You're still here?" Marius asked between panting breaths. Standing to brush the dirt from his clothes, he looked to the dark horizon. "Well, Dogon, what should we do now?"

Jonas

The morning sun blazed on his black armor. After dropping Nathaniel off at his deceased nemesis's former cottage, he needed to attend to his daily duties as the king's high commander. The journey proved more treacherous than expected. Aside from wandering through the darkness of the woods, they were attacked by umbra beasts twice. With Nathaniel's injuries, the battles proved difficult. However, Jonas's abilities and familiarity with the savage monsters made short work of the carnivorous fiends.

As he approached the castle's entrance, his thoughts dwelled on Adam Garrison. He didn't know why the mad knight decided to let him escape with Nathaniel, nor why he accepted the lame excuse Jonas presented for removing a prisoner from the dungeon. A novice knight wouldn't believe he intended to bring a prisoner to a secret location for "special interrogation," let alone an experienced knight such as Garrison. He knew of only two reasons the mad-man would believe a blatant lie; he intended to report the situation to his new friend Prince Godwin or use the information for later advantage. Jonas both assumed and hoped for the latter.

Upon entering the castle courtyard, a panicked-looking Paul Cormac halted his rapid stride to rush to Jonas.

"High Commander! Where have you been? The entire kingdom has been searching for you all night!"

"I had personal business to attend to. What is happening?"

"Personal business," Paul responded skeptically.

"Anyway, the castle was attacked last night."

"Attacked? By who?"

"Marius Vybian."

"Vybian? The high commander of Baxis? Why would he possibly do such a foolish thing?"

"No one knows. Lord Hardwood sent a messenger bird ahead of him to warn us that High Commander Vybian had lost his mind and intended to assassinate the king. Apparently, he had delusions that the beast races returned to Preclarium and that the only way to stop the beasts from destroying the kingdom was to kill the king that banished them."

"What happened?"

"He appeared out of nowhere. We posted guards in every corner of the castle, but he was suddenly inside the castle as if he stepped through a magical portal. He killed several guards as he tried to make his way to the king. With all the guards watching the city's entrances, he nearly made it too. Luckily, Adam Garrison was still in the castle. He confronted Vybian but lost the battle. However, Garrison bought enough time for the guards to return to the castle."

"Did they capture him?"

"No. The sounds of the returning guards must have spooked him. He didn't even try to make it to the king's chambers. Instead, he vanished as suddenly as he appeared. We scoured the castle trying to find him, but no one has spotted him."

"Where was he last seen?"

"A guard spotted him heading to the guest hall, but by the time they arrived, he was gone."

Jonas knew exactly how Marius Vybian entered

the city. The guest hall led to the secret escape tunnel that led out of the city. "You can cancel the search. Vybian is gone."

"How do you know that? So many secrets with you lately." Cormac narrowed his eyes.

"I do not have to explain anything. I am still the high commander. You'd do best to remember that."

"You can keep your secrets. I don't actually care. However, you returned at the right time. The king just requested your presence in his quarters."

"His quarters? Why there?"

"I don't pretend to know any more about his intentions than I do about yours."

"Fine. Thank you, Cormac. Oh, and please…"

"Yeah, yeah, don't tell anyone blah, blah, blah." Paul gave a dismissive wave as he walked away.

Jonas started his journey to the king's chambers, returning salutes and greetings along the way. His thoughts dwelled on Marius Vybian. He knew the man. He exuded honor, kindness, and loyalty. An attack on the capital seemed positively out of character. Although madness could cause any man to do foolish things, Jonas could think of no situation that could cause such a steadfast soldier to throw all common sense aside.

Considering madness, his thoughts turned to his own fate. Before himself, every death knight succumbed to the affliction, and Jonas was long past the age when insanity should have overwhelmed his mind. He attributed his mind's sturdiness to keeping focused on his goal of ensuring the king kept his promise. However, time conquers all foes, and Jonas's time ran short.

Standing erect at the door of the king's quarters, he took a deep breath. Meeting with the kingdom's sovereign always filled him with unease and dread. The knowledge that the man could kill Jonas with a wave of his hand certainly contributed to the anxiety, but not as much as the thought of bringing up the decades-old promise the king had yet to fulfill. With a pair of quick slaps to his face to re-focus his mind, he gave a knock at the king's door.

"High Commander?" The king asked through the door.

"Yes, Your Grace." Jonas returned.

"Come in."

Jonas entered the room, bowed, and fell to one knee with his fist over his heart in salute.

"Please rise."

Snapping to his feet, Jonas saw the king in an unfamiliar state. King Thomas Magicent stood in his usual regal manner. His chin held high, his shoulders pushed back, and his hands folded behind his back. However, the rest of his appearance contrasted with what Jonas expected upon seeing the nation's ruler. His salt and pepper hair faded completely to gray. His drawn cheeks sunk, and the bags beneath his eyes hung low. Instead of his usual regal clothing, he wore a silken robe over a nightshirt.

"Your Grace, what has happened?"

King Thomas took a few steps to close the gap between the two men. Standing in front of Jonas, he pulled up the sleeve of his robe, revealing a series of red blotches on the crook of his arm.

"Y-Your Grace!" Shocked, Jonas looked into his king's eyes. "Is that what I think it is?"

"The Pox, yes."

"Have you seen Doctor Hemming yet? I have heard he has made advancements in magical medical treatment. Perhaps…"

"I have not. Cedric Hemming sends reports on his

research regularly. I have read all of them. He has made no progress on curing this particular disease."

"We'll send messenger birds to the other provinces. There are many doctors in Preclarium. Perhaps one of the other doctors has made more progress."

"We both know the results of such an inquiry. The Pox has been around for centuries, and no doctor has come close to a cure."

Jonas's mind raced. With everything going on with the prince, he couldn't think of receiving worse news.

"Your concern for my health warms my heart, but that is not why I summoned you." King Thomas turned and approached his nightstand. Pulling open the drawer, he withdrew a rolled parchment, returned to Jonas, and presented the paper to him.

"What is this, Your Grace?"

"A promise."

Jonas's eyes widened. Slowly lifting his shaking hand, he took the parchment from the king. "Y-Your Grace, I-I"

"You may look it over if you like." King Thomas walked to his window, folding his hands to their usual place at the small of his back. "Let me inform you that there are conditions to fulfilling the contract. Your time has not ended yet. I feel that the kingdom will soon be in dire need of your talents."

"What do you mean...Your Grace?" The shock of the situation nearly allowed Jonas to forget to include the honorific at the end of his sentence when speaking to the king.

"A conflict looms on the horizon. I fear that war is at our doorstep once again."

"War, Your Grace? The kingdom enjoys its greatest period of peace. All the provinces remain loyal, and the people love you. Who could possibly want war with the kingdom?"

"The beast races. I fear their return is imminent." Jonas fell speechless. He couldn't fathom the possibility of the beast races returning. After a moment of contemplation, he organized his thoughts. "Your Grace, how could the beast races return? There are only two ports of entry in Preclarium. Even if they were to over-take Baxis or Prasillo, we would know immediately. Besides, there is no way they possess the numbers to overcome your army and bannermen. Do you know something I do not?"

"I cannot present any evidence. Let's just call it intuition, a…hunch. Have I ever been wrong?"

"No, Your Grace." Jonas meant his words. He had served King Thomas for over two decades, and during that time, never once saw the ruler make a miscalculation or poor decision. He seemed to predict any significant event that could bring harm to the kingdom. The king always possessed the foresight to predict conflicts, disease outbreaks, and even natural disasters. Even when his foresight failed to anticipate calamity, he reacted to any disaster expeditiously to prevent a true catastrophe.

"Once the war has ended, your duty shall be fulfilled. My son is aware of that parchment and shall honor its contents."

"Your son, Your Grace? You don't expect to survive until the end of the war? People live with the Pox for years before it takes their life."

"The disease has been ravaging my body for longer than you know. It is by sheer will alone that I have held out this long. I needed to see my son's coronation. There is nothing more important to me than being the one who places the crown on his head."

The news of the upcoming war pushed the thoughts of the prince's depravity from Jonas's mind. "When do you plan to hold the coronation, Your Grace?"

"In one week. Normally, the lords of province would be invited, but I fear my health will not hold out long enough for them to make the journey. Have messenger birds sent to inform them of the coronation. They will not be happy, but it cannot be helped. Include in the message that the lords should prepare for war. Warn them of the beast races imminent attack, and have them shore up their defenses. Also, have them halt all trade and have them keep their citizens within their cities. We do not know where and when the beasts will attack."

"What of the capital? Should I prepare our forces for war?"

"We will prepare for attack, but we will not inform the commoners of the upcoming war. Bring all of the citizens inside the city walls. We will allow them to think that they are being brought inside for the coronation. During the event, we will publicly announce the beast's return."

"Yes, Your Grace." Jonas slammed his fist into his chest before turning to leave. Grabbing the door's handle, he halted his exit. He knew this could be his last opportunity to speak with King Thomas about the prince. "Your Grace, may I speak with you openly about an important matter before I go?"

"Make it short, High Commander. I need my rest."

"Your Grace, it's about the prince. Why have you stripped me of some of my duties and given them to your son? Have I disappointed you in some way?"

"Of course not. My son will soon be king. He needs to understand a king's responsibilities as well as the responsibilities of his subjects. This change is only temporary. Is that all?"

"No, Your Grace. If you know of Prince Godwin's recent actions, why haven't you stopped him? He is killing your people in the streets." Jonas prepared himself. He knew confronting King Thomas with questions about his leadership often led to him activating the spell branded on every member of the king's army's chest. The intense pain it caused left the recipient in indescribable agony, but Jonas felt the kingdom's survival depended on him confronting the king on the uncomfortable subject. To his surprise, the king remained stoic.

"Jonas," King Thomas surprised Jonas by calling

him by his name, "I understand your concern. The responsibilities of a king are vast and overwhelming. Godwin is simply trying to find his way as the future ruler. He has lived within my shadow his entire life. He wants to leave his own mark on the kingdom's history without being only known as King Thomas's heir. Even I went through something similar when I first received the crown. Don't worry; he will soon abandon his foolish behavior."

"Your Grace, what of the rumor that Prince Godwin plans to abolish the use of runestones for anyone outside the royal family?"

"Godwin knows better than to enact such a foolish law. Even if he didn't, he would soon realize the importance of the lords of province and the armies having magic power when the war comes. I appreciate your concern, but Godwin will be a good king."

"Yes, Your Grace. Thank you for hearing my concerns." Jonas saluted again and left the king's chambers.

Heading down the hallway, he searched for the first vacant room he could find. He slipped inside an empty chamber and locked the door behind him. Whipping the king's parchment across the room, he let loose an exasperated scream. He didn't know what to expect when confronting the king about his son, but he'd hoped for more than excuses. He knew the king's misconceptions about his son would bring the kingdom to ruin. Jonas saw firsthand the atrocities the prince committed. The belief that a psychopath would outgrow acts of cruelty was both naive and dangerous. He knew only one path led to the salvation of the kingdom: regicide.

Clarissa

Clarissa stood on the executioner's platform. Looking out at the gathered crowd, she spotted Sir Kenneth in his paladin's armor. She wished he knew what happened. She pleaded with Lord Alcaldo to stay Sir Gabriel's execution, but her cries were ignored. She tried telling the Villam Lord what his son tried to do to her, but he dismissed her story as falsehoods. As punishment for slandering his son, he forced her to witness the execution of Sir Gabriel firsthand.

Two Villam guards flanked her. Francisco Alcaldo stood with his wife, Catalina, at his side. Their sons, Antonio and Carlos, stood beside their father. A wide smile spread across Antonio's face as he patiently awaited the death of the man that nearly took his life. His reattached arm rest in a sling that revealed the purplish hue of his fingers. Clarissa knew that color would soon return to the appendage, but the scar from Sir Gabriel's blade would remain. She hoped it would serve as a reminder of the repercussions of trying to force himself on a woman. Carlos's expression revealed his feelings about the execution. His eyes actively avoided the stocks that would soon hold the disgraced paladin, and his pursed lips revealed that he wished to be anywhere but here. It seemed like a cruel trick of fate that made Carlos the youngest Alcaldo instead of the eldest.

A murmur broke out in the crowd. Clarissa looked at the sea of people and saw a small group of men parting the waves as they approached the platform. The leader, an immense man, dressed in white armor large enough to fit two grown men, cut through the crowd with like-armored men trailing behind him. As he walked up the platform's stairs, Clarissa recognized the colossal man.

Everyone in Sanctum knew Severin Ward, better known as the 'Painted Shield.' The paladin's reputation spread throughout the kingdom. Clarissa cared little for the tales of a paladin's adventures, but the Painted Shield's tales of violence and brutality caught even her attention. The amiable sound of his epithet betrayed his true nature. When he accomplished a mission, it typically ended in gore and carnage. According to lore, every encounter with the man concluded with him bashing his shield into the face of his opponent until he crushed their skull. This means of execution didn't earn him the name; instead, his habit of leaving his adversaries' blood on his shield established his moniker.

Clarissa returned her eyes to the crowd to locate Sir Kenneth, but he no longer stood where she last saw him. She scanned the gathering for his white armor but could not spot the paladin.

The Painted Shield removed his helmet as he approached Lord Alcaldo. His gray-streaked hair, shaved bald on the sides and back, slicked back to the nape of his neck. A wiry gray bush of hair rested above his lip, as well as two more above his eyes, resembling caterpillars more than brows. Clarissa had met many paladins and knights in the twilight of their career. All of them showed signs of their battle experience: a crooked nose, a missing ear, at least one scar that decorated their face. Yet, not a single blemish adorned his aging skin. A sword that seemed as long as Clarissa's height hung from his hip, and true to his name, streaks of dried blood painted his massive shield.

Shifting her gaze to avoid looking directly at the fabled paladin, Clarissa trained her ear to eavesdrop on the conversation. She silently prayed that the Painted Shield came to free Sir Gabriel from the execution.

"Lord Alcaldo, I apologize for interrupting." The Painted Shield's deep, gruff voice rose above the crowd's roar. "We intended to arrive sooner, but we ran into some complications on the road."

"You are Sir Severin Ward, the Painted Shield, if I am not mistaken. To what do we owe the honor of your visit?" Lord Alcaldo responded with a hint of aggression in his voice.

"You know my name? My reputation precedes me. I am not here on any orders. I came of my own volition."

"I thought a contingent from Sanctum was scheduled to interrogate Sir Gabriel days ago. Since none arrived, I decided to move forward with the execution."

"Lord Bright decided to cancel the interrogation due to some issues with governing the city. I am here to present a request." A devilish grin spread across Sir Severin Ward's face.

"You wish to dissuade me from executing the

paladin? I cannot do that. Sir Gabriel has wounded my family's honor. That is something that cannot be forgiven."

"On the contrary, I am here to request that you allow me to carry out the sentence."

Clarissa's heart sank.

"You wish to carry out the execution? Why?"

"I personally trained Sir Gabriel. His failure is my failure. I would like to atone for my own sins by taking the head of one of my beloved students." Sir Severin taped his bloody namesake. "I'll add his blood to my collection to remind me of my negligence."

"You intend to behead him with your shield? That method would be far too gruesome for a crowd."

"For anyone but me, it would be. The bottom of my shield is bladed. It can do the deed just as easily as any sword."

"I'm not sure if pride or bloodlust drives you, but I don't care. If you want to carry out the sentence, I have no objection."

Moments later, six soldiers led by a man wearing a white mask exited the castle. At the center of the group, a nearly naked Sir Gabriel hobbled with his ankles and wrists bound by chains. His state betrayed the robust and handsome appearance she saw just days ago. His thin stature revealed his ribcage beneath his skin, and it appeared as though he lost over twenty pounds of muscle. His rugged facial features deteriorated, leaving a skeletal look on his face. His usual manicured golden locks looked like a mound of dirty straw, and dirt covered him from top to bottom.

The crowd roared at Sir Gabriel. They hurled rocks, mud, and rotten fruits and vegetables at him. Mockery and insults filled the air as some of the citizens attempted to break through the guards to assault the chained paladin. All the while, the noble knight kept his gaze fixed on the ground, even as he approached the stocks that would soon lock him into place.

The Painted Shield approached, bringing his face close to Sir Gabriel's ear. Clarissa could not hear the renowned paladin, but his words produced a profound effect on Sir Gabriel. His body shook, his jaw dropped, his eyes widened, and he gave Clarissa a quick glance before turning his gaze to his executioner. She could only assume that whatever the Painted Shield said included herself, allowing dread to creep into her heart.

"My people, hear me now." Lord Alcaldo spoke into a wind-runestone-empowered amplifier. The crowd hushed to hear his words. "We gather today to witness the execution of Sir Gabriel Nobilis, a former paladin of Sanctum, for the crime of unjustly attacking and permanently wounding my son, Antonio Alcaldo."

The crowd reacted with an onslaught of jeers aimed at the accused paladin. Clarissa saw a beaming smile spread across the face of the Painted Shield and Antonio as they absorbed the spectacle like a deranged sponge. Sir Gabriel kept his emotionless gaze fixed on the stocks.

"Sir Gabriel," Lord Alcaldo called, "as punishment for your crimes, you are hereby sentenced to death by means of beheading."

The soldiers pushed Sir Gabriel to his knees. He gave no resistance as they locked his head and wrists into the wooden openings.

Clarissa's breathing intensified. Beads of sweat formed on her arms and forehead. The beat of her heart drowned the crowd's roar in her ears. As the Painted Shield brought his massive shield above his head, a wave of panic consumed Clarissa, and her body reacted without her mind's permission.

"No!" She shouted as she rushed to stop the deadly blow. She only took a few steps before a pair of guards snatched her arms to halt her progress.

"Oh, don't worry, princess," the Painted Shield mocked, "You and I have our own matters to discuss after I take care of this business."

"What business could you possibly have with me?"

"One task at a time, princess, but don't worry. I am sure what I have to tell you will make you forget about this fool. Your life is about to take a dramatic turn after this mess."

Clarissa stopped fighting the guards. She couldn't fathom the meaning behind the Painted Shield's words. Her banishment didn't forbid her from entering Villam, and Sir Gabriel attacked the noble's son outside of her orders. A tidal wave of possible consequences flooded her mind, but she pushed the thoughts aside. Only ensuring Sir Gabriel didn't pay for defending her honor mattered.

Clarissa ripped her arms from the guard's loosened grip. She rushed to the Painted Shield, but

223

another guard blocked her path and grabbed her shoulders. Ignoring her, Sir Severin began his shield's descent to remove Sir Gabriel's head. However, the guard made a fatal mistake by leaving Clarissa's arms free. She traced out the runic symbol for the Holy Judgment spell on the guard's cuirass with lightning speed. A moment later, a beam of light descended from the heavens, bathing the guard in the destructive force of the most powerful spell known.

The shockwave blew Clarissa from the stage. The wooden platform erupted, spraying splinters in every direction. A cloud of dust and dirt exploded, filling the courtyard. Her body ached, her ears rang, and her mouth filled with a metallic taste from accidentally biting her tongue as she flew through the air.

Fighting the pain in her body, she propped herself up to scan the area. Through the haze, she saw that the spell eradicated the guard from existence. The entire Alcaldo family rolled on the ground covering various wounds with their hands. The Painted Shield lay unmoving on his back. She desperately searched for Sir Gabriel and soon confirmed her failure.

Sir Gabriel's headless body sprawled on the

ground. Dust filled her lungs, tears overwhelmed her eyes, and regret consumed her heart. She failed to save the man who rescued her, a man who remained loyal to her, even when the easier path to abandon her lay before him. The brave knight showed her nothing but kindness and concern, and the responsibility for his death fell squarely on her shoulders.

Beyond Sir Gabriel's headless corpse, black smoke rose from the ground. The shadowy wisps soon took shape to reveal the red-eyed specter's form envisioned the day Sir Gabriel attacked Antonio Alcaldo. She covered her ears in anticipation of the high-pitched squeal that emanated from it in their last encounter, but only the panicked screams of the scattering crowd filled her ears. Instead, the silent apparition raised its arm to point to the side.

Following the ghostly figure's gesture, Clarissa saw the Painted Shield rushing in her direction with his massive blade poised overhead. Rolling away, she narrowly avoided the strike that would have cleaved her in two.

"Look at me! I'll kill you!" The Painted Shield shouted.

The Holy Judgment spell charred most of the right side of his body. Blackened patches of skin floated upon a sea of pink flesh running red with blood. His bloodshot eye bulged from its socket, and only a hole remained where his ear once rested. His melting armor fused with his arm as smoke rose from the heated metal.

Clarissa knew the spell didn't directly strike the burned paladin, but his proximity to its devastating effects caused more damage than she expected. The fact that he even stood seemed too inhuman for even him.

The Painted Shield flexed his arm until the melted metal broke free, returning mobility to his elbow. Thrusting the tip of his sword at Clarissa again, he nearly skewered her, but before the blade found its mark, another sword knocked the strike away. Clarissa turned to see Sir Kenneth prostrating for a follow-up attack.

"So you're a traitor too?" The burned paladin blocked Sir Kenneth's attack with his mighty blade.

"You execute your own brother with a smile on your face, and I am the traitor?" Sir Kenneth's voice echoed within his helmet.

The two clashed blades, but the confrontation did not last. With extensive injuries, the Painted Shield soon found holding his weapon too daunting a task. His sword flew from his hand, leaving no option but to hide behind his blood-crusted shield.

Sir Kenneth drove his shoulder into the burned paladin's shield, knocking him onto his back. Raising his sword, it appeared that he intended to bring his blade crashing down. Instead, he leaned down and wiped the blood from the bottom of Sir Severin's shield. "You don't get to add his blood to your collection." Turning his attention to Clarissa, he reached out his hand. "Come on!" He shouted. Clarissa accepted the paladin's offer, and he yanked her up with a force that felt as though her arm nearly came out of its socket. "Follow me!"

The two began navigating through the panicked crowd. Clarissa stayed pressed against Sir Kenneth's back as swaths of citizens crashed against his shield. Once they cleared the masses, they found their path blocked by a line of soldiers.

"Halt!" One of the men shouted with his spear at the ready.

Through the opening in their helmets, Clarissa could see the apprehension in their eyes. No common soldier wanted to face a member of the famed paladins of

Sanctum, let alone a former high priestess with the ability to erase a person's existence. They soon found their fears realized.

The line of five cautiously crept forward. Before they could reach the pair, Sir Kenneth vanished. Shortly after he reappeared in front of Clarissa, the men fell to the ground clutching at their slit throats.

Sir Kenneth's breathing intensified. Clarissa understood the mechanics of the spell he just cast. Holy Dash allowed him to move at blinding speed, but only in a straight line, and the spell returned its caster to the spot of casting. To attack all five men meant Sir Kenneth cast the spell five times in rapid succession. Although the spell didn't require a substantial amount of energy to cast, the repetition would wear on anyone's constitution.

"Let's go." Sir Kenneth instructed Clarissa. "I have a horse prepared just outside the gate."

"How was the Painted Shield even moving? I've heard tales of his inhuman capabilities, but even he shouldn't be able to move with those wounds."

"He used the spell Pain Immune. It's a low-level spell with more risk than reward. It allows the user to push the body beyond its limits, but you can cause serious damage to your body without pain's warning. To my knowledge, he's the only paladin mad enough to use such a spell."

The duo dashed to the city's exit with little resistance. The few scrambling citizens that remained skirted their progress with fear plastered across their faces. A few random soldiers attempted to stop their progress, but Sir Kenneth dispatched each one with ease. Twice, an archer attempted to dispatch them from a distance, but each arrow sailed harmlessly over their heads.

Navigating through the obstacles, Villam's protective walls came into view and revealed their worst fears. Word of their deeds beat them to the city's exit, leading the guardsmen to lower the portcullis.

"What are we going to do now? If this exit is sealed, all the others must be as well." Clarissa kept pace with Sir Kenneth as they approached the closed gate.

"Just keep moving. We'll figure it out when we get there."

Arriving at the gate, Clarissa could see the operating mechanism through the wooden barrier's cross-shaped sections.

"Look out!" Sir Kenneth stepped in front of Clarissa with his shield raised. A whistling sound, much like a boiling tea kettle, tore through the air. With blinding speed, the object pierced through Sir Kenneth's shield, penetrated his armor, and buried itself deep into his flesh. The wounded paladin fell to a knee and grunted as he ripped out an arrow embedded deep in his shoulder.

"That's not possible! How can an arrow pierce armor?" Clarissa searched for the shooter but found none.

Sir Kenneth whipped the arrow to the ground as he stood, "Only one man could do this. The 'Enchanted Arrow,' Sandalius Arquero, is responsible. A few years back, he turned down the offer to become one of the Heads of Cerberus. He is a wind mage that casts his spells through his bow. Had I not raised my shield, the arrow would have torn through me."

"Perhaps you should cast a Barrier spell."

"I don't know the Barrier spell. Sir Gabriel knew the defensive spells; I knew the offensive spells. That's why we worked so well together as a team."

Clarissa's heart sank. Her unsuccessful attempt to save Sir Gabriel weighed heavily on her shoulders. The guilt of her failure would live with her until the end of her days.

"Get down!" Sir Kenneth shouted.

Clarissa dove to the ground as another whistling sound cut the air leaving an arrow buried in the stone wall behind her.

"Where is he shooting from?" Clarissa searched for the famed archer. The image of Sir Gabriel's headless body replayed in her mind. She knew that she should save dwelling on her failure for a more appropriate time, but she could not help it. Even in her dire situation, the remorse haunted her thoughts.

A puff of black smoke rose from the ground in the distance. Clarissa squinted her eyes to spot the apparition once again. It stood stoic and silent, pointing to an area behind a building.

"I know where he is," Clarissa knowingly whispered.

"What? How?"

"The building with the brown awning and closed shutters. He is shooting from behind its far corner."

"How could you possibly…"

Another whistling emerged, causing the both of them to drop back to the ground. The arrow buried itself into the stone wall again, this time going so deep that Clarissa could only see the hole left in its wake.

"Are you certain?" Sir Kenneth asked.

Clarissa looked to locate the specter, but it no longer stood in the street. Even with it no longer in sight, its message still lingered in her mind. "Yes, I am certain."

Sir Kenneth stood. With his shield arm, he began tracing out a runic symbol. Completing his spell, he thrust his palm forward, launching a tight ball of light. Clarissa knew this spell: Holy Bolt. Its properties resembled that of Holy Judgment, albeit far less powerful. The spell clashed against the building's corner and exploded the wall into rubble.

The mysterious archer emerged unharmed amidst the smoke and crumbling stone. As he approached, he fired another arrow that buried itself into the dirt near Sir Kenneth's feet. A moment later, bolts of lightning spread from the arrow in every direction like a giant electrical spider web, catching both Sir Kenneth and Clarissa in its spray. The attack caused little pain but served its purpose. The former high priestess and disgraced paladin fell to their knees, paralyzed as their muscles tightened and cramped.

"I have you!" Sandalius shouted, staying fifty stones away. "The effects of that arrow will wear off soon, but from this distance, you have no hope of evasion. If you move, I will shoot you."

Clarissa strained to look up. Seeing the archer for the first time, she made a note of his appearance. His silver, half-plate armor glistened in the sunlight. He stood at average height for a male human, and his thin composition didn't befit that of a soldier. His dark, chin-length hair blew violently from the swirling wind gushing from his magical bow. Although Clarissa had never heard his surname before today, his appearance relayed a relation to a noble family.

"As soon as you are able, lie on your bellies and wait until the guard arrives. This is your only chance for survival. Sir Kenneth, we have known each other for some time. You know that I will not miss. I don't want to kill you, so please do not force me to and do as you are told."

The lightning ceased, allowing Clarissa to regain the use of her limbs. Looking at Sir Kenneth, she could see the rage in his eyes. "Sir Kenneth, please do not do anything foolish. I cannot lose you as well. The archer is correct. We are trapped."

"The archer isn't who we need to worry about." Sir Kenneth stood, raising his shield and shifting his stance to brace for impact.

"You made your choice." The Enchanted Arrow began. "I told you I didn't want…"

Before he could finish his sentence, a flash of light erupted. The ensuing shockwave blasted dust and debris toward the Enchanted Arrow. His body launched and spun in the air. Flying the distance of forty stones, he crashed lifelessly to the ground. Clarissa could not tell if the blast killed him or knocked him into oblivion.

Clarissa's knowledge of light runestone spells served her well. Shield Bash, a spell typically utilized for defense, blasted a concussive force intended to deflect an attacker. The spell didn't cause much harm, as it usually served as a means to create an opening for a follow-up attack. However, this spell erupted with enough force to launch a man into the air. Looking to discover the source of the blast, she saw the Painted Shield marching with a contingent of soldiers in tow.

"I apologize, Arquero, but these two are mine and mine alone to kill." The Painted Shield slurred his speech due to missing half of his lips.

The soldiers sprinted ahead of their leader and formed two lines to block any escape. As the enraged paladin approached, Clarissa pondered how the man could even walk. Bits of his skull protruded through the gore of his wounded face, and smoke emitted from the melted metal that encased his arm. His eye turned to a pale blue, signaling its lost ability of sight, but he marched forward as if in perfect health.

"Thirty years. Thirty…years! That's how long I have served Sanctum. Never once has a warrior managed to leave a scar on my face. I have fought in wars, countless battles, skirmishes, and duels. I have defeated scores of renowned warriors. Look at me now. Burned by a spoiled princess. Do you understand how much shame and humiliation you have caused me? I'm going to kill you, but don't think it will be quick and painless. I am going to enjoy carving the skin from your bones."

Severin Ward raised his blood-encrusted shield. Clarissa ducked and covered her head in anticipation of another Shield Bash spell. Before the enraged paladin could trace the runic symbol, Sir Kenneth utilized Holy Dash to disrupt the incantation with a sword-strike. The blade clashed harmlessly against the blood-stained shield but successfully stopped the injured paladin from casting.

"Interrupt the spell. Who was it that taught you that tactic, Sir Kenneth?" The Painted Shield cracked a disturbingly bloody smile.

"I give you credit for that particular maneuver, but don't think you know all of my moves. Why don't you come over here and discover the strategies I learned outside your tutelage?" Sir Kenneth stood in front of Clarissa in a protective stance.

"You do know you're trapped, don't you? Even if you could defeat me, which you can't, you still have nowhere to run. Unless you plan to defeat the entire city's army. Face it, you are both going to die here today."

"Clarissa," Sir Kenneth whispered, "can you cast Holy Judgment on the gate?"

"No," Clarissa whispered in return, "the spell has to be cast directly onto a living person."

"Do you have enough energy to cast it again?"

"Yes, but only once."

"Alright, back up to the gate and wait. I'm going to force him against the gate. Once he is there, cast the spell on him. That should destroy the gate and give us our opening for escape."

"I don't mean to doubt your skill, but that's the Painted Shield. Do you think you can force him into position?"

"Normally, not a chance. But with those injuries, I think I can do it."

"Alright, I trust you, Sir Kenneth." Clarissa retreated to the gate.

The Painted Shield released a blood-curdling scream and rushed forward. Raising his shield, Sir Kenneth blocked the horizontal strike, but not without consequence. The blow swung with indomitable force, cleaving the shield in two and sending Sir Kenneth to the ground with a painful grunt.

Sir Kenneth spun to his feet and side-stepped the follow-up vertical swing. Swinging his sword, Sir Kenneth only struck metal as his adversary blocked the blow. Blood dripped from the wounded paladin's face as he thrust his sword at his adversary's abdomen, but Sir Kenneth nimbly leaped backward to avoid the stab.

"I should have predicted that you would have cast Strength on yourself before the battle began." Sir Kenneth whipped his broken shield onto the ground and shifted into a familiar stance that put his sword in both hands. His posture reminded Clarissa of the battle he encountered during their visit with the Assassin's Guild. "How long do you think you can maintain that spell, old man?"

"Your concern warms my heart, but we both know that this fight will be long over by the time my spell exhausts me enough for you to gain an advantage."

"Let's test that theory."

The Painted Shield continued with an onslaught of attacks. Each swing tore through the air with enough force to dice Sir Kenneth into pieces, but none found their mark. Sir Kenneth dodged in an elegant dance, bouncing from one foot to the other. He ducked, spun, and leapt with anticipation of each strike.

"You have the nerve to call yourself a paladin? We defend like a rock, not dance like a bird."

"I told you, I have learned much since the days of your teachings."

Sir Kenneth faked to one side before launching to the other with a one-handed strike aimed at the former mentor's unprotected head. With his sword blocking, the tactic knocked the over-sized paladin off balance. Sir Kenneth responded by spinning low to the ground and slicing his sword at his opponent's legs. His blade found its mark, clashing into the armor. The strike's force failed to pierce through the metal but kicked the aggressor's leg out from beneath him. The Painted Shield crashed to his back with an exhaled grunt.

Sir Kenneth stabbed his sword at the disadvantaged warrior, but the Painted Shield raised his namesake in defense. Thrust after thrust attempted to get past the steel barrier, but each attempt failed.

In desperation, Severin Ward dropped his sword, grabbed Sir Kenneth's ankle, and threw him away as if the fully grown man carried the weight of a small child. Sir Kenneth rolled on the ground, using the throw's momentum to spring to his feet.

Sir Kenneth plunged toward his opponent, launching a fury of strikes that forced Severin Ward to step back. The duo slowly approached the gate. With a final kick into the metal barrier, Sir Kenneth thrust his opponent into the lowered portcullis, giving Clarissa her opening.

The former high priestess took a step toward the Painted Shield, but before she could reach him, an explosion of light erupted from his shield. The Shield

Bash spell lacked the previous casting's power yet produced enough force to toss her and Sir Kenneth aside. The shockwave left Clarissa gasping for air as she clutched her chest. Rolling onto her hands and knees, she looked to discover her partner's condition.

Struggling to stand, Sir Kenneth used his sword as a crutch. Fighting his body's urge to keel over, he shifted himself into position to prepare for the approaching Severin Ward. As the assailant drew within range, Sir Kenneth swung his sword in a vertical strike, but the over-sized knight caught his wrist in mid-arc. Using his overwhelming strength, the Painted Shield wrenched the sword from Sir Kenneth's hand and stabbed the faithful paladin's side with his own blade.

Sir Kenneth released an agonized howl that cut short when a mammoth hand grabbed his throat. Using a single arm, Sir Ward lifted the stabbed paladin to the tips of his toes.

"It has been too long since I had an actual challenge." The Painted Shield gave a grotesque smile. "I thank you. It's a real testament to my abilities as a mentor."

"I...told you." Sir Kenneth squeaked through his

choking. "There…is a lot…you didn't teach…me."

Sir Kenneth grabbed Severin's face, stabbing his thumb into his one remaining good eye while digging the fingers of his other hand deep into his wound. The maddened paladin let loose a bitter scream, releasing Sir Kenneth to knock away his hands.

Severin Ward backed away, clutching his face. Sir Kenneth yanked the sword from his side and ran to Clarissa.

"Get ready." Sir Kenneth said as he traced out a runic symbol. Casting Holy Dash, he snatched one of the nearby soldiers and forced him against the gate. "Now!"

Clarissa ran to the man and drew out the runic symbol on his breastplate. "Move," she shouted as she dove out of the way. A moment later, a beam of light shot from the heavens. The light bathed the unassuming soldier and erupted a section of the city's barrier wall into a spray of rock and debris.

Releasing a pair of coughs, Clarissa helped her partner to his feet. Running through the cloud of dust, the duo escaped the city through the ruined wall. Sir Kenneth untied his waiting horse and climbed onto its back before helping Clarissa mount behind him. With a snap of the reigns, the pair escaped to the south.

In the distance, Clarissa heard the orders of pursuit.

However, those words worried her less than the blood seeping from Sir Kenneth's wound. She knew that he would soon lose consciousness from the loss of blood and that they needed to find a place to hide before that happened.

Brett

The complications of his mission kept piling up. First, Dorian, now a wanted criminal with his sword of extraordinary power, joined Brett and his band of travelers. Next, a young heiress to the city he never planned to return to joined them. Her presence brought even more risk than a wanted criminal. Most of the kingdom's citizens would instantly recognize any member of the noble families. If anyone were to see her among a rag-tag group that included a scoundrel, a former slave wild elf, and a mul, they would assume the group kidnapped her in search of ransom. Luckily, Lena's lack of a family crest on her clothing and general reclusive nature gave him a sliver of solace that they could creep in and out of Pasillo without being noticed.

The trip to Prasillo proved arduous yet uneventful. They crossed both the Fluit and Flumen Rivers by offering coins to fishermen in small towns. They followed the bank of Patera Lake, only traveling on the main road when necessary. They managed to get in and out of towns without Razuul brutally maiming a citizen who gave him a sideways glance or made a derogatory comment...mostly.

Brett wouldn't have typically considered entering a major city with this group of recognizable individuals, but he knew the city's citizens would be too preoccupied to notice them. The harvest moon approached, and with it, Prasillo's famous Azure Festival, the annual celebration of the Lazurite Beetles' migration. Every year, the blue bugs lit the night sky with their sapphire glow and brought in tow a harvest that allowed the city to prosper.

The harmless insects made the yearly migration west across the sea on the day of the harvest moon. No one knew how the insects knew to travel on this particular day, nor did they know their destination. The bugs just disappeared to the west every year to reach a landing that no ship ever discovered. However, the citizens of Prasillo weren't the only ones with the knowledge of this migration.

Every year, hundreds of thousands of fish

swarmed Prasillo Bay to feast on the insects that flew too close to the water. Before the migration began, Prasillo would raise a net at the bay's opening. The holes in the net allowed fish as big as a man to pass through. This net served to keep out the dangerous monsters that preyed on the fish. At the banquet's height, the Prasillo residents raised another mesh net that trapped the fish in the bay. Once trapped, the bay filled with enough fish to keep the fisherman busy all year. The festival celebrated this annual event, for without it, the city could not survive.

With the city's entrance before them, Brett could feel the excitement radiating from the straight-faced Dorian. During the trip, he spoke of little else other than the festival. He told the stories he'd read, full of history, traditions, and customs. He lamented about the incredible advancements in technology that first appeared at the Azure Festival. He relayed the stories told to him by his father about impressive displays of magic and theatrics.

Lena did not attempt to hide her delight. Far more ramped up than her usual enthusiastic self, she spent the last few days skipping, dancing, and twirling nonstop. Her nonsensical manner of speech gave clues about her childhood dreams of attending the celebration, although

Brett put little effort in trying to decipher her ramblings.

Razuul emanated a very different aura. He attempted to find an excuse to delay or avoid visiting the bustling city. He snarled at Dorian's stories. He remarked his displeasure at the thought of swimming in a sea of humans. He disputed anticipation for the festival's displays. Only through the companions' combined effort did they finally convince the former arena champion to release his trepidations. Even though his outward demeanor communicated his apprehension for attending the festival, Brett saw the slight smile the elven warrior cracked after hearing Dorian's excitement.

Brett hid the true reason he wanted to visit the city during this time. The festival brought people from across the continent. Many merchants came to open temporary shops to sell their various wares. Oddities, rare substances, exotic foods, and precious materials stood as some of the items sold at the Azure Festival. Most of the baubles, trinkets, and devices sold would later be discovered as nothing more than an over-priced counterfeit. Even with the negative reputation these swindlers garnered, it only took a single rumor of a great find sold at one of the mysterious shops to spread throughout the kingdom. Such gossip gave people hope of discovering a hidden gem that would bring them fame, notoriety, or wealth. Although most of the shops offered nothing more than charlatans attempting to make a quick coin, some presented sorcerers with a deep understanding of magic.

Brett needed to find one of these shops. During his travels, he'd developed an uncharacteristic caring for his companions. The guilt that caring brought weighed heavy on his shoulders. Unbeknownst to them, Brett relayed every event that occurred during their journey to the king through a secret communication device strapped to his wrist. More than anything, he wished he didn't have to keep betraying them, but the king left him few options. The magical brand the king placed on Brett's chest ensured loyalty. No matter where he went, the king could activate the brand, bringing on searing pain before melting its owner from the inside out. Only a magic-user of profound knowledge and skill could know how to counter the brand, and only the Azure Festival offered a place where such magic users gathered in one place.

He'd tried different methods to destroy the brand. He carved at the scar with one of his daggers, but the wounds immediately healed. He tried to burn the brand to misshape the magical pattern, but that only resulted in a torrid of self-suffering. He surmised that only a spell could counter the magical marking and swore not to give up searching for a solution that would allow him to stop stabbing his companions in the back.

"Brett," Dorian snapped Brett from his dwelling thoughts, "are you sure we will be safe here?"

"To be honest, no, I'm not. We're going to have to keep a low profile. Keep your hoods up and your heads down."

Brett turned to Dorian. "Since I can't convince you to leave it, no matter what, keep that sword in its scabbard. All it will take is for one person to spot that thing, and the entire city will turn on us."

Brett shifted his gaze to Razuul. "Please don't, you know…kill anybody. If someone gets on your nerves, take a deep breath and walk away."

Brett finished his instructions with Lena. "And you, don't be…yourself. We can't have another incident like we had two towns ago."

"That wasn't my fault. The dirt really wanted that man, and the bones were really springy. What was I supposed to do? Just let all the holes keep opening and closing? None of the dogs could have gone home to their families."

Brett rolled his eyes. "Again, I have no idea what you are saying. Just stick with Dorian, and let him do all the talking."

"Alright, but the bugs are going to dance like crazy." Lena twirled in place.

"Another thing," Brett moved on from the pointless conversation with Lena, "try not to spend any money. We are starting to get low on funds. I will try to find us a room for tonight, but I doubt anyone will have one available. Be prepared to sleep under the stars tonight. I'll look for all of you tonight to tell you what I found. Oh, and Lena, remember...Lena?" Brett spun in a circle but found no sign of the heiress. "You've got to be kidding me."

Dorian gave an exasperated sigh. "Don't worry, we'll find her."

"Just remember, try not to draw any attention to yourselves."

Brett parted ways with his companions and entered Prasillo. As expected, the city bustled with activity. Vendors begged bystanders to view their wares. Early drinkers stumbled through the streets. Children laughed and screamed as they darted through crowds of people. Entertainers put their talents on display as they swallowed flaming swords, juggled various objects, sang a melodious tune, and performed elegant dances. Booths of various sizes allowed customers to test their archery skills, arm wrestling, ax throwing, and ring tossing. Tables allowed participants to gamble away their earnings in games of dice, cards, and knuckle-bones, all rigged to the vendor's advantage.

Brett snaked through the crowd, picking the pockets of those showing signs of wealth. A coin pouch here, a necklace there, a random dagger that likely never saw the light of day; he found the marks too easy to resist. In his past, he would have spent all day thieving a relatively large sum of valuables, but his mission required him to focus on gathering information rather than treasure.

Brett's experience of dealing with less-than-scrupulous characters quickly allowed him to discern the swindlers from the honest. Few of the merchants claiming to possess ancient and powerful magics knew the difference between a runestone and a sleight-of-hand trick. He questioned every legitimate magical vendor he found, but even they never heard of a spell being branded onto a person's skin.

His search continued until an unusual stand caught his eye. A crowd of people gathered before the merchant, blocking Brett's view of the wares. Even though he could not see the goods the merchant offered, the bolts of lightning, sprays of flame, and clouds of frozen mist that fired into the air drew Brett to the dealer not selling the usual derelict merchandise.

Brett forced his way to the front of the gathering. A wooden barricade kept the crowd from approaching the merchant. At the center of the booth, a man stood behind a table covered in strange devices. At least one runestone embedded into each gadget, with a couple bearing all four elemental powers. Two muscle-bound men stood on either side of the merchant to keep scoundrels like Brett from stealing, and an assistant lingered near the merchant as he demonstrated the use of the various items.

"Now this item," the tradesman began, handing a gauntlet to his assistant, "does not require as much energy as many of the other devices."

251

The assistant donned the metal glove with a sigh. The color drained from the young man's skin as beads of sweat dripped from his chin. Heavy bags hung beneath his eyes, and his expression portrayed a man awash with exhaustion.

The young man pointed his gloved open hand at a thick log covered in burn marks. A wind runestone fixed into the metal on the back of his hand, and a small spike protruded from the center knuckle. Taking a deep breath, the assistant squeezed his hand into a fist. The crowd gasped as the spike, connected to the gauntlet by a thin wire, shot out of the metal glove. The spike drove into the log, and tendrils of lightning traveled down the wire as a strange humming emitted from the electrical current.

"I call this item the Shocker. The current will instantly incapacitate its target yet doesn't deliver enough charge to cause permanent damage or death. This leaves the user with plenty of energy to…" The man's sales pitch cut short after his assistant collapsed to the ground like a folded piece of parchment. "Oh, thimblewickets."

The disgruntled crowd dispersed to other enchanting booths. Brett heard some of the onlookers call the merchant "harebrained" and "preposterous" as they departed. Even the soldiers in attendance found the man's inventions absurd, even though the gauntlet seemed particularly useful to their occupation.

The merchant stroked the overgrown handles of his mustache. "Pickadillies and plums, not again."

"Hey, old man, you still have one customer here," Brett called.

"Oh! Well, heavens to heckbats, can I interest you in any of my amazing inventions?" The man squinted his eyes as though he struggled to see Brett even though he stood no more than ten stones away.

"What's with all the strange sayings? Heavens to heckbats? I've never heard anyone talk like that before."

"Oh, that's just an old habit of mine. My father taught me never to say things like 'by the gods.' He said it might offend our world's creators, and it's best not to upset beings of unfathomable power. So, I started coming up with nonsense words to keep myself from offending the gods."

"The gods? You really think they exist?"

"Why, of course! You only need to look at the runestones that represent the power of each god. They bless us with their benevolence, giving us just a fraction of their power for the betterment of our existence."

"If they exist, and they created us all, why do they allow their children to suffer? Why do they watch those in power cause such pain and agony and do nothing about it?"

"My good man, it is not our place to question the altruistic nature of the gods. They have given us life. Some are born with more than others. We can only do what we can with what we were given. It is the choices we make that define who we are, and only the gods can judge if we have lived our life in their light."

"Sounds like a bunch of nonsense to me, but I didn't come here to talk about the existence of omnipotent beings. I want to know more about those inventions of yours."

"Yes, of course. First, let me introduce myself. My name is Norman Temple." The old merchant stuck out his hand for a shake.

"Flint Merryman." Brett shook Norman's hand.

"Nice to meet you, Flint. Which of my inventions caught your eye?"

"I am traveling with some people with skills that are substantially greater than my own. I'm finding myself being left behind, and I'm looking for something that will help me catch up to them a little."

"If it's power you're looking for, I have this!" Norman gabbed a strange metal contraption in the shape of a barrel with one end tapering off into a thin pipe. "I call this the air cannon. Place the large portion under your arm, and point the thin portion at your enemy. Tap the wind runestone on the side, and watch your adversary wish he never met you. The runestone builds pressure in the large chamber and focuses that pressure into a single point at the barrel's end. The result is an air current with enough pressure to blow a hole straight through the trunk of a tree. The thought of what this thing could do to a person is enough to turn your stomach."

"How many shots can you get out of this thing?"

"Well…one. It takes a lot of energy, unfortunately."

"Pass. What else you got?"

Norman tossed the air cannon back onto the table before grabbing a crossbow, which he handed to Brett. "Take a look at this!"

Brett inspected the construction. "What's so special about this? It just looks like a regular crossbow."

"That's because the invention is the arrows."
Norman handed a quiver full of crossbow bolts to Brett.

"Each arrow is equipped with a fire runestone shard. The arrows explode on impact. Since they are so small, the amount of energy you use is minimal."

"Wait, if the runestones are on the arrow, doesn't that mean that each arrow can only be used once?"

"Well…yes."

"So when I needed more, I need to find you."

"Ahem, well, yes."

"Next."

"Alright. I have it this time." Norman tossed the crossbow on the ground. Rummaging through a pile of wood and metal objects, he turned back to Brett. "Here. Take this." With a beaming smile, he handed Brett the hilt of a sword.

"What am I supposed to do with this?"

"Touch the runestone."

Brett touched the fire runestone embedded into the hilt. A jet of blue flame in the shape of a blade shot from the guard, causing him to nearly jump out of his skin.

"As you can tell, this invention requires very little energy to activate."

"Whoa, this is amazing." Brett swung the sword to ensure the flame didn't extinguish.

"The secret is the canister inside the handle. It supplies the flame with a gas I invented called copper chloride. The gas exponentially increases the temperature and intensity of the flame. The canisters last nearly an hour, and I have many replacements that come with it."

"You should have started with this. This is amazing! So what happens if I clash it against a sword? Will it melt my foe's blade?" Brett extinguished the flame by touching the runestone.

"Oh, no. It doesn't burn that hot. If you tried to duel someone holding a blade, the metal would pass right through the flame."

"Then what good is this thing?"

"It looks very intimidating."

"Goodbye." Brett tossed the hilt back to Norman and began to walk away.

"Wait!" The old inventor called.

"I am actually trying to find a different kind of vendor anyway. I really need to move along."

"Before you go, allow me to show you one more of my inventions."

Brett shrugged and returned to the inventor. "This is the last one."

"Flibbitey flew, I really intended to hold onto this piece for one of the noble families, but I really need to make some sales." Norman reached behind his back, pulled out a peculiar-looking device and handed it to Brett.

The device resembled a sword's hilt but curved from the handle to form a thin, metal tube. Spanning the length of his forearm, the invention felt weighty yet light enough to hold for an extended length of time. Another cylindrical object, with the ability to rotate in place, hung from the tube. A small, etched fire runestone sat attached to the rotating section on the inside of the curve.

"What the heck is this thing?"

"I call it a gun. Hold it by the wooden section, point it at that log, and touch the runestone."

Brett did as instructed, causing a fireball to launch from the device's tube that crashed into the log and ignited it with fire.

"Whoa." Brett stared at the gun with wide eyes.

"Now, rotate that center section until it clicks one time."

Brett followed the old-timer's instructions. Turning the device caused the fire runestone to rotate away, and a water runestone sat in its place.

"Fire the gun now." Norman's face lit with anticipation.

Brett pointed and fired, causing a spray of mist and ice to launch from the tube. A dozen shards of ice buried deep into the log, and the mist extinguished the small flame that blackened the hunk of wood.

"If you rotate the chamber one more time, the gun also fires a limited range lightning attack that will continue firing until you release the runestone."

"You do realize that this is the only useful thing you've shown me, right?"

"Yes…I know."

"How many shots can you get out of it?"

"Well, that depends on the person. Everyone has a different amount of energy, and the lightning shot drains you faster depending on how long you hold the stone. If you are talking just regular shots, I'd say the average person can fire six to seven shots before fatigue starts to set in."

"How much do you want for it?"

"Five hundred gold."

Brett shoved the gun into the old man's chest. "Goodbye again."

"Wait, wait, wait. Slippery salamander, I really need to make a sale." Norman sighed and smoothed the point of his chin hair. "Fine, I'll let it go for two-hundred-fifty gold."

"No."

"Two hundred?"

"Nope."

"Blatherin' badgers, perhaps you should tell me how much you are willing to pay for it."

"Fifty gold."

"Fifty? That barely covers the cost to make the gun. How about one hundred?"

"Seventy-five."

"Eighty."

"Deal."

Brett paid Norman, took his new gun, and began to walk away. "Pleasure doing business with you."

"Are you sure I can't interest you in any other items?"

"I'm sure."

"If you ever want to see more, come see me in my home town Oppidum, in the Regiis province."

"Will do, old man," Brett replied as he returned to his mission.

Elendor

Elendor found it difficult to remember feelings of joy and happiness in his pit of despair. Aside from a select few who lived outside Parvus Arbor, Jocia, Galain, and himself represented the only free elves in the kingdom. As they pressed on with their mission, only his goal kept Elendor from slipping into madness.

His dwelling thoughts repeated in his mind. He could not help but wonder if he had not left the city to pursue selfish desires, would his involvement have prevented this tragedy? For generations, the arbormancer served as Parvus Arbor's staunch defender, yet Elendor abandoned his position. In his absence, the city lost its most powerful weapon. In addition, the loss of Jocia, a powerful mage, and Galain, a well-trained warrior, left their home vulnerable. Had they been there, Elendor doubted that Morace would have enacted his dastardly plan.

Now, with his arbormancy restricted to his wooden limbs, he doubted his presence would have made much difference. The instant stretching and shape manipulation of his wooden appendages proved useful but significantly less powerful than the ability to control surrounding vegetation. He lost count of the number of times he attempted to regain his ability. Each time failed. He even tried to remove his new limbs, but even that proved impossible. The roots that connected to his brain proved strong and deep; each attempt resulted in pain and suffering. Even though he achieved his life-long dream, the price of losing his ancestral home to the orcs, his ruined relationship with his friends, and especially the loss of his closest friend proved far too high a price.

As Baxis came into view, the trio spotted a pair of soldiers on horseback guarding the road that led to their destination.

"It is odd, is it not?" Galain asked.

"What do you mean?" Jocia turned to Galain.

"The soldiers. They are guarding the road. When we visited Tenebris, the guards stood posted at the city's entrance, but no one guarded the road that led to the city."

"I imagine every province possesses different customs and traditions. That likely includes military tactics." Elendor replied.

"True, but I find it odd. I also cannot shed a bad feeling about it. It may be nothing, but I feel as though we should remain on guard. Elendor, make sure to keep that wooden hand of yours hidden."

Elendor struck his hands into the pouch on the front of his shirt. He found his current clothing incredibly uncomfortable yet useful. The wool material irritated his skin, and the thought of using an animal's fur as clothing repulsed him. Even the leather boots on his feet felt unnatural. However, the pocketed pants and shirt, the durability of the material, and loose fit allowed for conveniences the silken attire of his homeland did not offer.

By the time the trio came into the soldier's view, their elven eyes could make out details about them. Each wore battered half-plate armor and seemed to be in the early years of human life. Both men carried a spear, and a sword bounced on their hips as they trotted their horses to meet the travelers.

"What is a group of elves doing so far from

home?" The first soldier raised his visor to reveal his youthful face.

"We are merchants." Galain began his lie. "We recently acquired some rare herbs and spices, and we are traveling the kingdom to see if we can find any customers."

"I don't see any herbs. Don't merchants usually travel with their wares?" The second soldier asked.

"The herbs we discovered are rare. If we travel with them alone, we are likely to lose our merchandise to bandits. We decided to travel to the other provinces to find buyers and draw up contracts. Once we have guarantees, we will prepare a stringent of guards to escort our products."

"Well, if you plan to visit Baxis, I'm afraid you are going to be disappointed. The city is closed to visitors right now."

"May I ask why?" Elendor jumped into the conversation.

"I am not at liberty to discuss." The soldier lowered his visor. "You'll have to find a new place to conduct your business."

"This is ridiculous. Parvus Arbor is part of the

accord that allows trade between…"

"It is fine," Jocia interrupted, "Baxis is not the only province that will be interested in what we have to offer. We certainly do not want to cause any unnecessary trouble."

"You need to listen to that one, elf." The soldier tipped his chin at Elendor.

"You are correct, Jocia. The other provinces will surely be much more appreciative of what we have to offer."

Jocia placed both hands on Elendor's shoulders and flashed a wide, fake smile at the guards. "Please disregard my friend's attitude. The road we have traveled has been long and difficult. We are all longing for a warm place to rest our weary bones. Do not worry. We will respect your orders and find a new place to visit."

"You're lucky you brought her, elf. Move along, and do not try to visit Baxis again."

The soldiers turned their mounts to depart as Elendor silently simmered with rage. As the guards rode, they began conversing, underestimating the power of elven hearing.

The second soldier leaned into the first. "I thought

the beasts already took over Parvus Arbor."

"Jocia!" Galain shouted as he darted toward the soldiers.

Understanding his orders, Jocia drew out a runic symbol. A moment later, a long rock wall rose from the ground that blocked the soldier's path. Elendor also understood Galain's intentions. Following behind his friend, he drew back his wooden arm and shot it at the first soldier. Before the wooden tentacles reached their target, Galain shot an arrow at the turning soldiers, burying one deep into the second soldier's skull. The wooden arm spread wide, wrapping around the first soldier's limbs, and plucked him from his horse to suspend him in the air.

"What was it your companion just said?" Elendor retracted his arm to bring the soldier closer to him.

"What kind of magic is this? Let me go!"

Elendor manipulated his appendage to form two more tendrils that poked into the man's nostrils. "You better start talking, or I am going to bury those into your brain."

"Alright, alright! I'll tell you! Lord Hardwood made a deal with the beast races. In return for permitting access to Baxis, the beasts are going to take over the kingdom and place Lord Hardwood on the throne."

"What? That makes no sense." Elendor replied. "If the beast races intend to conquer the kingdom, why would they not take the throne for themselves?"

"Something about the humans not accepting a non-human ruler. I don't know. I'm just a soldier!"

"Why would a soldier who has sworn loyalty to King Magicent go along with such a plan?" Galain asked.

"When the war is over, Lord Hardwood is going to move the entire city to the capital. You have no idea what it is like living in Baxis. The city is old and run-down. We barely receive enough food to sustain ourselves, and the harsh weather takes more citizens every year."

"So you would allow a war that will kill thousands so you can live fat and happy? How do you even call yourself a soldier?" Elendor crept the tendrils deeper into the man's nose, causing panicked yelps. Only a follow-up question from Jocia stopped him from shooting the wood through the man's brain.

"So Baxis is currently overrun with beasts?"

"No. Only a small regiment remains in the city. Most of them are currently marching to Prasillo."

"How many are there?" Galain asked.

"Thousands."

"How does an army of thousands of beasts plan to travel across the kingdom without being noticed?"

"Actually," Galain answered Elendor for the soldier, "with Parvus Arbor fallen and Tenebris closed for repair, an army could circumvent the capital and make it to Pasillo unnoticed. It would be a difficult journey, but not impossible."

"How long ago did the army leave?" Elendor slightly withdrew his wooden fingers from the soldier's nose.

"Over a week ago."

"That means they should arrive soon." Galain's gaze fell distant.

"What should we do?" Jocia asked. "There is no way we could get to Prasillo before them. Perhaps we can find a way to send a messenger bird?"

"Even if we did," Galain began, "there is no way we could find a town that has messenger birds and then have one arrive there in time. Unfortunately, Prasillo will have to defend itself. The best we can do is make it to another city and prepare them for the invasion. We need to get to the closest city…Durrum."

"Durrum?" Elendor addressed Galain. "Heece specifically told us to avoid the dwarves because they hate elves."

"Think about what we learned from the specter. If this continues, no one is safe. The specter's words affect the dwarves just as much as the elves."

"We cannot tell the dwarves about the specter," Jocia responded. "They would think us mad."

"I know that, but they cannot ignore an invasion by the beast races."

"I doubt they would even believe us about the invasion," Elendor added.

"Do you see another option? Parvus Arbor and Baxis have fallen. Tenebris's forces are severely depleted. Sanctum is too connected to Regiis, and it would take far too long to get to Villam. Durrum is our only choice."

"Uh, if you are done, maybe you can let me go?" The soldier begged. "I-I promise, I won't tell anyone about you. I'll tell my captain that my partner fell off his horse and…"

Elendor shot the wooden tendrils through the soldier's skull. "Well, Durrum, it is then.

Marius

Marius lost track of which direction he headed. Even the amount of days that passed since he escaped from the capital eluded him. Not that it mattered. He didn't have a destination in mind. By now, he knew the rumors of his madness and assassination attempt traveled to all corners of the kingdom. No matter where he went, someone would recognize his face, and instantly he would be pursued. Every plan he concocted in his mind ended with the same result: he would be captured or killed.

However, he refused to relent. He recalled the words of Thomanthus, the centaur that freed him from the Baxis prison. If Marius didn't soon find a way to prevent the invasion from spreading past Baxis, the entire kingdom would erupt into a war. Even though he was very young during the Beast Wars of twenty-five years ago, he remembered the devastation it brought. At the beginning of the original war, the beast races remained separate, with each one acting in accordance with their interests. Once they eventually united, the kingdom began to lose ground, and the situation became dire. The nation only survived due to the heroic actions of a dwarf named Thane Kinsman.

Marius wished he could find the fabled hero now. He had heard rumors of the old dwarf opening a weaponsmith shop in Regiis but knowing that information did little for him. The capital city stood as the last place Marius could revisit after his epic failure in attempting to warn the king of the invasion.

Even more than Thane Kinsman, Marius wished he could speak with Richard. The conversations he held with his lover always produced positive results. Even when Richard offered no useful advice, the simple act of talking with him always helped Marius come to the correct conclusion, regardless of the problem he faced. Something about his gaze put Marius at ease. Something about his voice soothed Marius's soul. The list of Richard's traits that helped Marius succeed spanned long, much longer than that of his current travel companion.

Dogon refused to leave Marius's side. Even after

the creature flew off to hunt prey, it always returned. Marius could not fathom why the dragon-dog followed him. He'd done nothing to help, save or feed the thing. Yet, it acted as though they shared a master-beast relationship that spanned the past several years. Not that Marius would complain. He consistently talked to Dogon. He knew the scaly dog did not understand him, but it felt good to unload his concerns onto something with ears.

Dogon's strange growl-bark interrupted Marius's dwelling thoughts, and at first, he dismissed his companion's yelps. It seemed to bark at anything from a bug buzzing to a rock that vaguely resembled the shape of a four-legged beast. This time the barks seemed more urgent. With every yelp, it spun in a circle and barked in the direction behind them.

"What is it, boy?" Marius squinted. In the distance, he saw a small group of people heading his way. He purposely stayed away from the commonly traveled roads to keep from being spotted, so seeing anyone came as a surprise. Creatures of varying degrees of threat wandered the woods and plains far away from the roads, and the entire kingdom knew this fact. This led Marius to the only possible conclusion: these people searched for him.

Marius darted to the nearby rock cropping to hide. "Come on, Dogon," he said as he ducked behind a large formation. His companion responded with a single bark before trotting off in the opposite direction. "Ugh, definitely should have expected that."

Keeping himself hidden, he prayed the travelers had not spotted him. The loss of his dagger left him defenseless. Even if he still possessed his weapon, he held little desire to cause more bloodshed.

Marius peeked around the cropping, making sure to expose as little of himself as possible. After waiting for an extended period without seeing the travelers, he assumed they took a turn that led them away from his position. Slowly, he began to creep out from his hiding place, but before he made much progress, a spell-bound attack stopped him in his tracks.

Six rock spikes shot from the ground, stopping their progress a finger's length from his throat. The rocky protrusions surrounded Marius's neck, preventing him from moving in any direction.

"You move, you die. Who are you and what are you doing way out here?" The youthful male voice inquired.

Marius traced the voice to see an elf standing atop a nearby boulder with a drawn bow and arrow pointed in his direction. The look on his face communicated the seriousness of his threat. His long, black hair blowing in the wind gave the only indication of his age. The lack of white or silver strands meant he aged anywhere from eighty years to eight hundred. Marius met very few elves in his life. He knew the basics about their characteristics but little about their culture. Even with his limited knowledge, he spotted something quite odd about this elf.

"Your clothes," Marius began, "I've never seen an elf in human clothing."

"You are hardly in a position to be the one asking questions." A female voice said from the opposite direction.

Turning to spot her, he found another elf with her hand extended to maintain the spell that kept Marius in place. Also dressed in human clothing, the look on her face seemed far less threatening than that of her companion.

"Look, kill me or let me go. I have somewhere important to be, and I don't feel like sharing my life's story with a couple…"

"It is just as I thought." A third voice emerged from behind Marius. "He must have been sent from Baxis to kill us. Why else would he have hidden the moment he saw us? We must kill him before he kills us."

Marius turned, ensuring to stay steady to prevent himself from accidentally impaling his neck on the stone spikes. The elf he saw this time seemed different from the other two, standing slightly tall for his race and seemingly intent on keeping his arm hidden in his tunic pocket. Even when he stumbled on the rocky ground, he refused to withdraw his hand to maintain balance. He, too, dressed in human clothing, but none of his strange appearance compared to the aura radiating from him. His smug face relayed an arrogance about him that exceeded the stereotype of the elven confidence. His eyes flashed with rage, and his voice filled with bloodlust.

"Wait," Marius processed the words from the third elf. "Did you say Baxis? Why would Baxis send someone to kill three elves?"

"As if you do not know," the hidden-arm elf began, "you will not trick us. Jocia, end this so we can move along."

"No, Jocia, wait…" Marius racked his brain for the words that would save his life. "Heece! I know Heece, the High Commander of Parvus Arbor. Do you know him? He would vouch for me."

The elves reacted to Marius's words. The black-haired elf lowered his bow. The female elf dropped her hand, allowing the rock formations to retreat to the ground. The third elf's face angered as he stormed at Marius.

"Do not say his name!" The third elf ripped his hidden arm from his pocket. Marius expected to find a small dagger. Instead, he found a wooden hand. The elf cocked back his wooden appendage and shot it forward, splitting it into wooden tentacles. The tendrils wrapped around Marius, pinning his legs together and his arms to his side. "You do not deserve to utter his name."

"Elendor! What are you doing?" Jocia pleaded with Elendor. "He only said his name."

"Do you not see? He is lying! The entire kingdom knows the high commander of Parvus Armor's name. He is trying to use Heece's name to get us to drop our guard."

"I do know Heece. We drink together at every king's tournament."

"You lie." Elendor squeezed the wood around his captive.

Marius tried to reply, but the pressure from his bindings left him gasping to draw air. It felt as though his bones would soon snap. Blood rushed to his head, bringing light-headedness that forced him to fight to remain conscious.

"Elendor, stop!" The black-haired elf jumped down from the rocky formation and began pulling at the wooden trappings.

"Galain, I am only trying to keep us safe. You do not see what I see. If we allow this man to live, we…"

Jocia interrupted Elendor's words by slapping him hard across the face. "I do not know who you are anymore!"

The wooden arm released Marius and returned to its original form. Coughing as the air rushed back into his lungs, he crumbled to the ground.

"You would kill a man for saying a name?" Tears began streaming down Jocia's face. "What has happened to you?"

"Are you alright?" Galain squatted down next to Marius.

"I-I'll make it." His arms and legs throbbed, his lungs burned, and his head pounded.

"Can you tell us your name now?"

"Marius, Marius Vybian."

"What?" The three elves replied with disbelief.

"What did I say?"

Dennis Medbury

Ramon

Ramon trotted his stallion down the streets of the area commonly referred to as Shack Town. Officially, the sector possessed no name, as it only endured due to overpopulation in the capital city. Shack Town was never meant to exist. The defensive walls of Regiis spanned much further than that of any other city. Its design was meant to house hundreds of thousands of citizens. However, the city architect, whose name only ancient history books could relay, failed to foresee the city's massive population growth. Centuries ago, when the poor and destitute began constructing the ramshackle homes outside the city walls, the Magicent family ordered their soldiers to burn the place to the ground. The king of that time insisted that Shack Town's citizens either find a place within the castle walls to live or find a new domicile elsewhere. Shack Town's burning repeated for many years until eventually, the town grew to the point that burning it would cause a blaze that would threaten to spread too far and wide to take the risk. These days, Shack Town encircled the entire city and housed as many citizens as the rest of the city.

Most of the homes looked as though a strong breeze would knock them to the ground. The sturdier-built shanties stood as the base for the hovels constructed above. Some even stacked as high as four floors without a staircase or ladder to connect them. Ramon always wondered how the squatters safely entered and exited the elevated shanties. Normally, upon an armored contingent of soldiers entering the area, a litany of down-trodden citizens would line the streets to beg for coins or scraps of food. Today, only mangy dogs, tattered cats, and disease-ridden rodents roamed the streets of Shack Town.

"What is going on here?" Diana asked. "Do you think Shack Town came under attack while we were gone?"

"Perhaps disease finally wiped out this area." Luis scratched at the facial scar he received from their battle in Tenebris.

"Unlikely," Ramon scanned the area, hoping to

find even a single person. "None of the buildings are burned, and no bodies line the streets."

"Well, whatever happened here, it feels really creepy." Diana gripped the handle of her sword.

Ramon nodded his agreement. It felt as though the ghosts of Shack Town still inhabited the area. Hole-ridden clothing still hung from lines. Tattered blankets, pottery shards, rusted plates, and broken baskets lay scattered in the streets. All signs pointed to the citizens leaving in a hurry.

Ramon approached the lowered portcullis of Regiis. In all his time serving in the king's guard, he had never seen the city close itself off from visitors.

"State your name." The soldier beyond the wooden barricade demanded.

"Commander Ramon Alcaldo. What is going on here?"

The soldier ignored Ramon as he rummaged through a stack of parchment. "How many soldiers are in your company?"

"Twenty-three."

"That isn't the number I have written here."

"I do not have to explain anything to you. I am a

commander in the king's guard. You will open this gate, now."

"My orders come from the prince. No one is allowed entry without permission. You are on the list, but I need to confirm your identity."

Ramon looked at Luis, who shrugged his shoulders. Looking at Diana, he found her face turning the shade that earned her the moniker the 'Red Lady.' Turning back to the soldier, he reluctantly responded. "We left with thirty-eight. I lost fifteen soldiers during the skirmish in Tenebris."

"I was about to ask you where you were returning from, but you just answered that one. Your entry is permitted. Please report to High Commander Werner. He has been awaiting your arrival. Raise the gate!"

As commanded, the portcullis lifted. Ramon and his company dismounted as several servants rushed to take their horses to the stables. Upon entering the city's outer wall, Ramon stared in slack-jawed disbelief.

The mystery of the missing citizens of Shack Town revealed its answer. Thousands upon thousands of people packed into the city like a herd of sheep awaiting slaughter. The doors and shutters on the surrounding buildings lay in shambles due to the stampede of people searching for a place to breathe. Even the rooftops were overcrowded with people. Cries of displeasure overwhelmed Ramon's ears, and the stench of the crowd flooded his nose. Massive stone barriers lined the road that led to the inner city, leaving the street as the only area not packed with bodies.

"This is insanity! Why would the prince do this?" Diana asked.

"I don't know, but I intend to find out." Ramon began his trek to the inner city.

Arriving at the second ring, he found this section in a similar state as the previous one. This area housed people of moderate wealth. Those with enough coin to comfortably support themselves, yet not enough to support political influence. Although the side streets contained a mass of citizens, there remained enough room for people to squeeze through the crowds. Most of the buildings looked intact, but many showed signs of vandalism.

Entering the third and final ring revealed a section of the city unaffected by overcrowding. This section held housing for the capital's elite. Business owners with widespread power and influence and relatives of noble families resided in this area. Although Ramon belonged to the latter category, he never felt that he belonged with them. The fact that they sat comfortable and content in their massive homes while people struggled to find a place to lay their heads in the lower ring bothered him. Seeing extra guards posted at the upper wall while citizens assaulted and stole from one another to survive turned his stomach.

Ramon stopped at the castle courtyard and turned to his two captains. "Take the men to the quarters and have them get some rest. Do not dismiss any of them. I suspect we will be receiving new orders very soon."

"What about the men that didn't come with us to Tenebris? Should we round them up?" Luis asked.

"No, they should be under orders from Captain Bentley. Best to leave them be for now. Make sure to gather as much information as you can from the soldiers you come across."

Ramon headed for the castle. He knew the high commander rarely remained in one spot, but one man, in particular, kept track of everyone's whereabouts that held considerable political influence. Upon entering the

Throne Room, a rat-faced man named Putnam Callidus greeted him.

"Greetings, Commander Alcaldo. You are certainly taking the long path to get to the commander's meeting."

"Commander's meeting? I only just arrived. I didn't know the high commander organized it. How long ago did it begin?" Ramon knew that Putnam possessed no need to know this information but expected the gossiping man to acquire it regardless.

"I believe they are awaiting your arrival. I wouldn't keep them waiting if I were you." Putnam's creepy smile eased across his face.

"Very well. Thank you, Callidus."

Ramon ignored whatever snide remark Putnam spewed and headed for the Commander's Council. Upon entering his destination, he found three familiar faces seated at the commander's table, along with one man he didn't recognize.

First Division Commander Sathak McDohl barely acknowledged Ramon's entrance. The first division, commonly referred to as the infantry division, included nearly half of the king's guard numbers. As tradition demanded, a dwarf helmed the leadership role of the infantry.

The young McDohl seldom spoke during these meetings and rarely took his responsibilities seriously. As the fourth son of Lord Rorn McDohl, he routinely used his family name as an excuse to escape as many assignments as possible.

Second Division Commander Gregorio Corilla gave Ramon a beaming smile. The second division consisted of the archers of the king's guard. Although Parvus Arbor's elves possessed the finest archers in the land, the king's second division recruited an elite unit with far more versatility. Due in no small part to Gregorio's leadership capabilities, the division boasted advanced hand-to-hand skills to accompany their long-range abilities.

Gregorio took command shortly before Ramon founded the fourth division of magic knights. Since the day they met, the commander acted as a mentor of sorts to Ramon, although Ramon never saw him that way. As Ramon's cousin and his father's nephew, he gained the opportunity to fill the second division commander's vacant seat. However, without the Alcaldo surname, he stood as the only commander to earn his position through hard work and determination.

Third Division Commander Yrsa Harken gave Ramon a frustrated look. Consisting of slightly more members than the magic knight unit, the third division only allowed sorcerers to join its ranks. Studying, training, and research absorbed most of their time, although their commander regularly volunteered the unit for any mission.

Ramon didn't know Yrsa very well. She radiated contempt toward him. He assumed she hated that Ramon created a division that also utilized magic, although she never voiced her reasons. Her father, the disgraced Oscar Harken, provided her with the namesake required to hold her position. Whether her sex or reputation as the daughter of a coward drove her ambitions, Ramon did not know, but he always held respect for her desire to prove herself.

Beside Yrsa, a timid-looking, middle-aged man sat staring at the table. Ramon never met this man before, but the chimera emblem embossed into his armor's breast signified his relation to the Hardwood family.

At the end of the table, High Commander Jonas

Werner seemed set to deliver his orders. Flanked beside him, two of the Three Heads of Cerberus and another unfamiliar face lingered.

With his fire runestone eye and pointed beard, Paul Cormac stood with his usual lackadaisical look on his face. To the left stood Adam Garrison. Leaning against the wall, he stared out the window with a look of fury upon his face. His nose looked recently broken, and dents and scuff marks decorated his usual pristine armor. Ramon couldn't imagine who put the mad-man into such a state, but he wished he could shake the man's hand.

The unfamiliar face stood rigidly at attention with a strange double-bladed staff in his hand. His expression seemed blank, as if he were a horse and cart without a driver.

"Commander Alcaldo, I'm glad you're here. Now we can begin the meeting." The High Commander gestured for Ramon to take his usual seat.

"It seems I have missed quite a bit while I was away," Ramon remarked.

"Yes, there is much to discuss." Jonas pinched the bridge of his nose and took his seat at the head of the table. "First, I would like to introduce Commander Livius

Saxa. He has taken the fifth division command, the cavalry unit, due to Cassius Drake's disappearance."

"Th-thank you, H-High Commander." Livius slowly stood. "It is an honor to be…"

"Shut up, Saxa." Jonas interrupted the new commander. "There is much to discuss. We don't have time to hear your pitiful life story."

"Y-yes, High Commander." Livius returned to his seat like a beaten dog.

"Next, I'd like to introduce the newest member of the Heads of Cerberus, William Yates."

The commanders all gave Jonas the same shocked expression. Only Yrsa possessed the bravery to speak first. "This is the new Head of Cerberus? How old is he? I have dresses in my wardrobe older than this piece of sh…"

"You shut up too, Yrsa. The prince made this decision. If you have an issue with who he selects as a Head of Cerberus, I suggest you take it up with him."

"Excuse me, High Commander," Gregorio began, "I thought the selection of the Heads of Cerberus was up to you. We all assumed you would select Captain Isaac Bentley as the new Head."

"Isaac Bentley, that reminds me." Jonas turned to Ramon, ignoring Gregorio's statement. "Commander Alcaldo, the Frost Blade, was injured on a mission during your absence. He no longer possesses his left arm."

"What? What happened? Who could have injured him?" Ramon voiced the questions on all the commander's minds.

"I will debrief you on that after this meeting. For now, I must move this along to business that I am sure will shock you even more. The king has contracted the Pox."

Each commander took the news differently. Sathak dropped his jaw. Gregorio leaned into his chair with wide eyes. Yrsa stood, slamming her fist onto the table and demanding to know how long Jonas knew this news. Livius peaked his intertwined fingers and placed them on his chin. While just as shocked as the others, Ramon kept calm and began contemplating the repercussions of the king's inescapable death.

"Calm down," Jonas said, mainly directed to Yrsa. "I only recently discovered this information. King Thomas has been keeping this secret for many months. He approaches the final stages of the disease."

"How is that possible?" Sathak demanded. "The Pox shows many signs of its infection. How did no one notice his health deteriorate?"

"The king has always worn clothing that covers him from neck to toe. Count in his reclusive nature, and he found it easy to keep his secret hidden."

"How long does he have?" Ramon asked.

"He believes he will not last the month."

The commanders murmured exasperated replies. "Please remain calm, as I have yet to give you the biggest news of all. Due to the king's failing health, he has decided to proceed with Prince Godwin's coronation. He desires to be the one who places the crown on his head before the disease takes his life."

"Is that why the citizens of Shack Town were brought into the city? For the prince's coronation?" Gregorio asked.

"Yes, and no."

"When is the coronation?" Livius found the courage to speak.

"In two days."

"Two days?" Yrsa slammed her fist onto the table and stood again. "That is nowhere near enough time to prepare."

"What of the lords of province?" Sathak added. "They could not possibly arrive at the capital in two days. They will be offended if they are not invited to such a momentous occasion."

"The coronation isn't the big news you spoke of, is it?" Ramon could tell that Jonas kept another secret he felt reluctant to share.

"No." Jonas took a glance at all the faces around the table. "The beast races have returned."

All the commanders stood, filled with a barrage of questions. How is that possible? How does he know? Where are they now? Where do they plan to attack? How did they enter the continent?

"Stop!" Jonas smashed his fist on the table, breaking off a section of wood. "Sit down, and shut up! I don't know how, but the king predicted the beast race's return a few days ago. I immediately sent scouts to the provinces, but Baxis and Parvus Arbor's scouts have not returned. The other scouts returned with nothing to report."

"So Baxis and Parvus Arbor have already fallen?" Ramon asked.

"It would appear so."

"We need to counter-attack!" Sathak insisted. "Send an army to one city or the other and liberate them. Then…"

"No." Jonas interrupted. "We have reason to believe their army is on the move, but we don't know their destination."

"All the more reason to liberate one of the provinces. If their army is on the move, we need to attack while their defenses are depleted." Yrsa's voice lost some of its confidence.

"What if the army is moving here? If we make a move now, the beasts may attack the capital. Then who will defend the king?"

"So we do nothing?" Gregorio asked.

"For now, yes. When the beasts make their move, we can send the guard to eradicate whatever forces they have remaining from the attack. If they come from Baxis, their most likely target is Durrum, as it is the closest. The dwarves live within the Hygard Mountains. Their defenses are among the best in the kingdom. No force could over-take that city before we could attack them from the rear."

"My people would never surrender their home. If the beasts plan on attacking Durrum, they will soon learn the folly of invading the land of the dwarves." Sathak proudly announced.

"I do not believe," Jonas continued, "they are departing from Parvus Arbor. If they were, Ramon would have seen signs of a moving army on his trip home from Tenebris."

"Oh, yes," Yrsa turned to Ramon, "I forgot about your recent mission. So it is true? Centaurs did attack the land of the dead?"

"I found evidence of a centaur attack, but…well, it's hard to explain and inconsequential at the moment. Right now, we should focus on what we will do instead of what has already happened."

"Well said, Commander Alcaldo." Jonas commended.

"So that is the true reason all the citizens are in the city." Ramon thought aloud. "You wanted to protect the people and curtail panic. You told the citizens that they were being brought inside for the coronation."

"Correct. Excellent deductive reasoning, as expected from you, Commander Alcaldo."

The other commanders, especially Yrsa, shot Ramon a sour look.

"Cormac," Jonas addressed the other Head of Cerberus, "get the map of Regiis and help the commanders strategize their defense of the city. Commander Alcaldo," Jonas turned to Ramon, "step outside. I have a different matter to discuss with you."

Once in private, Jonah began in a hushed tone. "I have a special mission for you. There is someone I need you to hunt down and kill."

"You don't want me to help with the defense of the city?"

"This mission is just, if not more, important. There is a mul out there carrying a weapon that yields great power. If he were to join forces with the beasts, the balance of power would shift to their side."

"You want me to hunt down a single mul? What type of weapon does he possess that could be this disconcerting?"

"He wields a sword that can utilize two runestones in unison."

"I thought that was impossible."

"As did I, but there is more. The mul is the son of

Thane Kinsman."

"The hero? Shouldn't we want the hero of Preclarium's son on our side for this war? Especially if he holds a weapon of such immense power."

"The mul despises the king. He feels the kingdom betrayed his father by not fulfilling some promise the king made before the Beast War's end."

"But I thought…"

"Yes, yes, we all thought Thane retired from the king's guard of his own volition, but apparently, he told his son a different story. Now he is out for revenge against the kingdom."

"Alright, I understand. How many of my men should I bring?"

"All of them."

"You want me to bring over sixty men to hunt a single mul?"

"Do not underestimate the power of the mul's sword. That is how your Captain Bentley lost his arm. Besides, there is another obstacle to bringing this mul down. He travels with Razuul, and they seem to have formed an unusual bond."

"Razuul? The pit fighter that earned his freedom

by ripping the heart out of a dragon?"

"One in the same. The wild elf has cultivated whatever power he utilized to kill the dragon. He is far more dangerous now than he was during captivity."

"I'd imagine he also holds some animosity toward the kingdom after being in the arena for all those years as well."

"Exactly. I know you probably want to be involved in the city's defense, but I cannot stress the importance of this mission."

"Understood. Tell me, what is the mul's name?"

"Dorian, Dorian Kinsman."

Dorian

Dorian sneezed. Dust sifted through the air as thousands of people swarmed the streets. The enticing aroma of various sweets, baked goods, and honey-based candies wafted from every direction. Jubilant cheer, laughter, and merriment echoed within the city walls as the citizens gathered for their annual celebration.

Dorian experienced a strange mixture of excitement and anxiety. Street performers delighted him and filled him with awe. The prospect of winning games of chance thrilled him. The thought of tasting a new confectionery invention tickled him with delight. Still, being surrounded by an immense crowd of people set his nerves on end. He felt that any one of them would attempt to steal from him at any moment. With every bump into a stranger, he felt his hood would drop and reveal his half-blooded ancestry. The thought of strangers staring at him with hatred made him want to turn tail and run. Even though his father's teachings told him to avoid such a large gathering, he pushed through his fear, staying close to Razuul while searching for their missing companion, Lena.

"Everyone! Gather around!" A performer shouted from a nearby stage. "Come and witness the most amazing spectacle of magic you will ever see. Prepare yourselves, and burn what you are about to see into your memory so you can pass it on to your children and your children's children."

Dressed in a red flowing robe, the man flashed a charismatic smile. The lack of hair atop his head reminded Dorian of himself, even though a pair of bushy eyebrows and a full set of lashes decorated this man's face. The raised stage provided an angle of sight that made him appear tall, although the Dorian estimated he stood not much taller than himself when on even ground, making him quite short for a human. His narrow eyes and flat nose reminded Dorian of Elijah, but this man presented a healthy figure, unlike his former friend's hefty visage.

Dorian halted Razuul by the arm. "Let's watch

this for a minute."

The performer continued his dialogue. "My name is Odo Lister, and I am the most powerful fire mage in all of Preclarium."

Odo traced out a runic symbol and turned his palms skyward. A moment later, two swirling funnels of flame jettisoned from his hands. The tornado-flames began to dance, bending and swaying in perfect harmony. Aside from Razuul, the entire crowd gasped in awe.

"Fire, the most destructive of the elemental magics, is wild, fierce, and unpredictable when found in nature. Its insatiable hunger allows it to consume everything in its path. It is akin to starving malum ursa, and a fire mage must devote all of his power to tame the beast."

The columns of flame combined, twisting and turning until they became the shape of a lion. Dorian never imagined that a mage with such immense skill existed. The onlookers applauded with amazement as the lion began prancing through the air.

"It takes years of practice for a fire mage to learn how to bend a flame. Many mages have spent their entire life unable to control the flame's ferocious nature. Under my power, fire is no more than a harmless, playing kitten."

The lion shrunk until it resembled a kitten. It hopped, skipped, and trotted through the sky. It swiped its front paw as if played with a feather on a string. It rolled onto its back and kicked its paws as if it held a ball of yarn.

"Remember, folks, even under my power, fire is dangerous. Why else would the mighty dragon have chosen it as its weapon of choice?"

The kitten morphed into a dragon and began soaring high and dipping low through the air on blazing wings. As it flew, streams of fire erupted from between its flaming fangs.

"As the world's most powerful fire mage, even the dragon is no match for my skill. Watch as I tame even the mighty dragon and show it who the real master is."

Odo traced out another magic symbol and a flame that resembled a whip shot from his hand. Every time the dragon flew close, the mage cracked the whip at the flaming beast.

"Watch out, folks, this one is a real fighter, and it looks angry."

The crowd screamed as the dragon dove overhead. As it approached the ducking audience, Odo's flame whip caught its neck before it could make contact.

"Have no fear! I have it now."

The dragon flew through the sky as though it fought against its flaming restraint. Odo tugged and pulled at the flame as though he fought against a massive fish on a line.

"Oh no, this one is too strong! Look out everyone, I can't hold it any longer, and it looks hungry!"

The flame whip dissipated. The dragon flew high in the sky before it turned its sights on the crowd. It dove over the people with its flaming mouth open wide, and Dorian swore he heard a roar release from its maw. The threat of the attack panicked the crowd. Parents pulled their children close. Grown men screamed in fear. Everyone covered their heads to brace for the impact, save for Razuul, who still stood unmoved and unimpressed.

A moment before the flaming dragon crashed into the crowd, it exploded into dozens of small, blazing balls. The fireballs shot into the sky as they twisted and twirled, entwining each other. When the flaming orbs reached a

303

height that nearly escaped sight, each one bloomed into flower-shaped designs in a series of audible pops and snaps.

The crowd cheered, clapped, and praised Odo with a barrage of compliments. The mage seemed to bathe in the adoration as he smiled and bowed.

Dorian joined the cheering before turning to Razuul. "You didn't like that? I thought it was amazing!"

"I hate magic."

"Aye, I know, but you had to be at least a little impressed. I mean, when that dragon dove at us, weren't you even a little scared?"

Razuul looked at Dorian with a half-smile. "I'm not afraid of dragons."

Dorian chuckled. "Aye, of course you're not. Where should we go next?"

"I don't…" Razuul stopped mid-sentence. Something in the distance grabbed his attention.

"What is it?" Dorian stood tip-toed, trying to spot whatever entranced his wild elven companion.

"I'm…not sure. Someone is in that direction." Razuul began to follow his gaze.

"Hey, wait for me," Dorian called, but Razuul didn't seem to hear.

Dorian weaved through the crowd to keep pace with the wild elf but lost sight of his mentor. He wanted to call out his name but knew that doing so would bring unwanted attention to the arena champion. Dorian spun wildly, searching for a clue to his whereabouts. On the skirt of his vision, he saw the mysterious doors appear amongst the crowd, but they disappeared once again when he focused on them. Disregarding the image, he began to wade through the masses when an unmistakable sound alerted him to the correct direction.

Steel clashing against steel rang nearby, followed by someone crying out in pain.

"Oh no," Dorian said to no one.

During their travels, he had heard that exact string of sounds more than once. In nearly every town they visited, inevitably, someone angered Razuul. He always gave his opponent the chance to draw their weapon, and it always ended the same. Their weapons clashed once, followed directly by the moans, screams, and cries of the person foolish enough to upset the Dragon Fist.

Dorian pushed through a group of onlookers to find an unusual sight. A square-shaped ring, barricaded by wooden planks, prevented outsiders from entering. At the center of the ring stood a man holding a peculiar sword in both hands. As a weaponsmith, Dorian forged blades of every shape, size, and length imaginable, or at least that's what he thought. The slightly curved blade stretched longer and thinner than most blades. It lacked a sharpened edge to prevent permanent injury to his opponent, but even it was sharpened, its design allowed for it to cut from only one side of the steel. Instead of having the usual cross-shaped design, the guard resembled a disk. The grip looked unusually long, and it lacked a pommel to prevent the sword from flying out of its owner's hands.

The man's appearance seemed foreign to Dorian. A long ribbon tied his hair into a ponytail at the top of his head rather than the customary style of tying hair to the base of the neck that males typically used. Rather than the rounded features of standard armor, his bore an angular design with pauldrons that resembled shingles on a roof. He seemed human, although his narrow nose, face, and frame signified an unknown descent. His body structure, armor, and sword seemed odd to Dorian but not nearly as unusual as the fact that he stood in a fighting ring with a strip of cloth bound tightly around his eyes.

At the man's feet, a man writhed in agony, clutching his forehead.

"Another challenger falls!" A man announced as he stepped into the ring. "Is there anyone else brave enough to face the greatest swordsman? For those just joining us, the rules are simple. Wager as much money as you like. If you manage to beat him wearing a blindfold with an arm tied behind his back, you can double your money. If you can beat him wearing a blindfold only, you can triple your money. For those who are truly confident in their abilities, you can challenge him without any handicap and win the entirety of the winnings he has earned today. At the moment, that sum is well over five hundred gold coins."

For Dorian, the opportunity seemed too good to pass up. For countless nights, he'd sparred with the greatest swordsman, Razuul. The lessons he learned through his training dramatically increased his skills. Although he knew he needed to sharpen his abilities further, he doubted even Razuul could defeat him blindfolded at his current level. Considering that his currency ran thin, he doubted he could find a better opportunity to replenish his supply.

He thought about his goal, killing Jonas Werner. He could feel Shadowflame on his hip, begging to be drawn. The thought of confronting his father's killer stirred a blinding rage inside Dorian. He pulsed with an overwhelming desire to unleash his pent-up fury on a strong opponent, one that could resist his power and put up a fight.

Dorian began to raise his arm when a hand clasped his wrist and forced it back down. He found Razuul standing next to him with his gaze solidly fixed on the blindfolded man.

"You don't want to do that." The look on Razzul's face perplexed Dorian. Whatever thoughts juggled in the wild elf's mind, whether confusion or intrigue, Dorian never saw him in such a state.

"He's blindfolded. I've been training so hard, and I've gotten a lot better. No matter how good he is, there is no way he could beat me in that state."

"You're wrong."

"How do you know?" Dorian's raging inferno reduced to a flickering flame.

"I don't know how…I just do. Besides, did you forget? You are a wanted man. Do you really think it's a good idea to bring that kind of attention to yourself?"

"You're right. I don't know what came over me."

"No one?" The man in the ring addressed the crowd. "Surely someone is brave enough to face him."

"Why don't you take him on Razuul? There's no way he could beat you."

"If the fight weren't for entertainment, I would. I swore to never fight for anyone's amusement ever again."

"Aye, I forgot. Sorry."

"Is there no one brave enough to face the mysterious swordsman Syken Hygimora?" The announcer scanned the crowd.

"I'll take him on!" A large man parted the crowd. He attempted to step in between the ring's planks, but his massive girth prevented entry.

"Allow me." The announcer man opened a gate to grant access.

The crowd began to murmur. Dorian heard whispers of the 'Cleaver' in reference to the over-sized man. People talked of his exploits, rise through the military's ranks, and thirst for violence. From what

Dorian could gather, the man possessed a reputation that earned him fear more than respect.

With a full head of hair and lack of gray in his bristling beard, he seemed in the prime of his life. A minor belly began to emerge at his midsection, but he appeared in decent shape otherwise. Dorian could smell ale emanating from the man, but his balance, lack of glossed eyes, and unslurred speech meant he hadn't reached inebriation yet. He stood above the average human's height with a thick build, but the sword strapped to his back looked too large even for him.

"Welcome challenger," the announcer gave the Cleaver a broad smile, "which handicaps would you like give our champion?"

"All of them. I've been itching to put the hurt on someone."

"Very well, and how much would you like to wager?"

The man shoved a bag of coins into the announcer's chest. "There are fifty gold coins in there. You had better not try to scam me when I win. If I count ninety-nine coins in my winnings, I'll come back and chop and you in two."

"My, my, fifty gold coins? You must be very confident in your abilities." The announcer man replied.

"I am impressed," Syken spoke for the first time. "Fifty gold coins become one hundred. Chopping a man in half divides one into two. Your propensity for mathematics is impressive."

Dorian's secluded life prevented him from learning the different dialects and speech patterns of the provinces. In the past few months, he had traveled a great distance and met many people of varying origins, races, and social standing. None of the people he met sounded anything like Syken. He pronounced his words with emphasis on the final letter and inflected his voice in strange places.

"That's right! Wait, are you making fun of me?" The brutish man demanded.

"I shall allow you to make that determination for yourself." Syken walked to the corner, where a set of attendants tided his arm behind his back and tightened the blindfold.

The Cleaver's breath intensified. "Hey," he shouted at the announcer, "you going to get me a practice sword or what?"

"Oh, no need," Syken replied for the announcer, "feel free to use the one on your back."

"Your funeral."

The two combatants approached the center of the ring. Syken's stance looked strange without the use of one arm. He squared his shoulders at his opponent and held his blade with the handle pointing toward his stomach. Dorian's studies on swordsmanship taught him that single-handed fighters usually stood sideways with their sword-arm extended to give their opponents as little striking surface as possible. The Cleaver withdrew his over-sized blade and held it in both white-knuckled hands.

The announcer raised his arm and sharply chopped it down."Begin!"

The Cleaver brought his sword down with a primal scream. Instead of blocking the blow, Syken withdrew his blade and pivoted to avoid the strike. The Cleaver followed with swing after swing, but the blindfolded man easily side-stepped each attempt in a manner that reminded Dorian of a leaf falling from a tree.

"How is he doing that?" Dorian asked.

"Watch his feet," Razuul responded.

Dorian followed his mentor's instruction. He observed elegant footwork like that of a dancer; however, it didn't take long for him to realize what Razuul intended him to notice. Each step the blindfolded swordsman took happened before the Cleaver swung his sword. His toes pointed in the precise position needed to escape the blows as if he knew which strike his opponent would attempt next.

"That-that's not possible. It would be one thing if he could see, but he's actually predicting where his opponent will strike. It's like he can see into the future."

"That's not exactly correct. He's using the same power that I have to feel his opponent's stance and shifting his own in response." Razuul's expression angered.

"I didn't know anyone had that power other than you. I've read dozens of books on swordsmanship and the abilities of the greatest swordsman in history. None of them mentioned a power that enhances your senses, strength, and speed. I thought you were the only one ever to discover the ability."

"Me too, but there's more." Razuul's frustration grew. "He's using it more...I don't know the word. It's as if he turns it on and off in quick bursts to conserve energy. He focuses his senses to only one place, so he isn't picking up on anything other than what is necessary."

"The word you're looking for is efficient, but how do you know all this?"

"I can feel it. I don't even need to use the power myself. I just know. And I'm betting he can do the same thing. Keep your eyes on the swordsman." Razuul closed his eyes and took a deep breath. In Dorian's experience, this meant that the wild elf intended to enter his own enhanced state.

Keeping an eye on Syken, Dorian witnessed the exact moment Razuul entered the heightened state. For a moment, the blindfolded man's attention shifted away from the opponent to Razuul.

"Die!" The Cleaver shouted with a horizontal swing of his mighty sword. The blow nearly landed, but Syken jumped back in barely enough time.

"Alright, I am done playing with you now." Syken retook his strange stance.

"We'll see about that!" The Cleaver, panting from exhaustion, attacked with an overhead strike.

Syken remained motionless until the last possible moment and disappeared, leaving the opponent to strike nothing but dirt. In a flash, the blinded swordsman reappeared behind the Cleaver with his back facing him; his attention focused on Razuul.

"How the…" The Cleaver began to speak when Syken swung a backhanded strike to the forehead that knocked him out cold. All the while, he never shifted his focus from Razuul.

"Come on, let's get out of here." Razuul turned and began to walk away.

"Not again. Razuul, wait!" Dorian followed after the wild elf.

Catching up to him, Dorian struggled to keep up with Razuul's long strides without jogging.

"Where are you going? Don't you want to know more about that man?"

"No."

"Why not? He might know some things about your power that he can teach you."

"I don't care."

"He was obviously interested in you. You could at least talk to him."

"No."

"But, why?"

"Because he's human!" Razuul stopped to shout at Dorian. "I don't want to learn anything from a human!"

Razuul looked around at the surrounding people starring at him. Pulling his hood down low over his face, he turned and walked away.

Dorian felt ashamed. He knew that Razuul held animosity toward humans, but he didn't realize his hatred ran that deep. The wild elf despised drawing attention to himself. For him to shout before a massive crowd meant his feelings boiled over enough to forget his usual policy of not drawing attention to himself. All because Dorian could not stop poking his nose where it did not belong.

Pulling his hood down, Dorian trailed Razuul to an area near the city's walls where few people lingered.

Dorian approached his angered mentor. "I'm sorry. I shouldn't have pressed."

"No, you shouldn't have, but it's fine. I know you were only trying to help."

"So, you hate all humans? Even Brett?"

"I don't know if he qualifies as human."

Dorian chuckled. "You know, I am half-human."

"I know. That's the half I don't like."

The two shared a laugh.

"Excuse me." A familiar voice came from behind them.

Dorian turned to see Syken Hygimora approaching. He no longer wore a blindfold, revealing his bright, yellow eyes.

"I apologize for interrupting you, but please give me a moment of your time." Syken's accent thickened in his excited state.

"Go away." Razuul insisted.

"Hold on a second, Razuul," Dorian suggested.

"Did you see his eyes? He might not be human."

"Is that why you left? You hate humans?" Syken pinched at the skin on his neck. "I can relate. I am not too fond of them either. Unfortunately, I am indeed a human."

"I don't care. Just get out of here."

"Please, just hear what I have to say. It will not take long, and once you have heard my words, I promise to leave you alone."

After a moment of awkward silence, Dorian spoke up. "Well, he hasn't attacked you yet, so I think this is your chance."

"Well, first, my name is Syken Hygimora. Well met, Master Razuul."

"I am no master and don't use the elven greeting. You are not an elf."

"I meant no offense. Hear my tale so that I may take my leave. I am from a land far away from here. In my country, I am the last remaining member of a proud clan of swordsmen. Since birth, we have been taught the way of the sword and trained to use Hakai."

"Hakai?" Dorian asked.

"It is an ability that allows a person to gain access to incredible power. For a short time, a Hakai user is granted an immeasurable increase in strength, speed, and senses."

"Just like you, Razuul! So, it's called Hakai?"

"That is what my people call it. Does it have a different name here?"

"It doesn't have a name here. As far as we know, Razuul is the only person who can do it."

"I see. Then it is fortuitous that I came to this land."

"This is all very interesting, but can you please get on with it so you can leave us alone." Razuul rolled his hand, signaling to move the conversation along.

Syken returned to pinching the skin on his neck. "Yes, of course. As I said, I am the last member of my clan, and when I die, a millennium's worth of knowledge dies with me. A few years ago, my homeland was ravaged by war. We also have runestones in my country, but we have advanced much further in technology than the people here. A few years ago, a man invented a new type of weapon that shifted the balance of power. It allowed anyone to possess the most powerful mages' destructive capabilities. My clan shunned the runestones, but this did not exclude us from being caught in the devastation.

"At the war's end, most of our population was decimated. I roamed my homeland for years, trying to find someone who could learn the secrets of Hakai. However, even within my clan, the ability is rare. I found no such prospect.

"Lacking other options, I found a ship and set sail. I hoped to discover a new land. One that could offer a warrior with the potential to continue our proud tradition. It took many months, but finally, my ship spotted this land. As soon as we approached, several sea monsters attacked our ship and pulled it to the bottom of the sea. I used Hakai to swim to land but became exhausted and drifted from consciousness. I woke here, on the shore of Prasillo. I still do not know how I survived.

"For a while, I roamed your land to find a warrior that could inherit my clan's techniques. To survive, I used my ability to perform jobs. I would hunt down a monster or track down a band of thieves. All the while, I challenged warriors to test their skills, but none showed potential.

"Then I heard about a festival—one where thousands of people gather. I thought if I opened a challenge that allowed fighters from across the land to earn a great deal of money, I would find the warrior I sought. That is when I felt you in the crowd, and my heart filled with happiness. I finally found someone that could learn my clan's techniques, and their knowledge could be passed along."

"Why not find someone young? Dorian asked. "If you trained someone from a young age, you might be able to awaken the ability."

"Unfortunately, I do not have enough time for that. Using Hakai comes with a cost. It shortens one's lifespan, and I rapidly approach the age where members of my clan traditionally perish."

"Wait, Hakai shortens a person's lifespan?" Dorian looked up at Razuul.

"A small price to pay for the elven race. I only learned of the elf's existence since arriving here. From what I understand, an elf can live more than a thousand years. Unless your friend here has been using Hakai for the past eight hundred years, I doubt you have much to worry about."

"So you want to teach me your techniques? I have been fighting with my own style for too long to learn yours."

"I do not wish to teach my fighting style, only the many uses of Hakai. Without a teacher, I imagine using Hakai exhausts you, possibly causes you to pass out if you use it for too long. I can teach you how to regulate and refine the Hakai so that you can use it for hours at a time. Since you already have the ability, I can teach you these techniques in a short amount of time. It will take you more time to master them, but you can practice without any assistance once I have taught you. What do you say?"

"I think..."

Before Razuul finished his thoughts, a loud bell rang in the distance. Soon another bell followed, followed by another and another. The chimes echoed throughout the city until they drown out all other sounds.

"What is that?" Dorian yelled, covering his ears.

"Dorian! Razuul!" A barely audible voice called over the bells.

Dorian turned to see Brett gesturing his arm to signal them to follow him. Running up to him, Dorian asked, "What is going on?"

"The city is under attack!" Keeping his fingers in his ears, Brett turned in every direction. "Did you find Lena?"

"No. Who could possibly attack the city?" With all the excitement, Dorian forgot about the young heiress.

"We are going to have to leave her. We don't have time. If we don't get out of here, the beast races will kill us all!"

Clarissa

Clasping Sir Kenneth's waist, Clarissa sat behind the paladin atop their trotting horse. With the sun setting at her back, she knew they headed east, but she didn't know their destination. After everything that happened, she hardly cared. No city remained that wouldn't arrest them on sight. Clarissa knew by now word of their treacherous actions spread throughout the kingdom like a wildfire. If caught, Sir Kenneth would be brought straight to the executioner's block. Clarissa's fate would be far worse. During the trial that resulted in Clarissa's excommunication, the king ordered her never to use the Holy Judgment spell. Instead, she used the spell two times in one day to escape the detestable Alcaldo family. Due to her treasonous actions, she felt confident that the king would publicly torture her to send a message to all the people that disobeying the king's orders resulted in a fate worse than death.

"Sir Kenneth, how is your wound?"

"I'm fine. We just need to find…" Sir Kenneth slumped forward and slid off the horse.

"Kenneth!" Clarissa found her dress saturated with blood. She knew Sir Kenneth's wound caused him more pain than he admitted, but she failed to realize the extent of the damage.

Hopping down from the horse, she began unstrapping the armor from his limp body. Sir Kenneth insisted that the blow he received only grazed his flesh during their escape, but he lied. The sword stabbed through his side, likely piercing a bodily organ.

During her training to become high priestess, Clarissa only learned two spells that befit her title, a prerequisite to her position. As such, she never knew the healing spells common among light runestone mages. Holding the prestigious title meant she would not see a battlefield up close. Learning both spells required intensive study and practice due to their complex and intricate requirements. Holy Judgment offered no help to their current situation. Still, the other spell stood a chance at saving Sir Kenneth's life: the Forgiveness spell, a mass healing spell intended to revive an entire squadron of soldiers. The high priestess studied this spell in case of dire circumstances. If her home city, Sanctum, ever came under attack, the high priestess could cast this spell from any tower within the castle, ensuring the ruler's safety while enabling her to keep her soldiers in battle.

In any other situation she would not question using Forgiveness, but casting it brought severe risk to the duo. The spell rained dozens of soft-light beams from the sky. Doing so would alert those hunting them to their position. Furthermore, Forgiveness required a vast amount of energy, and since she recently cast Holy Judgment twice, she didn't know if she possessed enough energy to cast the taxing spell.

Clarissa reflected on Sir Gabriel. Her reluctance to take a risk in Villam resulted in the loyal paladin's death. She dwelled on the different scenarios she could have taken that may have resulted in saving one of the only two people who remained at her side during the most challenging time in her life. Now, the only person remaining loyal to her lay dying. She cursed herself for considering to not take action.

Clarissa sat back on her knees and focused on

gathering every bit of magical energy held within her body. She traced out the runic symbol for Forgiveness with her finger and poured the accumulated energy into the spell. A moment later, several beams of light bathed the area. The surrounding grass sprouted, each blade stretching high enough to bend under its weight. A nearby apple tree sprouted countless fruits that grew to two fists' size before dropping to the ground with a heavy thud. Clarissa looked down at Kenneth to watch his gaping wound close, leaving nothing behind but dried blood and a minor scar.

Dizziness consumed Clarissa's mind and her body weakened. Unable to overcome her weariness, she dropped to her back. Shadowy fingers crept at the edge of her vision, threatening to drench the world in darkness. Using all of her willpower, she fought to force back the tendrils of unconsciousness, but she slowly lost the battle. As the darkness nearly enveloped the world, her surroundings suddenly shot back into view.

Clarissa sat up with a yelp. She no longer felt the exhaustion from the spell. Her mind felt clear and alert, and fatigue completely escaped her body. Her physical state felt as though she would soon drift into the air like embers floating up from a fire. She delighted in the freeing sensation, but only for a moment. Looking to her surroundings, the shock of discovering her new environment settled in.

She sat in her old room in Sanctum. Everything in the room remained exactly as she remembered. Piles of pillows sat atop her bed just the way she liked it, and her favorite silken sheets spread across the mattress without a single wrinkle. The ornate mirrored wardrobe stood in the corner, and a three-log fire burned in the hearth just the way she always insisted.

She approached the window that overlooked the city. Peering through, she found nothing but smoke and darkness. Not a single streetlight, lit window, nor lantern of a roaming soldier pierced the darkness. Clarissa could not imagine any weather phenomena that could blank out the entirety of Sanctum's glow.

A clanging startled Clarissa. She spun around to find the same specter she'd seen in Villam. Seeing its ghostly figure rose the heat in her cheeks. Rage stirred in her chest like an inferno. Clenching her fists, she narrowed her eyes at the armored wraith.

"What do you want from me?"

The apparition remained motionless.

"Are you friend or foe? You show up, pierce my ears with a howling scream one day, then save my life the next! I can't take this anymore. Just tell me why you keep visiting me, then leave me alone!"

The apparition denied Clarissa's request with silence.

Clarissa retrieved the poker from its stand near the hearth. Approaching the phantom, she swung the impromptu weapon at its head. The apparition remained unmoving, and Clarissa discovered why it did not fear the blow. Instead of striking its head, the poker passed through its hooded visage, trailing a line of smoke in its wake. She repeatedly swiped, aiming at every section of its armored body. Each attempt passed through as though she swung her weapon at the smoke of a fire.

Clarissa dropped the poker. "Just tell me what you want."

The high-pitched scream released from the other-worldly figure. Clarissa covered her ears, but the sound quickly faded. Soon, the noise sounded similar to a crackling log in a fire.

Clarissa slowly removed her hands from her ears.

"Are…are you trying to talk to me?"

"Find…elves…" The whispered words seemed to consist of many voices speaking at once: male, female, young, and old.

"Elves? What elves? What are you saying?"

"Find…elves…" The specter repeated in the same echoing voices.

Suddenly, the ghostly being grabbed the sides of its hooded, smoky head. Bending over, it writhed as though it experienced excruciating pain. The crackling voice intensified, and soon the high-pitched scream returned.

Clarissa covered her ears again. It felt as though a million needles stabbed at her inner ear. Her muscles cramped, her head throbbed, and her eyes burned. As she thought she would soon lose her sanity, the screaming ceased.

Returning to her feet, she glanced around the room. The apparition disappeared. Not a single sign of its existence remained. She turned to continue her search when the entire room vanished.

Clarissa fell into an empty void. Fear gripped her heart. She attempted to scream, but no sound came.

Twisting her body, she searched for an end to the pitched void, but only blackness existed. Tears streamed upwards from the corners of her eyes. The wind howled past her ears. Before long, her destination came into view. The ground rushed toward her as she plummeted through the void. In the distance, she saw two people lying on their backs in a field of overgrown grass. The field grew closer until the identity of the bodies became apparent. The larger of the two belonged to Kenneth, while the smaller she identified as her own. Surrounding the bodies, a group of shadowy beings sat atop horses with spears in hand. Each of the beings crept toward the bodies and pointed their weapons at Clarissa and Kenneth's bodies.

Clarissa's fall ended when she crashed into her own body. Taking a sharp inhale, as though she emerged from the water after nearly drowning, she bolted upright. Hot daggers of pain stabbed into her temples, and her blurred vision perceived the world as looking through a drinking glass. The darkness began to envelop her sight again. She barely made out the attackers' visage before the shade of night overcame her vision.

Four horse-backed figures approached with spears drawn. As she crumbled to the ground, she managed to utter a single word before slipping into darkness.

"Elves."

Marius

The journey to Durrum proved difficult, but the addition of travel companions made the trip more bearable. The dangers intensified as the distance to their destination shortened. The rocky terrain threatened to break an ankle or trap a person in a hidden pit. Beastly attacks increased in frequency. Twice, a pack of malum ursa attempted to dine on their innards. Three times, a swarm of minuscule trumkins attacked, and the entire group nearly met their end when a klora tried to liquefy them with venom.

Each attack ended with his elven companions making short work of the monsters. They graciously provided Marius with a knife, but he felt useless in battle without his usual enchanted dagger. Jocia squished, slammed, and impaled with her earth magic. Galain utilized his superior athleticism and incomparable bow skills to dispatch any threat. Elendor stretched his strange magical arm to stab, squeeze, hit, entangle, or whip any attackers.

Marius found Jocia and Galain quite pleasant, but Elendor's demeanor left him uneasy. He lacked apprehension in situations that garnered fear for self-preservation. He spoke with arrogance about subjects of which he knew nothing. His comments left everyone uncomfortable, and he shunned any ideas that weren't his own.

Marius learned much from his companions, but he could tell they kept something hidden. He learned about the attack on Tenebris that they helped defend. They told him about the fall of Parvus Arbor at the hands of their own chief. They even informed him how they achieved the use of Elendor's magical limbs, but certain subjects seemed taboo.

Any mention of the king caused them to change the subject quickly. During one of their conversations, Jocia mentioned an incident in Nigereous Forest, but the others insisted that she say no more. He yearned to know more of what they learned during their travels but resigned that he needed to earn their trust further before they would relent their secrets.

In return, Marius gave up all the information he knew. He told them how Baxis fell in nearly the same fashion as Parvus Arbor. He appraised the tale of how he tried to inform the king about the invasion, only to be labeled as a treasonous assassin. He even told them about Dogon, but they didn't seem to believe him. He couldn't blame them for their apprehension. Even he found the strange creature's existence hard to believe, especially since it hadn't shown itself since Marius met the elves.

"Marius, do you know how much further until we arrive at Durrum?" Galain asked.

"A little more than a half day's walk." Marius estimated.

"Good. I think we should camp here. That gives us time to gather wood for a fire and get a good night's rest. We may need all of our strength for when we enter the land of the dwarves." Galain dropped his gear onto the ground.

"Do not worry. If the dwarves wish to close their ears to our words, I will force them open." Elendor split and stretched his arm to gather enough rocks to encircle a fire pit in one grab.

"I recommend you don't try to force the dwarves

to do anything. Your magic is strong, but even you couldn't handle the thousands of dwarves that live in the Hygard Mountains." Marius began gathering kindling for the fire.

Elendor scoffed. "You have no idea what I am capable of."

"Regardless, when we arrive, you should let me do the talking. I'm sure you are all aware that the dwarves still hold a great deal of animosity toward the elves."

"That is if they do not arrest you on sight." Jocia unfurled her sleeping pack. "We can only hope that word of your assassination attempt has not reached the Hygard Mountains."

"Normally, I wouldn't even question it. Something like that would spread across the kingdom faster than a starving elf gathering berries."

All three elves shot Marius a disconcerting look.

"Sorry…it's just a saying. Anyway, I'm betting that all communication between the provinces has been focused on the invasion. Any messages not bearing the king's war seal has likely been pushed aside." Marius threw his gathered kindling into the pit. "There is something we can do to help prevent me from being recognized." Marius pulled out his dagger and juggled it in his hand. "Have any of you ever cut hair?"

"You want us to shave your head?" Galain finished sparking the flint to start the fire. "That blade is not nearly sharp enough. You do realize that it will hurt?"

"I do, but it's the safest approach. The dwarves rarely travel outside their mountain, and I haven't been to Durrum in many years. No one there should know me well enough to recognize me without hair. It's not a perfect disguise, but it's the best we have."

"Only the humans and dwarves are superficial enough to not recognize someone due to a haircut," Elendor remarked.

"True, but at least it's an advantage we wouldn't have otherwise." Marius shot an unamusing smile at Elendor.

That night, after a painful hour of head shaving, the group laid down to sleep. Marius closed his eyes, but his irritated scalp kept him from entering slumber. For hours, he tossed and turned. After the elves drifted off, Marius got up to find a place to relieve himself. Just as he finished, a pair of hands grabbed his shoulders.

The hands yanked Marius off his feet and pulled

him into the sky. He flew at an incredible speed. Trees blurred past, the whipping winds filled his ears, and he found it difficult to breathe. He tried to see who pulled him, but as soon as he faced forward into the wind, his eyes filled with tears.

Just as suddenly as it started, the trip ended. The hands released his shoulders, sending Marius rolling in the dirt. His body ached from impacting the ground, and his head spun from the unexpected jolt and subsequent flight, but he emerged otherwise unscathed.

Staggering to his feet, he searched the area to find a woman sitting straight-backed and crossed-legged on the trunk of a fallen tree. Her snow-white hair, pulled back into a braided ponytail that resembled the bones of a fish, draped over her shoulder. Her skin, nearly as white as her hair, revealed blue, spiderweb-like veins beneath the surface. Her eyes, lips, and fingernails shone blood-red, and her white blouse, velvet vest, and leather pants presented a refined appearance. Her presence felt ominous yet alluring. Part of him wanted to remain in her presence. The rest of him wanted to run away in terror.

"Hmm, you seem resistant to my charms. How very interesting." Her words seemed to echo with two voices. One sounded much deeper than the other, yet both possessed a seductive, feminine quality.

"Your charms?" A bevy of questions entered his mind, yet he felt compelled to respond only to her words.

"Yes, most men succumb to their passion and grovel at my feet upon seeing me. I think perhaps a male member of my family would have had better luck with our persuasive abilities."

Marius shuttered with a chill, as though someone released an icy grip from his mind. "Wait, what is going on? Who are you? How did..."

"Shh." The woman suddenly appeared in front of Marius with her finger pressed against his lips. "This will be much easier if I give you the information you seek."

Marius wanted to protest but felt overwhelmingly compelled to follow her orders. The woman strolled back to the tree and returned to her previous posture.

"My name is Aleece Valencia. My family heads the Assassin's Guild. That is all I am willing to tell you about myself, so all further questions are forbidden. I have been tasked with finding people who have an understanding of what is happening within this kingdom. We have come to understand that something significant is occurring, and we know you are involved, but we don't know how."

"The beast races have invaded the kingdom. They plan on…"

"Yes, yes, we know all of that." Aleece waved a dismissive hand. "The information I seek is more…magical in nature. Something is disturbing the flow of magic in the land. We have sensed it."

"Elendor? He managed to combine his earth runestone with darkness runestone shards. They also told me of a mul that…"

"We know of the elf and the mul already as well. Whatever is occurring is far more significant." Aleese released a disappointed sigh. "Well, it seems you do not have the information we seek. Perhaps we will meet again."

"Wait!" Marius called, but the strange woman vanished. Marius turned in circles, but no trace of her remained. "Where am I?" He shouted to no one.

Jonas

The day of the coronation arrived. Jonas stood at the rear of the platform to keep watch on the ceremony. With his hair freshly groomed, his armor polished, and his face clean-shaven, he felt uncomfortable. The feeling didn't come from his fresh appearance; rather, it derived from the knowledge of his failure. He hoped to discover a way to end the prince's life before the king's demented son took the crown, but the opportunity never arose. The prince consistently surrounded himself with hordes of admirers. Adam Garrison never left his side, and even when he did, a gaggle of women and servants clung to him. Even when he slept, the prince of paranoia ensured guardsmen stayed at his bedside.

King Thomas Magicent stood at the foreground of the platform. Dressed in a silken shirt trimmed with shimmering gold threads, his regal appearance befit his royal lineage. A cape lined in luxurious fur draped across his shoulders. Rare, sparkling gems adorned his fingers and hung from golden chains wrapped around his neck.

To his right stood Aaron Bright, the out-of-place High Priest of Sanctum. His white robe glistened like the sun reflecting off the ripples of a pond. His thin, blonde hair shifted in the breeze, and his gaunt face showed the effects of inheriting his demanding title.

The king's council stood on both sides of the platform, dressed in their finest ceremonial attire. Each wore gaudy baubles on their fingers, facial hair, heads, and necks. In an attempt to outshine one another, the council members wore flashy outfits embellished with giant feathers, frills, exotic furs, and even freshly cut flowers.

The crowd packed the courtyard. No standing room remained as people sat on roofs and hung out windows to witness the celebration.

Before the king, a pair of servants hauled a podium with a wind-runestone-powered amplifying device attached.

"Welcome, subjects." The crowd's roar diminished to a hush. "As you know, we gather today to celebrate the coronation of Prince Godwin Magicent. I count myself lucky. Most of my ancestors died before they could place the crown on their offspring's head. Like the setting sun brings the promise of a new day, my time as king comes to an end while my son's reign begins. I could not be more proud. I have watched Prince Godwin grow into a proud, charismatic, and honorable man."

Jonas felt lucky that no one could see him roll his eyes beneath his helmet.

"I feel confident that I leave the kingdom in the best possible hands. Under Prince Godwin's rule, I believe the kingdom shall prosper. You may all look forward to a thriving age filled with honesty and justice."

Jonas felt he could fill his helmet with vomit.

"Without further ado, I give to you, Prince Godwin."

The crowd erupted and poured adulation onto the prince as he emerged from the castle doors.

The prince shot a sly smile at Jonas as he approached the podium. Dressed in a crushed velvet shirt with gold buttons, he confidently strolled to his father. A red shoulder-cape covered the right half of his body, and a jewel-encrusted sword rested on his hip. Keeping true to his simplistic style, not a single ring rested on his fingers, and not a single chain hung from his neck.

Approaching his father, he placed his fist over his heart and took a knee. A man dressed in a white robe, embroidered with the Bright family crest, carried a lavish pillow holding the king's crown to Aaron Bright. The high priest, in turn, ceremoniously handed it to King Thomas.

"By the…" Aaron's voice cracked."Ahem, by the power vested in me as High Priest of Sanctum, I bless this coronation. Prince Godwin Magicent, may your rule be just, as taught by our god Metera. May you respect all those that have passed, as the god Morthem instructs. May the winds given to us by the god Ventus fill the sails of the fishermen that provide meals for the hungry. May the soils given to us by the god Terram be fertile and produce bountiful crops. May the fires given to us by the god Ignitus keep your people warm during the cold. May the water given to us by the god Markka be provided to all those that thirst. Most of all, may your rule be filled with the wisdom of the father of the gods, Doleum."

"From this day, and until your last," King Thomas raised the crown high, "you shall bear the title of king." Placing the crown on his son's head, King Thomas offered his hands to help Godwin to his feet. "Arise, King Godwin."

The crowd erupted in cheer. People jumped to get a better view of their new ruler. One man fell out a second-story window as the people behind him accidentally pushed him out by trying to get a good peek at the newly crowned king. Godwin turned to the gathering with his arms held wide, absorbing the adulation.

Taking the podium, King Godwin began his speech. "My people, today begins a new era in Preclarium. I can only hope to be a ruler as kind, just, and caring as my father before me."

The crowd cheered for their former king.

"However," King Godwin's voice deepened, relaying a serious tone that grabbed the crowd's attention, "certain changes must be made. Since I returned to the capital, I have seen too many injustices. Even with the enforcement of my new strict and harsh policies, criminals continue to harm my people. They rape, they steal, and they kill, all in the name of selfish desires. From this day forward, I am increasing the number of patrolmen and am authorizing the use of deadly force toward anyone who dares defy the kingdom's laws."

The crowd's murmur intensified until one brave man approached the steps. After climbing two steps, several guards halted him by threatening with the tips of their spears.

"Your Grace!" The man called. "What of the beast races? Word has spread that they have returned and are currently attacking our cities."

"My good man," Godwin flashed his wide smile, "These rumors of the beast races returning are just that...rumors."

"That's not how we heard it." A woman took to the stairs, but the guards halted her as well. "We heard that you brought us inside the walls because you expect an attack. You hid this information by telling us we needed to attend the coronation."

"My people, your safety is my primary concern. Not just for those here in Regiis, but for all of the citizens in all of the cities. If the beast races attacked any of the provinces, we would send an army to eradicate them immediately."

"You lie!" A red-faced man made it to the fourth step before being threatened. Jonas drew his sword and stood next to his new king to ensure his safety. "You talk about punishing criminals, yet you allow the beasts to run rampant in the countryside. What game are you playing?"

The crowd communicated their agreement by defiantly throwing trash and debris at the stage. A few more citizens tried to approach the platform, but a line of guards rushed to protect the crown's new owner.

"Your Grace," Jonas spoke in Godwin's ear, "perhaps it is best if you return to the castle for now."

The king turned to Jonas, his face twisted with fury. "Nonsense!" He turned back to the amplifier to address the crowd. "You trash! How dare you…"

The sound of flesh smacking stone interrupted Godwin. Jonas turned to see the former king lying on the floor, limp. Rushing to his side, Jonas knelt and leaned his ear against the former ruler's chest to check for a heartbeat. Not able to hear above the surrounding roars, he looked up at the guards that rushed to encircle them.

"Did any of you see anything? Did someone do this?"

"No, High Commander," one of the guards responded, "he just collapsed."

"You and you," Jonas pointed at two guards, "go

get Doctor Hemming and escort him to the king's quarters. The rest of you, help me get him to his bed."

As he stood, lifting the former king's faltered body, a hand grabbed Jonas's arm. He turned to see Godwin's enraged face. "I think you mean my bed."

Jonas ripped his arm from the king's grip. "Your Grace, now is not the time."

Ignoring the newly appointed ruler, Jonas helped carry Thomas to the king's chambers. After laying him down, Jonas ordered the men to leave the room.

Taking off his helmet and whipping his gauntlets to the floor, Jonas took his liege's hand. As soon as their skin touched, Thomas's eyes fluttered open.

"J...Jonas?" The former king spoke in a weak voice.

"I'm here, Your Grace."

"M-My son. I-I must s-speak with my son."

"Right away, Your Grace."

Jonas exited the room to summon the newly appointed king. As soon as he shut the door behind him, Godwin approached.

"High Commander, how dare you make any orders that involve my quarters. If it weren't for..."

Jonas interrupted Godwin's beratement by slapping him across the face. The king cradled his cheek with a shocked expression.

"Your father lies dying, and you talk about a room? For all of your pompous declarations about caring for the kingdom and its people, how about you show some respect for the one that gave you life. He has asked to see you anyway. And don't worry, you can hand out any consequences for my actions after you've said your goodbyes…Your Grace."

"Oh, there will be consequences." Godwin squeezed past Jonas to enter the chamber. "You better prepare yourself!"

Jonas leaned against the wall. He knew slapping a king across the face would incur severe penalty, but he did not care. Afflicting any pain on the neurotic, pretentious, psychopathic king felt better than he expected.

Pulling his gloves on, Jonas prepared to rejoin his men in the courtyard. The crowd's boisterous roaring in the courtyard escalated, and he doubted any of his captains possessed the wherewithal to disperse the angry mob.

He thought about King Thomas as he descended the stairs. Although he never felt close to the king, he still respected him. During his greatest need, the man helped Jonas and named him High Commander when the entire kingdom expected a different candidate. Echoes of the past replayed in his mind as he recounted the events that lead to his appointment. Nearly at the stairwell exit, he decided to change his course and re-ascend the stairs to say his final goodbyes to the only man he could ever envision himself calling king. As the king's door came into view, Jonas found a sight that made his heart skip a beat.

An intense light poured from the door's perimeter. Even with the glow shining only from the cracks, it lit the entire hallway. Jonas darted up the stairs. The door violently shook as though someone desperately pulled at it from the other side only to find it locked. Jonas turned the knob and pushed at the door, but it refused to open. He pounded, kicked, and rammed his shoulder into the wooden barrier to no effect, all the while screaming the king's name. Drawing his sword to hack at the door, a faint voice emerged from beyond the doorway.

Jonas leaned in, trying to perceive the voice's

message. The muffled ramblings sounded pained and desperate, but he could not discern the words. The tortured voice undoubtedly belonged to King Thomas or his son, but he could not tell which one.

"Your Grace! Your Grace!" Jonas screamed at the top of his lungs, driving his sword into the door's frame to attempt to pry it open. Just as he began working the blade, the light dissipated and the hall fell silent.

"Your Grace! What is happening?"

"You may enter, High Commander." King Godwin replied.

Jonas turned the doorknob, and the door easily swung open. Walking into the room, he found a strange sight.

King Godwin stared out the window with his hands folded behind his back in a familiar posture. All of his father's rings adorned his fingers, and his stance resembled that of his predecessor. On the bed, King Thomas's body laid motionless and seemed decayed far too much for a man that passed only moments ago.

"Your Grace, what happened in here?"

King Godwin turned to Jonas. "My father has passed. We will need to begin the funeral arrangements.

Unfortunately, since the beast races have returned, I do not believe it is prudent to perform the Rites of Passage in Tenebris. We will need to make other arrangements."

"There was a light! The door wouldn't open, and I swear I heard someone screaming."

"I do not know what you are talking about. Are you feeling well, High Commander? Perhaps you require some rest. Maybe the stress of fretting over your mother's condition is getting to you."

"My mother? Have I ever told you about her, Your Grace?"

"No, of course not, but I am king now. It behooves me to know all I can about my closest subjects." King Godwin turned back to the window and resumed his contemplative posture. "Now, I believe the guardsmen require your assistance in dispersing that crowd. Afterward, get that rest we spoke about."

"Yes, Your Grace." Jonas began to leave the room. Before he closed the door, he peeked into the quarters.

"Your Grace, may I assume that all is forgiven?"

"Forgiven?"

"For striking you before you entered the room, Your Grace."

King Godwin reached up and touched his cheek.

"Ah yes, I do feel a slight sting. Do not worry. I seem to remember emotions were high. My father lay dying after all. No one saw the strike, so I believe we can forget this incident."

"Thank you, Your Grace."

Elendor

Elendor awoke to a call of his name. Sitting up, he rubbed his eyes to find Jocia searching the area.

"Jocia, what is happening?"

"Marius, he disappeared!"

"What?"

"Just look! All of his things are still here, yet he is nowhere to be found."

"He likely just found a place for privacy." Elendor laid back down and shut his eyes.

"I have thought of that already. Galain has scouted the immediate area, and he is widening his search, but it seems unlikely that he would venture very far. He is without his usual weapon. His safety relies heavily on our escort."

Elendor rose to his feet, rubbing his sleepy eyes. "I agree with your assessment. Perhaps one of the many beasts we have encountered took him in his sleep."

"How can you say that in such a cold tone? Marius is a living being. We should show caring and compassion for all living creatures."

"He is a living being, but he is human. The entire kingdom is better off with fewer humans."

Jocia shot a narrow-eyed glare. "I do not know what has happened to you, Elendor, but I do not like it."

Elendor did not know either. The words that escaped his mouth sometimes surprised even himself. He could not explain it. He did not hate anyone outside Morace, the man that imprisoned the entirety of their home city. However, everyone outside his two friends seemed insignificant.

"You are correct, Jocia. The situation seems odd. I shall join in the search."

"No need," Galain stated as he approached, "I found his tracks."

"Where do they lead?" Jocia lit with relief.

"At some point during the night, he left the camp and traveled south. He did not go far, as his tracks stop in front of a bush. That is where it is difficult to determine what happened next. There are drag marks where the tracks end. It seems that something dragged him from his feet."

"Just as I said, some beast must have abducted him. Possibly a klora?"

"That would be a sound assumption, but there is something else very odd about the tracks, or rather the lack thereof."

"What do you mean, Galain?" Jocia asked.

"There are no tracks for his captor. Even a klora would leave impressions in the dirt. I searched everywhere for signs of the abductor, but there is nothing."

"Perhaps a group of bounty hunters captured him. If what he told us is true, then there is likely a large reward for his capture." Elendor began gathering his travel pack.

"That is possible but unlikely. A group of bounty hunters would know how to cover tracks, but Marius is not easy prey. There is no sign of a struggle. He possesses enough skill to best Heece in tournaments three out of six times. Would you believe that a group of bounty hunters could capture Heece without a fight? No, something is very wrong here. It is as if he were plucked out of the sky."

"So, what do we do now?" Jocia clasped her worried hands at her chest.

"What else can we do? We must move on." Elendor threw his pack over his shoulder.

"You want us, three elves, to prance into the dwarf's territory?" Galain began to pack up his gear. "Seems like a fool's errand. The dwarves will have no interest in what we have to say."

"I see no other choice. We do not have the supplies to make it to anywhere else. We will just have to convince them to hear our words." Elendor began the trek to Durrum.

Jocia and Galain caught up with Elendor. The trio traveled for hours without incident until they approached a worn path surrounded on either side by a perfectly carved stone cliff.

"Have you ever seen a more perfect passage for an ambush?" Galain peered up at the rocky outcropping.

"No. We should certainly tread lightly. Jocia, please keep your magical senses sharp. I suspect a rock avalanche is the best form of attack from this high vantage point." Elendor reckoned.

The moment the three friends entered the passage, a voice called from seemingly all directions. "What business do you have in Durrum, elves?"

The trio searched the area for the voice's source but found no one.

"We are here to speak with Lord McDohl," Elendor responded. "We have information that is imperative to the kingdom's survival."

"If you are talking about the beast race's invasion, we are already well aware of the situation. So you can go about your business elsewhere." The voice replied.

The friends looked puzzled.

"What should we do now?" Jocia whispered.

"That is only part of the information we bring. We have other information that threatens the existence of all the races, including the dwarves." Elendor's voice echoed within the canyon.

Galain grabbed Elendor's wrist, "What are you doing? You know they will never believe us."

"Threatens our existence, eh?" The voice unmistakably came from the path ahead.

A moment later, a dwarven man emerged from behind a cropping. Heavily armored with an ax gripped in both hands, he stood at an average height for a dwarf. Several small braids of hair hung from his cheeks, with one thick braid hanging from his chin, appearing more like a rope than hair.

"Whatever information you have, you can give it to me."

"I apologize, but we cannot do that. This information is time-sensitive, and it is pertinent that we deliver it directly to Lord McDohl himself."

"Just who do you think you are?" The dwarf began marching toward the elves. "You come here, to our land, demanding to speak to our lord. Are you some form of nobility, or do all elves find themselves so self-import that they can demand an audience with a lord of province?"

Elendor's temper flared.

"That's exactly what I would expect from an elf." The dwarf came within striking distance. "Your entire race finds themselves so far above everyone else. Tell me, do bugs ever fly up your nose when you turn it up at everyone else, or do insects shy away from your natural flowery scent?"

Elendor clenched his fists.

"Oh, am I making you angry, elf? I didn't know your race ever got upset. Careful, if you squish up that pretty face of yours, you might crack that perfect skin. We all know that the elves care more about their appearance than they do anything else. Besides, what are you going to do? I see no weapon. You think you can best me with your fists? I would like nothing more than to stick my ax right up your perfectly manicured arse. So go ahead and make your move...elf."

Elendor could no longer contain his rage. He cocked his wooden fist, intending to impale the dwarven man through his skull. Just as his arm began to shoot forward, a blunt object struck the back of his head, causing the world to go dark.

Elendor opened his eyes to discover his environment changed. His head laid on a scratchy pillow, and a thick blanket covered his body. Staring up at a stone ceiling, he shifted his eyes to find himself enclosed by granite walls. He sprang to a seated position, but the swiftness of the act caused stabbing fingers of pain to squeeze the back of his brain.

"Thank Matera. You are finally awake." Galain's voice took him by surprise.

Elendor found his friends seated at a table with over-sized stone mugs resting in front of them. Jocia grabbed her flagon and brought it to Elendor.

"Here, drink this. It will help you to feel better."

Elendor took a sip. The moment his tongue took in the flavor, he leaned and spewed the liquid onto the floor. "What is this? It is horrible!"

"The dwarves call it honey mead. I find it quite enjoyable."

"Dwarves? Are we in Durrum?"

"Yes, no thanks to you," Galain remarked.

"Me? They attacked me. My head still aches." Elendor gently rubbed the back of his head,

"The dwarves did not attack you. Jocia struck you to stop you from doing something monumentally stupid."

"Jocia? You did that?"

Jocia took a swig from her flagon to avoid verbal confirmation.

"It is best that she did. You were so focused on the dwarf spurring you on that you failed to notice a dozen dwarves above us with their bows aimed at our heads. If you had struck that dwarf, we would all be dead right now."

Elendor felt ashamed. "You are correct, Galain. Thank you, Jocia, for knocking some sense into me. My friends, I humbly apologize for losing my temper."

"In a way, we were lucky that you did. I doubt we could have made it into Durrum otherwise." Galain released an ironic chuckle.

"Yes, how did the dwarves allow us entry?"

"After Jocia knocked you out, the dwarves found her actions so amusing that they burst into laughter. What she did next earned her their trust."

Elendor looked at his friends. Galain struggled to keep from bursting into laughter. Jocia's face reddened as she turned away with a chuckle of her own.

"Well, do not keep me in suspense. What did she do next?"

Galain fought to keep his laughter at bay. "After the hit, she walked to your body, gave it a couple quick jabs with her foot, and said, 'by the gods, elves are such pansies.'"

Elendor's friends buckled with laughter and he could not help but to join. Even though the joke came at his expense, it felt incredible to laugh once again. It felt like ages since the group enjoyed a pleasant moment together. Memories of their former life surged in his mind.

"Remember the time Jocia stole a bushel of cherries from the storehouse?" Elendor reminisced.

"Of course!" Galain excitedly replied. "We stayed up all night eating them, then ended up getting sick from eating an entire month's supply."

Jocia chuckled. "I did not steal. I permanently borrowed."

"Elder Jalaana had you picking cherries for months to make up for the lost supply." Galain hugged his stomach from the laughter.

"You should not talk, Galain." Jocia grinned a sly smile. "Remember the time you switched the labels on Telianna's cinnamon and red pepper spice jars?"

"I do!" Elendor guffawed. "A dozen elves burned their tongues so bad; I thought they would exhaust the village's entire water supply!"

Galain's face lit with a memory. "Elendor, do you remember the time you used your arbormancy to bloom the radish crop instead of the cornfield you were supposed to do?"

"Ugh," Jocia covered her mouth, "if I never see

another radish, it will be too soon. Every meal involved radishes for an entire season."

"That was not my fault. Vaylon brought me to the radish field and insisted the Crop Master told him to bring me there."

The laughter diminished. Mentioning Vaylon's name reminded the elves that their departed friend no longer accompanied them.

"I miss him." Jocia wiped a tear from the corner of her eye.

"Me too," Galain added.

"As do I." Elendor gently touched the knot on the back of his head.

The awkward silence broke when a dwarf entered the room. "Consider yourselves lucky. Lord McDohl has agreed to see you."

"That is wonderful!" Jocia folded her hands at her chin. "May we see him now?"

"Aye, come along."

The trio followed and entered a massive cavern. Statues of dwarves, atop spiraling columns, stood with their arms raised to give the appearance they held up the ceiling. Carved into the walls, dwarves of renown posed with their weapons. Each figure's intricate design looked incredibly life-like, as if they would step out of the wall at any moment. A lit fireplace, larger than Elendor's old room, warmed the colossal space. The waxed stone floor reflected the hearth's dancing flames as well as the torches lining the twelve dimly lit tunnels that led to unknown destinations.

None of the cavern's beauty compared to the chiseled spectacle at the center. A waterfall poured into the room from the ceiling. Catching the water, an over-sized female dwarf, with a gentle smile, held a massive pot on her shoulder. The pot poured a stream of water from twelve holes punctured at the bottom. Each stream poured into smaller pots held by dwarven children. These smaller pots overflowed into a circular pool carved into the floor. Twelve expansive waterways ran from the pool down each tunnel like a wagon wheel. Taking a moment to observe, Elendor found that the fountain served a dual purpose, demonstrating the dwarves' artistic abilities and ingenuity.

Numerous helmet-clad dwarves roamed the cavern. Men, women, young and old, all wore thick, leather singlets with a leather apron. Pickaxes and shovels leaned against their shoulders. As they disappeared down the tunnels, they pulled wagons made of a material unfamiliar to Elendor. The dwarves loaded various supplies into the carts, pushed them into the water, and walked alongside them as they floated lazily down the dwarven-made rivers.

The elves stopped to admire the view. Elendor and his friends stared in bewilderment. The books, scrolls, and tales told in Parvus Arbor gave a false representation of the dwarves. Each painted a picture of the dwarven people as brutish curmudgeons who cared for little outside gold and riches. It warmed Elendor's heart to learn the elven teachings' fallacy, leading him to wonder how many other erroneous lessons they had been taught.

"Are you three going to stand there and gawk, or would you like actually to meet with Lord McDohl?"

"I apologize," Jocia responded, "this hall is simply astounding."

"Hall?" Their guiding dwarf laughed. "This is just the work center. This place pales in comparison to the Great Hall of Durrum."

As they followed, their awe-struck look remained as they barraged their guide with questions.

"Where do all of these tunnels lead?" Galain asked.

"That's a tough one to answer. Each tunnel branches off to more tunnels, and those tunnels branch off to more."

"Do you know how many there are?" Jocia asked.

"Nay. There are hundreds of miles of tunnels in Durrum. No one knows all of them by heart."

"How do you prevent from getting lost?" Elendor asked.

"We have a group of map makers. They routinely inspect the mines and update the maps accordingly. They then post the maps at every intersection within the city."

"What about the children? I do not mean any offense, but I saw some young ones heading into the mines. Are they forced to work?" Jocia timidly asked.

"Of course not. The children work in the mines because they enjoy it. Most dwarves love to dig."

"What of the ones that do not enjoy digging?" Galain's eyes darted about as he observed his surroundings, trying to absorb everything within sight.

"Durrum has plenty of jobs to offer, and any dwarf can choose any vocation they please. We have map makers, stone carvers, soldiers, mages, and of course, our renowned blacksmiths and weaponsmiths. We even recently decided to try our hand at farming when we discovered a hidden valley with rich, fertile soil. Soon, Durrum will be completely self-sustainable."

The trio followed their guide into the Great Hall and discovered the truth behind the dwarf's words. Twice the work center's size, the hall's artistry amazed the elves. Scenes of famous battles carved into the walls bore astonishing detail. The use of colorful dust and shards of gemstones brought the landscape scenes and posing warriors to life in vivid color. Statues of dwarves in various dress dotted the hall. Some wore armor and brandished weapons, others in floor-length robes read from scrolls. Even miners held representation as they held their tools, giant hunks of gold, or valuable gemstones. Three fireplaces warmed the hall, with one nearly the size of Parvus Arbor's Great Hall. Above the massive fireplace, an ax with an earth runestone embedded hung in reverence. Above the ax, a carving of a dwarf stood with arms folded and a canny smile. Between the ax and the dwarf, a nameplate read, 'Torbin the Wise.'

"Caught ya gawking again." Their guide chuckled.

"Come on. We're almost there."

Elendor and friends followed the dwarf to a spiral staircase. The ascending stairs seemed to climb to the heavens, leaving Elendor dizzy at the sight.

"Don't worry," their escort mentioned, "we don't need to go to the top."

As they traversed the perfectly carved stairway, Elendor admired the workmanship the dwarves poured into even something as simple as a staircase. The artisans honed each step in perfect symmetry and carved elaborate patterns into the polished, centuries-old wooden handrail.

"Allow me to apologize for us asking so many questions," Galain remarked. "I imagine we are the first elves to visit Durrum in hundreds of years."

"Hundreds? Ha!" Their guide's laugh echoed in the hallway. "More likely thousands, and I think that visit wasn't exactly as friendly an encounter as this one. I don't mind answering your questions. I rather enjoy it. We are told that elves are so stuck-up that they consider any culture other than their own beneath them. I find it amusing that you three are so enamored in ours."

"Well," Jocia began, "I think those teachings are accurate to some elves, but certainly not all."

"Yes, one elf, in particular, would not be impressed," Elendor added in reference to their homeland's chief.

After a brief climb, they entered an office carved into the mountainside. The space featured far less artistry than the previous rooms, although several busts of dwarves lined the walls. At the center of the room, an oak desk shined in the light of the lanterns hanging from the back wall. In the corner of the room, a young dwarf sat reading a dusty book. A wizened elderly dwarf, with an embroidered family crest of a mountain on his shirt's breast, sat behind the desk amongst a pile of scrolls.

"I must say, it has been quite some time since I met with any elves." The old dwarf circled the desk to greet the visitors.

Rings of gold and gemstones decorated his braided white beard that swept the tips of his sandaled feet. A thick mane of white hair encompassed his face, giving him the appearance of an elderly lion. His bulbous nose and beady eyes gave him a picturesque look from the books in Parvus Arbor, but his kindly smile and friendly demeanor betrayed the dwarven reputation in the elven community.

"My name is Rorn McDohl." The dwarven lord leaned on his ancient hand-carved wooden cane as he gestured to the young dwarf in the corner with an open hand. "This is my ward, Harbum Kinsman."

"Well met, My Lord." Galain bowed. "My name is Galain, and this is Jocia and Elendor.

"Kinsman?" Elendor narrowed his eyes as he racked his brain. "I feel that I have heard that name before."

"There are many in Durrum with the surname Kinsman. Those with lineage relating to the McDohl name but have no claim to the title of lord take the surname Kinsman. Harbum here is my nephew."

"W-well met!" Harbum stammered his words as he bowed with the traditional elven greeting.

Harbum's bright red beard barely sprouted, showing his young age. His hair tied neatly at the back of his head, and his unassuming clothing betrayed his noble lineage. Slouching his shoulders, he fidgeted with his hands and avoided eye contact, relaying his timid nature.

"Well met." The three elves returned.

"Now, my guards inform me that you have information that is imperative to our race's survival."

The elves looked nervously at one another. "Yes, My Lord," Galain spoke first. "Our tale may sound…far-fetched, but every word of it is true."

The elves relayed the events that lead them to Durrum. Beginning with the death of their dear friend Vaylon, they told the old dwarf everything that transpired during their trip to Nigereous Forest. Elendor could tell that the mention of the specter brought doubt to his mind, but Lord McDohl graciously allowed them to complete their story uninterrupted.

"That is quite a tale." Rorn stroked his beard. "Tell me, do you have any proof that what you say is true?"

"Actually, we do," Elendor replied. Jocia and Galain looked at him with a confused look. Taking off the glove he received from their time with Marius, Elendor presented his wooden hand and wiggled his fingers. "This should provide all the evidence you need."

Razuul

Boulders flew overhead, smashing into buildings that crumbled under their crushing weight. Balls of flame streaked through the sky, exploding on impact with homes and civilians alike. People ran in every direction to escape the onslaught, trampling the small and weak without regard. Screams of horror mixed with the jangling of armor as soldiers scrambled to gather their weapons and return to their post. Already, the smell of death permeated the air with the scents of blood and burned flesh.

"This way!" Brett shouted over the terrified screams. "Follow me!"

"Brett," Dorian yelled, "The guards are guiding everyone to the docks. Shouldn't we follow?"

"There aren't enough ships to fit this many people. If we go to the docks, we'll be like fish in a barrel.

There's an entrance to the city on the southern side that is only known to thieves. The attacks are coming from the main gate, so we should be able to get out."

"Please," Syken approached, drawing his blade, "allow me to accompany you, and I shall lend you my sword."

"Who in the bloody hells are you?" Brett ducked as a volley of arrows rained down just beyond them. "You know what? I don't care."

Brett led them through the city. Hugging the city's outer walls, Razuul witnessed countless people fall as the onslaught continued. As they approached the city's southern side, the crowd thinned. Soon, the path cleared enough for them to jog without colliding with scrambling citizens. Reaching Brett's destination, they tossed aside a stack of logs to find Brett's secret entrance patched with fresh brick and mortar.

"Hells!" Brett pounded the wall with his fist. "I swear the hole was here just two years ago."

"What are we going to do now?" Dorian scanned the area.

"If I may." Syken placed his hand on the wall.

"This barrier is thick, but if we combine our

efforts, we should be able to break through."

"How?" Razuul drew his swords.

"Please back away." Syken requested Brett and Dorian. Guiding Razuul out of the wall's striking distance, the foreign warrior took his fighting stance alongside him. "I must give you the instructions now, for once we enter the Hakai state, we shall lose our hearing. I need you to focus your energy into your blades. Compress the energy as if you are squeezing it into the center of the metal. Once you have done that, force the energy into the tip of your blade. When you are ready, nod, and together we will release the energy at the wall."

"We are too far away from the wall. Shouldn't we get closer?"

"No. If we are too close, we will be caught in the explosion. You must trust me."

"You better know what you are doing."

Razuul closed his eyes. Entering the Hakai state, the surrounding carnage became sickeningly evident. People's life force extinguished at an alarming rate. The copper scent of blood, mixed with the odors of burning wood, straw, and flesh, overwhelmed his nose and threatened to turn his stomach. Outside the city walls, he felt the presence of innumerable beings. The sheer number of aggressors interrupted his focus. Taking a deep breath, he redirected his concentration and resumed Syken's instructions.

The sensation differed from his previous uses of the Hakai state. He felt a higher degree of control. In the past, the energy felt like an explosion, a raging inferno ready to consume everything in its path. This time felt similar to a tranquil wave, a calming aura radiating from him like the glow of a flickering candle. He focused his energy into his sword, squeezing it until only a thin line remained down the center of the blade. The power flowed like a droplet of water that picked up other droplets in its path until only a massive drop remained at the tip.

Razuul opened his eyes and gave the nod to Syken. The mysterious warrior raised three fingers. Dropping them one-by-one, the two raised their weapons and slashed at the air. Razuul felt the energy jettison from the blade in an arc.

Two scythes of energy launched at the wall. Upon impact, the stone exploded in a mass of rubble. Once the smoke cleared, Razuul saw the massive crater the two warriors created.

"Razuul! That was amazing!" Dorian exclaimed.

"We can all be impressed later." Brett stepped through the hole. "For now, let's concentrate on staying alive."

Razuul approached the wall, but before he reached it, a familiar voice called out.

"Wait!"

He turned to see a bald man emerging from behind a nearby stack of wooden boxes. Razuul recognized the robed man as the mage that performed the fire magic display at the festival.

"Please, take me with you." The man ran to Razuul and dropped to his knees with folded hands. Tears streaked his face as he begged. "Please, I have a wife and children at home."

"Who is this?" Brett peered through the hole.

"His name is Odo," Dorian responded. "He is a powerful mage. He can help us get out of here."

"How many strays are we going to pick up?" Brett gestured his arm for everyone to follow him. "Enough jawing, let's go!"

The group followed Brett. Outside the wall, Razuul absorbed the scope of the attack. The beasts launched a hundred arrows for every arrow the guards returned.

Monstrous, sand-skinned creatures with tusks jutting from their lower jaw, rushed at the gate carrying rickety ladders. Others of the same race remained back, launching spells and giant arrows over the city walls. A group of men with horses for a lower half marched to the gate with their shields raised. The half-horse men pulled a strange wheeled device with a massive, pointed tree trunk suspended vertically by ropes at the center behind them. Alongside the contraption, immense men with the head of a bull pushed with all their might. Thousands of small beings with black, slimy skin rushed across the field on all fours and scaled the walls like a swarm of insects. Among the creatures staying back for an aerial assault, two different monstrous beasts launched giant rocks as easily as a child throws a ball. The smaller of the two, gray-skinned and hunch-backed, possessed bulky arms that hung to the ground. The larger one's proportions matched that of a human, although only one eye and a horn existed above their noses.

Brett led them away from the battle. As they topped a small hill, Razuul saw many tusked and slimy-skinned creatures rushing toward them.

"Odo!" Dorian shouted. "Hit them with some fire!"

"Y-y-yes. O-of c-c-course."

Odo drew out a runic symbol. Fountains of flame spurted from his hands to form the shape of a dog in front of him. The spectacle mesmerized the attacking beasts, causing them to halt in their tracks.

"Hound of hell, attack!" Odo pointed his finger forward.

The fire-dog ran at the beasts. Raising shields, ducking, and covering their heads, the attackers braced for impact. The spell leaped in the air and crashed at the contingent's center, exploding in an outward expanding circle, leaving all bathed in flame. Once the fire dissipated, Razuul saw the small army unscathed with a few patting out flames and embers on their clothes.

"What was that?" Dorian asked in a frustrated tone.

"I-I can manipulate the shape of the flames, but they lack heat or power," Odo spoke with shame.

"So, you're completely useless. Great." Brett reached into the waist of his pants and withdrew a strange cylindrical piece of metal. "I'll show you how it's done."

The beasts renewed their attack. Brett touched the angular metal crook before they approached, causing a pair of fireballs to launch from its barrel. The flames found their mark, smacking into the face and chest of two attackers. Each screamed in pain, and each dropped to the ground smoldering to death.

"What is that thing?" Dorian asked.

"It's called a...gum? Gurn? It doesn't matter. I got it at the festival, but I can only fire it a couple more times."

"Seems like we have no other choice then." Dorian withdrew Shadowflame, instantly igniting it in black flame.

Odo dropped to the ground in fear. "What kind of magic is that? Are there two runestones on that sword?"

"I'd explain the intricacies of how this sword's magic works, but I think we have bigger problems at the moment."

Razuul ran to meet the attackers. Staying out of the Hakai state to conserve energy, he clashed steel with the beasts. One, two, three fell. Razuul checked on his companions, starting with Dorian. Four and five met the tip of his swords. His half-dwarf companion fought, turning three enemies to ash with his sword. Six, seven, eight, and nine lost their lives to Razuul's skill.

Checking on Brett, he found the thief staying back from the battle, firing bursts of lightning with his strange weapon at those that got too close. Ten, eleven, and twelve more no longer posed a threat. Glancing to Syken, he found the swordsman taking down just as many foes as himself. Numbers thirteen through twenty found their end as Razuul utilized a small amount of Hakai to finish off the attackers.

"Is everyone alright?" Brett gulped heavy breaths.

"Where is Odo?" Dorian searched the area.

"Here." Odo emerged from behind a nearby bush.

"So glad we brought you along." Brett scoffed.

"More approach." Syken took his fighting stance.

To their left and right, more enemies crept up. Joining the two previous hostile races, a group of half-horse men Razuul finally remembered as centaurs joined the fray. He took a step to engage, but before he could meet them, a troop of skeletons popped up from behind the attackers and slit their throats with rusty blades.

"Lena!" Dorian shouted.

Razuul turned around to see the young heiress emerging through the hole in the wall he and Syken created.

Skipping up to them, Lena flashed a bright smile. "Isn't this wonderful? So much death!"

"Where did you go?" Dorian asked.

"Well, there was a dog that hopped like a bunny, so I went to say hi, but then all these people started mumbling. So, I poked at the apron, then all this fire started making new play things, and I..."

"We don't have time for rambling nonsense." Brett interrupted. "We have to get out of here."

"Razuul, Hakai!" Syken shouted.

Understanding the warning, Razuul returned to his enhanced state and sensed a volley of arrows soaring toward them. As the projectiles approached at a perceived snail's pace, he and Syken cut each one out of the air.

"Thank you, Razuul." Dorian wiped the sweat from his brow.

"No time for pleasantries. Here comes more." Brett aimed his weapon.

Razuul spotted roughly a hundred beasts. Centaurs, tusk people, slime skins, and a new strange fur-covered, four-armed creature stampeded. The four-armed creatures launched themselves high into the air and landed in the middle of their group.

"Kill." The four monsters spoke as one.

Razuul hacked at one of the beasts, only to have his blade get stuck in the creature's dense hide. In response, the hairy brute punched him in the chest, sending him flying back.

Razuul rose to his elbows to see his companions. Brett backed away, firing fire, ice, and lightning shots, but the creatures seemed utterly unfazed. Just before the strange things could pounce on Brett, Syken entered the Hakai state and removed their heads. The effort visibly wore on Syken. Bending over to lean on his knees, he gasped for breath.

Dorian faced the final two four-armed monstrosities. Using a move Razuul taught him, the half-dwarf shifted to one side and dragged his blade across the creature's midsection. Expecting it to turn to ash, Dorian turned to face the remaining creature. However, the first beast failed to subdue to Shadowflame's unusual power. The beast struck Dorian's arm, sending him rolling to the ground. Lena responded by aiming bone spears at the creatures, but each one bounced off their hide with no effect.

Even from his distance, Razuul heard the bone in Dorian's arm snap from the impact. Using Hakai, he sprinted at the attackers. As he rushed past, he slit the first beast's throat and stopped as he ran his blade through the heart of the second.

Remaining in his state, Razuul turned to the rest of the attackers to see them barreling at them. He began to rush in their direction to take out as many as possible, but a strange sensation stopped him in his tracks.

A cold aura behind him shot out like a shockwave. Razuul turned around to see Dorian standing up. The son of Thane seemed far different from any of Razuul's previous experiences with him. The center of his eyes completely vanished, leaving only a milk-white, deadened glare. Magical energy burst from him in epic proportions. Razuul saw Dorian use the magic of his sword before, but this felt different. Usually, the blade caused its user to emit an aura of passion-fueled rage. This time, Razuul felt a bitter chill of malice and murderous intent. If evil itself possessed an aura, Razuul felt it exploded from his half-blooded companion.

Dorian pointed his sword at the beasts. His broken arm swayed like a flag in a light breeze, but he didn't seem to notice. The moment the blade reached its apex, an icy wind shot from Dorian in all directions. Razuul squinted and blocked the wind with his hand. The black flames on Shadowflame burst into an inferno and launched to the center of the attackers. A circular void, blacker than the darkest night's sky, opened at their feet, swallowing dozens of beasts.

The terrifying spell continued to evolve. A pair of hulking skeletal hands emerged from the void and slammed onto the ground. The hands pushed into the ground, causing black flame-emitting fissures to crackle outward. A moment later, the skeletal body rose from the chasm and roared a chilling scream into the air. Only the upper half of the undead apparition emerged, but it towered twice the one-eyed beasts' height. Black flames shrouded it like a cloak with a hood that surrounded its fanged skull.

The skeleton faced the beasts and released a bone-chilling screech. Wind poured from its mouth, pushing back their hair and causing ripples in their skin. With terrified expressions, the beasts began their retreat, but they did not get far. The skeleton swooped its arms through the crowd. The bony appendages passed through their bodies as if they possessed no physical form, but every hide it touched burst into midnight-colored flames, reducing each to ash. In all, over a hundred beasts fell to a single spell.

With its job finished, the skeleton sank into the void. The moment its cloaked head dipped beneath the opening, the chasm sealed. The field from which it emerged returned to its previous state, leaving the scattering ashes of their enemies as the only sign of its existence.

Dorian dropped his sword and collapsed. His skin took a blueish hue, and his chest rose with shallow breaths.

The other companions entered a state of shock. Brett and Syken stood wide-eyed and slack-jawed. Lena's eyes also widened, but she seemed more excited than scared. Odo trembled with his hands folded at his mouth, and a puddle of urine circled his feet.

Razuul ran to Dorian's side. "Dorian? Dorian!" He shook the half-dwarf's body but received no response.

"He is fading." Lena approached from behind.

"The flame of life is nearly extinguished."

"Can you do something?" Razuul felt a strange sensation, one he hadn't felt in decades. His eyes watered and threatened to spill from the corners.

"I am a necromancer, not a healer, but..." Lena walked to Shadowflame, picked it up, and placed it in Dorian's hand. In response, his hand instinctively tightened without the rest of his body reacting. Unlike usual, no flames ignited on the blade. "The flame of life stopped dying. It's as if the sword is keeping him alive."

"Will he recover?" Razuul rubbed his eyes with the palms of his hands.

"That is up to him. If his will is strong, the flame of life may burn once again."

"No matter what, we need to get him somewhere safe." Brett approached. "Razuul, can you carry him?"

"Yes." Razuul lifted Dorian's limp body.

"Come on, Dorian cleared a path for us. Let's not waste it." Brett began leading the group south.

Each member of the party, save Odo, looked near the point of exhaustion. Syken limped from a wound Razuul failed to see him receive. Brett clutched his arms around his chest. His new weapon, while effective, drew much of his energy. Lena walked her normal gait, but she did not skip, demonstrating her lack of stamina.

"Stop," Razuul said upon spotting two enormous figures.

Stepping into the light of the moon, two of the massive gray-skinned creatures blocked their path. Each bore an enormous club the size and weight of a man. Snarling their faces, they presented their pointed teeth as sign of their intent.

"Trolls." Brett pulled his weapon, but Razuul knew he didn't have the strength to fire it.

Razuul assessed the others. Lena drew out a runic symbol. Three skeletons rose from the ground, but they instantly crumbled to dust. Syken drew his sword, but he struggled to support its weight. Odo cowered in place, but seeing him gave Razuul an idea.

"Odo, come here."

"M-me? You saw that my magic has no power. What can I do?"

"Just get over here now."

Odo complied. As soon as he reached Razuul, the angered wild elf snatched him by the front of his robe. "Listen to me. You will kill those…things." "Trolls,"

Odo muttered.

"Shut up, and listen. You can manipulate the size and shape of your flame, correct?"

"Y-yes."

"Well, what if instead of making them big, you make it small."

"H- how…"

"I said shut up." Razuul looked at the trolls to see them start to jog in their direction. "It's just like the instructions Syken gave me when we broke through that wall. Compress your flames into a single point instead of spreading it out. If you put all the power into one point, it should do what flames are supposed to do."

"That might work!" Syken added.

"I-I can t-try."

Odo drew out a runic symbol. Pointing at the trolls who nearly bore down upon them, a bright but small ball of flame flickered at his fingertip.

"Compress it more," Razuul instructed. "Push it until the flames stop flickering. Make it look like a miniature sun."

Odo furrowed his brow in full concentration. The ball of flame shrunk, but its brightness intensified.

The trolls raised their clubs to hammer the fire mage. In terror, Odo fell backward and released his spell. A beam of compressed flame shot from his finger. His finger accidentally shot forward during the fall, catching both trolls in its wake. The beam sliced the first troll in two and beheaded the other. In three consecutive thuds, the trolls fell to the ground.

"I-I did it!"

"Hey, sissy fire guy. Want to keep your voice down? That is unless you want to attract more of those things."

Odo covered his mouth with both hands, but Razuul could still see the smile beneath.

For hours, the group moved south. Overhead, the event that inspired the festival occurred. Rolling clouds of beetles painted the sky, emitting their soft glow. Individually, the insect's light barely registered even to elven eyes, but together, they lit the night in every conceivable shade blue. Like a million sapphires drifting in the air current, they bathed the world in an azure luminescence. The leaves of trees, the blades of grass, and the rocks at their feet all took a shade of blue. Under the same light, the differences between the six travel companions seemed less significant. The shape of their faces, their bodies' size, and shade of their skin all seemed homogeneous. Even though the morning sun would soon display their contrasts once again, Razuul relished in their shared parallels.

The melodious hum of bug's wings raised and lowered in pitch, replacing the ensuing battle's horrid sounds in the distance with their sweet song. The twang of loosed arrows, the roar of animalistic battle cries, the boom of giant rocks destroying hopes and dreams, and the screams of terror as thousands drew their last breath all succumbed to the beating of countless, tiny wings.

Razuul wished he could stop and admire the magnificent splendor, but Dorian threatened to drift off into eternal slumber in his arms. Brett and Syken offered to help support Dorian, but Razuul refused their help. He didn't know why, but he felt that he needed to bear the burden solely. Odo begged to rest, but Razuul insisted they keep moving.

"Look! The bugs are burning!"

Brett looked upward. "What are you talking about? The bugs aren't burning."

"Not those bugs, those bugs!" Following Lena's

pointed finger's direction, the group saw a campfire a stone's throw away. Surrounding the flames glow, Razuul observed a small group of humans setting up camp.

"See! I told you. The burning bugs fly up."

"Lena, I believe those are embers." Syken turned to Razuul. "What should we do? They may have some medical supplies."

Razuul thought for a moment. He did not trust humans, and none of their group possessed enough strength to face them if they refused aid. Seeing no other option, he elected to ask them for help. "Let's go."

When the weary warriors approached the fire, a pair of armored soldiers approached them.

"Whoever you are, you need to leave." The soldiers readied their spears.

"We mean no harm." Brett raised his open hands. "Our friend is in dire need of medical attention. Do you have any herbs or medicines that can help?"

"Didn't you hear me? I said, get out of here!" The soldier demanded.

"You are going to help us, or you are going to die," Razuul warned.

"Wait!" A voice came from the camp.

The voice's owner approached. Razuul recognized the man but couldn't place him in his memory. He stood at roughly six stones, and his demeanor presented himself as a leader. Gray streaked his black hair, and his beard faded completely to gray. His armor shone even in the dim light of the fire, and the intricate designs on the hilt of his sheathed sword relayed a man of wealth. The etching of a fish in front of a pair of spears on his breastplate rang with familiarity in Razuul's recollection of his past.

"You two, put those spears away unless you want to die. Even carrying that young man on his shoulder, he would kill you before you could blink." The man chuckled.

"Do you know this wild elf, M'Lord?" One of the soldiers asked.

"You don't recognize the famed Dragon Fist? Let me introduce Razuul, the only person ever to free himself from the arena."

"You!" Razuul placed the man's identity. Lord Harken, the man who sent him to the arena all those years ago.

About the Author

Dennis is a veteran of the United States Navy after serving in his country for fourteen years. During his service, Dennis developed PTSD, which resulted in insomnia. Not willing to take prescription or over-the-counter medication, he began constructing a story in his mind to find a natural method to fall asleep. After fifteen years of development, and countless sleepless nights, he finally decided to put the story into words. This story is the result of him turning a debilitating condition into something positive.

Dennis is a native of the Buffalo, New York area, where he was raised by his parents, Lawrence and Barbara, alongside his sister, Kelly. He currently lives in the Atlanta, Georgia area with his loving and supportive wife Kimberly and three children, Hailey, Joseph, and Breanna.

Excerpt: Book Four

Silla's face angered. "I would like to remind you, that while you may be the high commander, you are not of noble blood yourself. Watch how you speak to your betters."

"My betters? How about I…"

"Enough, Jonas!" King Godwin cut off Jonas's words.

"Yes, Your Grace."

"The high commander's temper aside, he is correct. Our next move is imperative." King Godwin folded his hands behind his back.

"Your Grace," Jonas began, "I shall meet with my commanders. The other provinces can offer a combined forty-thousand troops. If we add that to the forty-thousand troops in the capital, we can easily eradicate the beasts. It will take some planning, but I believe we can be ready to march within three days."

"No." King Gowin replied.

"No, Your Grace?"

"We will not march. I want all of you to send

word to your provinces. Have them keep up their defenses. Increase the production of weapons, and make sure all civilians are armed. We shall wait until the beasts make their next move and allow them to smash themselves against our walls."

"But…" Oscar muttered.

"Your Grace, this plan is foolish!" Jonas couldn't keep his words inside any longer. "What of the people of Prasillo? They suffer while we wait. The beasts have invaded the kingdom. We must act!"

King Godwin's face angered. "High Commander, I have given my orders."

"Please, Your Grace, military operations are my duty. I know we can end this war. If you'll just allow me to…"

"Enough!" The young king shouted. Adjusting his throat, he pinched the bridge of his nose and returned his hands behind his back. "This council meeting has ended. Everyone, carry out your orders. High commander, you may have a point. I will hear your strategies. Stay behind, and we will discuss this further."

The council gathered their belongings and exited the War Room. Before Oscar closed the door, he turned to

Jonas and mouthed "thank you" to him.

With the council departed, Jonas began to relay his plan. "Your Grace, if we gather our forces, and…"

The brand on Jonas's chest burned. Intense waves of pain radiated throughout his body. He dropped to the floor, curling into a ball. He tried not to scream, but the agony forced him to cry out. His breakfast hurled from his mouth, his muscles cramped, and it felt as though his eyes would soon pop out of his head.

Leaning over, King Godwin looked Jonas in the eye. "Thank you, High Commander. It has been too long since I tortured someone. Now, let me remind you of your place."

Other books in The Secrets of the Runestones series by
Dennis Medbury:

Book one: Secrets of the Runestones
A Book Excellence Award Winner

Book two: The Price of Vanity

Contact Dennis Medbury:
dpmedbury@gmail.com
Instagram @dpmedbury
Twitter @DennisMedbury
www.amazon.com/author/dennismedbury

Made in the USA
Middletown, DE
15 September 2021